All For Her

By the Authors

Gun Brooke

Romances

Course of Action

Coffee Sonata

Sheridan's Fate

September Canvas

Fierce Overture

Speed Demons

The Blush Factor

Soul Unique

A Reluctant Enterprise

Piece of Cake

Thorns of the Past

Wayworn Lovers

Insult to Injury

Ice Queen

Limelight

Science Fiction

Lunar Eclipse

Renegade's War

The Amaranthine Law

Supreme Constellations series

Protector of the Realm

Rebel's Quest

Warrior's Valor

Pirate's Fortune

Exodus series

Advance

Pathfinder

Escape

Arrival

Treason

The Dennamore Scrolls

Yearning

Velocity

Homeworld

Novella Anthology

Change Horizons

J.J. Hale

Truly Wanted

Truly Enough

Truly Home

Synchronicity

Aurora Rey

Published by Bold Strokes Books

A Convenient Arrangement

Frosted by the Girl Next Door

Built to Last

Crescent City Confidential

Lead Counsel
(The Boss of Her collection)

Recipe for Love:
A Farm-to-Table Romance

The Inn at Netherfield Green

The Last Place You Look

Ice on Wheels
(Hot Ice collection)

Twice Shy

You Again

Follow Her Lead
(Opposites Attract collection)

Greener Pastures

Hard Pressed

Roux for Two

Cape End Romances

Winter's Harbor

Summer's Cove

Spring's Wake

Autumn's Light

Renovation Romances

Sweat Equity

Good Bones

Published by Bella Books

Love, Accidentally

New Leash on Love

All For Her

by

Gun Brooke, J.J. Hale,

and Aurora Rey

2025

ALL FOR HER

ISBN 13: 978-1-63679-713-7

This Trade Paperback Original Is Published By
Bold Strokes Books, Inc.
P.O. Box 249
Valley Falls, NY 12185

First Edition: January 2025

Credits
Editor: Cindy Cresap
Production Design: Stacia Seaman
Cover Design by Tammy Seidick

All For Her

Her Boss's Wife

Gun Brooke

Chapter One

January Wild couldn't remember ever having felt this uncomfortable. On one side of the enormous walnut desk, halfway out of his leather executive chair, Peter Sundh looked like a furious bear, ready to strike down his prey.

On the other side stood Mallory Davigne, Peter's wife, clearly not about to back off so much as an inch. Her hands were firmly planted on the desk, and her classically beautiful face showed rage, but her voice was calm when she addressed the man she was about to divorce.

At the side of said desk, after backing up a few steps for self-preservation, January clung to her tablet. She was there to take notes to assist Peter, her boss, but so far, she hadn't been able to hear more than a fraction of what they were saying. Peter because he was spitting the words out like razor blades—Mallory because the angrier she got, the more soft-spoken she became.

"If you think you're going to get away with this latest stunt of yours, you'll find that you're sorely mistaken! You're entitled to exactly zero of my mother's estate," Mallory growled, finally raising her voice a few decibels. The tone reverberated through January's abdomen. No matter how intimidating Mallory was, there was no doubt she was classy and stunning. Her light brown hair was meticulously treated at a famous salon. Golden highlights reflected the light from the lamps in Peter Sundh's corner office. Mallory was dressed in a chocolate brown skirt suit, and on top of that, she carried a camel-colored trench coat flung over her shoulders. Black four-inch heel pumps completed the outfit together with a black Chanel handbag.

As usual, it baffled January how Peter didn't seem to notice his wife's beauty as he glowered at her, his color accelerating from pink to crimson. Whatever had made him fall in love with Mallory at some point was apparently long gone and all he saw was a bitter adversary. He looked at Mallory with such disgust, January feared he might suffer a coronary. What Mallory saw when she looked at her soon-to-be ex-husband was anybody's guess.

As if he realized January was focusing on him, Peter snapped his head around, nailing her with his dark brown eyes. He was a handsome man, and when he and Mallory were still happy together, they had been considered one of the best-looking couples in Seattle. He was tall, thin, and had those distinguished gray temples that so many women swooned over. There was nothing handsome about the way he redirected his wrath to January at the moment, though.

"January! I asked you a question!" Barking the words and adding emphasis by slapping his palm onto the desk, he looked exactly like what his opponents in court called him—a predator. This look was the same as when he cross-examined witnesses in court. January knew she didn't have to accept being spoken to like that. She reminded herself that all she had to do was stick with her job as his assistant for another few weeks. Then her tenure at the law firm would be over and Peter would provide her with the promised glowing letter of recommendation that would open every door she needed it to in Seattle. She would be several steps closer to her dream job. Now, this said, she wasn't Peter Sundh's punching bag, and he better remember that—quickly.

"Yes, Peter," January said mildly, and hoped neither of them could tell how hard she held onto her tablet. Only an onset of discoloration of the screen made her ease up on her death grip before it cracked. "It's just that when you raise your voice like this, HR has told me I should just back off. It is not in my job description to tolerate these decibels."

Peter opened his mouth and then shut it again. "Damn," he said and sounded marginally calmer. "Of course, you're right. Can you please pull out the documents from the prenup agreement? My lawyer insists he overnighted it."

"I think there might have been a delay on the hard copy, but I have access to a digital copy of it and can send it to your email. Will that be sufficient for you as well, ma'am?" January turned to Mallory and lost her train of thought for a moment. Where the woman had been seething only seconds ago, she now regarded January with something close to relief. Then she blinked and her blue eyes went back to being opaque.

"By all means." Mallory gave an elegant shrug. "It won't matter in the long run, of course, but if there is something my lawyer needs to deal with, she will do so immediately. You're not dragging this out any further, Peter." Apart from sounding annoyed, there was something else, something like fatigue, tingeing Mallory's words.

"We'll be meeting under completely different circumstances next time," Peter said. "It was hardly appropriate to spring this surprise visit on me in the middle of a workday like this. We shouldn't meet at all without our lawyers. I know you're not a lawyer, but I'm sure your attorney has conveyed this, Mallory." The condescension was back, but this time Mallory didn't bite.

"Oh, I'm fully aware. You were meant to be out of the office today." Here Mallory shot January a disapproving glance, as if it were her fault that yet another rainstorm prevented Peter from his weekly game of golf. "I used to work here, and I kept boxes of old photos around."

"Even old photos need to be shared. You can't just waltz in here and grab stuff." Peter sat down and straightened his blue tie. "As for working here, that's hardly accurate. You used two of the rooms for your little projects."

January wanted to smack Peter with her tablet. How could he talk like that about a foundation that helped feed homeless people and furnished small, new apartments that other organizations built for the most vulnerable in Seattle. The foundation employed at least twenty people full-time. They were now housed in a new, better office space in the center of the part of Seattle that was their target area.

"Exactly. And the photos are from the work we do, from my college and university years, and of the dogs. You've never been interested in any of those things before." Exasperation filled Mallory's voice as she took her trench coat from her shoulders and put it on. She tied the belt hard around her waist with jerky movements, her knuckles as white as January's. "The boxes are already in the trunk. If you truly feel it is worth suing me for photos of beach bonfires and the dogs on the boardwalk, you know where to find my lawyer."

And with that, she gave January a long, withering look and left.

❖

Mallory got into the back seat of the waiting car. In the driver's seat, Rita, her chauffeur, turned around and studied her closely.

"Home?" Rita asked.

"Yes. Home, for God's sake." Mallory thudded her head against the neck rest. She was still enraged, but it wasn't just about Peter and his infuriating methods of fucking with her. It was so much more. She had spent the last five years trying to make things work between Peter and her, going against a lot she believed in, just to keep the peace. Still the man acted as if she was the one who was trying to screw *him* over. He was the one with the mistresses, the insanely long business hours, and the one to make plans for holidays and parties without talking things over with her, or even bothering to find out if she was able to attend.

She could have dealt with all this if he had shown her the least bit of respect. He hadn't loved her for a long time, and she had fallen out of love with him as a result of this coldness, but the way he acted these days was…unhinged.

Mallory was glad to be back in the car. It had been tormenting to be on the receiving end of Peter's fury, but mostly because January Wild, Peter's assistant, was there to witness it all. It was clear that January had wished she were anywhere but caught in the crossfire of Peter and Mallory, but the young woman had stood her ground. Even if she had clung to her ever-present tablet like her life depended on it, she hadn't allowed Peter to bully her.

The image of her soon-to-be ex-husband's assistant lingered, and Mallory allowed her head to fall back against the neck rest as she closed her eyes. Normally, she was good at pushing unwanted imagery away, but now she allowed her brain to roam freely.

January Wild. What a suitable name when it came to the diminutive blond woman. How old was she? Twenty-five? That would make her fifteen years Mallory's junior. Still, there was something in those blue eyes, which were unusually dark. Yes, determination and a fearlessness that Mallory certainly hadn't possessed at that age. Back then, she had just met Peter and been swept off her feet. For five years, she had thought she lived in a happy marriage, where both of them lived the dream of fulfilling private lives and careers. After her thirtieth birthday, the cracks began to show, and no matter how she tried to repair them, to a degree where she completely went against her grain and humiliated herself, it was in vain.

The turning point had come when Mallory moved offices a year ago and became completely independent of Peter and his ability to drape himself like a wet blanket on top of everything she did. Her foundation soared, she networked well outside hers and Peter's circle of friends and business associates, and reached such success, any thought of trying to appease Peter left her. She wasn't sure when Peter had realized he'd lost her years ago, but when he did, she filed for divorce—and all hell broke loose. At that time, January had worked for Peter for one year and Mallory had dealt more with her than her husband. Peter wasn't above using his assistant as a shield, which wasn't fair on anyone. January had gone from looking like the proverbial deer-in-the-headlights to vaguely exasperated employee in mere months.

When Mallory's foundation moved offices and began hiring more staff, Mallory had almost offered January a job as her assistant but stopped herself in time. January was loyal, even if it was obvious that she found Peter difficult. She would never agree to work for Mallory as she would find it a conflict of interest.

At one point, when Mallory had arrived at Peter's office to collect her two golden retrievers, after finally getting Peter to agree to give full ownership of them to her, she stumbled into a scene that lingered in her mind since then. The dogs, Corma and Hera, sat on either side of January, who was suffering through one of Peter's dress-downs.

"And I shouldn't have to tell you how important it is to never, ever leave the desk unmanned. Clients, damn it, clients that are more important than you could ever dream of, know they can depend on reaching this office at any time. You weren't there and now Richard Castell is unhappy. Most unhappy."

Corma, the more impulsive of Mallory's dogs, began to growl deep in her throat. January sent the dog a quick glance but didn't move.

"I apologize, Peter, but—"

"There's no excuse!" Peter bellowed, and Mallory gaped at the way the arteries at his temples stood out like thick ropes. "The Castell account makes more than fifteen percent of our revenue. As my assistant, you know this!" Peter glared at Corma, whose ears lay flat against her head. "What the hell's wrong with the dog?"

Perhaps it was the way he stared at the dogs, but now Hera joined in, actually pulling her lips up a fraction of an inch. Mallory knew Hera didn't like when someone locked their gaze on her. What was different, though, was how they pressed their bodies against January's legs. Taking the tense situation as her cue, Mallory stepped into the office and broke the dog's focus on Peter.

"I'm here for the dogs." Mallory patted Corma, who came over to greet her, her tail wagging. Hera didn't budge. She had stopped growling, but remained by January's side and didn't take her eyes off Peter.

"Ms. Davigne." January sounded relieved. "I'm glad you're here. I have tended to Corma and Hera, but I fear Hera may have come down with a stomach bug, or perhaps swallowed something that didn't agree with her. She threw up on the outer office floor earlier." She shot Peter a disgruntled look. "And that's why I was absent for a few moments, as I had to clean it up. It was that or letting some of your other important clients step all around the poor dog's vomit."

Peter sighed. "Damnit. All right. Not your fault this time, January." As expected, he turned his annoyance toward Mallory. "Take your damn dogs with you. They've cost me enough as it is today. We don't run a dog daycare here."

"They wouldn't be here if you hadn't fought me every step of the way for custody of them." Mallory accepted the leather leashes from January and attached them to the dogs' collars. "Thank you for looking after them. I will make sure Hera's all right."

"No problem, Ms. Davigne. They're lovely dogs." January ran her hand over Hera's head. "Feel better, sweetie."

Hera tilted her head, angled her ears forward, and drew her eyebrows together, which meant she was listening intently to January. Neither of the dogs gave Peter so much as a glance when Mallory left the office with them walking at heel. When they reached the elevator, Mallory stealthily glanced back at the open door to Peter's office. January was still there, standing ramrod straight with her tablet pressed to her chest.

Mallory shifted restlessly in the back seat of the car. She had often wondered what sorcery January possessed that made it possible for her to work for Peter for two years without strangling him. It couldn't be the pay, as an assistant's salary was barely above minimum wage.

As Rita maneuvered rush hour traffic with ease, Mallory closed her eyes, as always exhausted after dealing with Peter. She hoped there would come a time when all this wouldn't haunt her so mercilessly.

Chapter Two

January was relieved to step onto the bus. She was lucky that there was a bus stop right outside the office building she worked in and also just one block from her apartment complex. The ride took about half an hour, depending on traffic, and for her it was a perfect time slot to down yet another mug of coffee in the morning and decompress a bit in the evening. Not that anyone was waiting for her when she came home, but she still liked to enter her private domain in as good a mood as possible. There were some days that working for Peter Sundh made that impossible, and today certainly had all the markings for such a day. Drawing a deep breath through her nose, she let the air out via her mouth.

"One of those days, eh?" a male voice said from across the aisle.

Jumping slightly, January looked over at an older, rather distinguished-looking man, dressed in a navy trench coat and holding a briefcase on his lap. He looked friendly enough, but January wasn't much for striking up conversations during her efforts to relax. "Yes." She nodded politely and then focused on something outside the window.

"I can see that I'm intruding," the man continued, unperturbed. "I don't mean to impose, but your gloves are on the floor."

January saw that her new leather gloves indeed had slipped off her lap and ended up on the floor. "Thank you," she said, warmer now, and bent to collect them. As she straightened up, the bus made an unexpected sharp turn and came to a stop. Only her quick grip saved January from falling off her seat. The man across the aisle wasn't as lucky. He lost the grip on his briefcase, which fell to the floor and skidded several feet along the aisle.

January watched the man slip halfway off the seat and acted without thinking. She let go of her gloves and bag, stood up, and pushed against his side, effectively shoving him back onto his seat.

"Now that was fast thinking, my dear," the man said, his eyes wide. "I think you may have saved me from breaking my hip." He shook his head. "Thank you."

"Are you all right?" When the man nodded, January looked toward the driver, who was in an argument with some of the passengers up at the front. She wondered what just happened but wasn't going to insert herself in any more arguments today. "Hang tight." She collected the man's briefcase, her bag, and—again—her gloves, and returned to his side. "Here you go, sir." She handed over his briefcase.

"Ah, thank you, my dear. But please, call me Constantine." He smiled broadly. "After all, you're my savior."

Reluctantly charmed, January remained standing beside him, starting to feel responsible for the older man. He looked like he might be in his early eighties. Him fearing a fracture wasn't unwarranted. "I'm January," she said and watched his smile widen further.

"Now that suits you perfectly," Constantine said. A frown appeared between his eyebrows. "I hope we won't be too delayed."

"I second that." Looking around, January saw that most of the other passengers were slightly familiar faces of fellow commuters, which made the elegant Constantine stand out, as she had never seen him before. "Where's your destination?"

"I'm changing buses four stops from here. I'm on my way to my granddaughter's. As a surprise." Constantine gripped his briefcase harder. "Perhaps I should have taken a cab after all."

"It's not too late." January placed a gentle hand on his arm. "I live at the hub where you're supposed to switch to another bus. What if we call a cab when we get there?"

Constantine brightened. "Now, that's a clever idea. My sweet girl will approve. I meant to surprise her with not just coming to see her, but also to show her that I can still function independently." He straightened his tie. "Although she's one of the few in my family who thinks there's still life in the old man." A tinge of sorrow flickered through Constantine's hazel eyes.

"I don't mean to pry," January said slowly, "but does anyone know that you're on an adventure, Constantine?"

His expression grew mild. “Not really. I’m a widower, living alone. I have some assistance with house cleaning and meal preparations, but mostly, I reside in that big old house alone. My sweet girl has asked me to move in with her, but I value my privacy, and nowadays, so does she. So, no, this surprise is just that—a surprise.”

“Why the bus? You look like you can afford a cab.” January winked to remove any hint of criticism from her voice.

“I know, but—I wanted to see people. Be among people. See this city before they change things again. I’ve lived here all my life, and you wouldn’t believe how much has changed. It’s a surreal experience.”

The bus started moving, but a lot slower than before. The driver used the speakers and informed them that he was going to let everyone off at the next stop due to technical difficulties, and that a replacement bus was on its way.

“Damn.” January looked out the window where snow had begun to fall. “This isn’t ideal. Why don’t we call a cab right away and we share it.” January hardly ever splurged on cab fares, but she felt responsible for Constantine, and sharing the cab would make it less expensive.

“That sounds excellent. I think I’ve seen enough of Seattle for now.” Constantine nodded.

“Let me call one from the company my boss uses. They’re fast to arrive.” January pulled out her phone and pressed the speed dial for the company. Talking to the same woman she’d gotten to know over the last two years, January smiled in relief when she disconnected the call. “The dispatch is redirecting a cab as we speak. It won’t be long.”

“You’re a miracle worker.” Constantine shot her another blinding smile, but it was obvious that he was starting to get tired. He was leaning toward January, and she placed her body to keep him from sliding off the seat. The woman sitting next to him by the window nodded approvingly.

Only two minutes later, the bus turned off the busy lane and into the bus stop. Something underneath was obviously broken, as it gave ear-piercing, metal-against-metal screeching sounds.

“Good Lord,” Constantine said and shook his head. “Glad we didn’t get into an accident on top of all this.”

“For sure.” January waited until all the other passengers had gotten off before she offered her arm to Constantine. “You all set to go find our cab?”

"I am." He disregarded her arm at first and heaved himself into standing up, but then he fumbled for her, his eyes unfocused. "I apologize. I seem to be a little dizzy."

"Lean on me." January took small steps next to Constantine as they maneuvered through the bus toward the back exit. The woman who had sat next to him turned out to be another helpful soul, and January drew a deep breath of relief when they were all safely outside. Once she felt large, wet snowflakes land on her head, only to melt and run beneath the collar of her coat and onto her back, she pulled Constantine closer. "Hold on to me."

"Same goes for you, dear." Constantine squinted at her through the rain. "This is quite the change in weather."

January had to smile at his perpetual politeness. Looking around, she saw a taxi approach and pull in behind the bus. To her dismay, a large group of people swarmed it and pulled at the door handles. Fearing they might lose their ride, she raised her hand and tried to get the driver's attention. He didn't see her, but he was smart enough to keep his doors locked as he got out enough to call out. "January Wild! This cab's for January Wild."

"Here!" Jumping up and down to make it possible for him to see her behind the mob, January waved her free arm.

"Gotcha!" the driver called out and then simply pushed through the crowd and approached them. "Got ID?"

"I do." January had already pulled out her driver's license and gave it to him, hoping they could get into the cab before Constantine caught his death in the relentless snow-mixed rain. "This ride's not to be charged to Sundh, Ferris, and Ferris Jr. I'll be settling the cab fare personally."

"All right. No probs." The driver, a stocky man in his forties, smiled at Constantine. "Need some support to get through this mob, Grandpa? But perhaps you risk drowning more than being trampled in this weather. I was sure the forecast said snow. This is slush."

January closed her eyes in exasperation at the "grandpa" comment, but Constantine merely returned the grin. "I think that would be safer, yes. It might change fully into snow yet." He turned to January. "Will you be all right plowing through them on your own, my dear?"

"I will." January turned to the woman who had helped them. "Can we drop you off somewhere?"

The lady shook her head. “You’re sweet to ask, but this is my stop, so I’ll be fine. Take care of him. I’d say they don’t make men like him anymore.” She patted January’s shoulder. “But then again, I didn’t think they made girls like you anymore either.”

January blinked. “Um, thanks?” She hurried after the cab driver and Constantine and made herself ignore it when several people became rude when she wouldn’t let them in on the ride. “We don’t know them,” she murmured as she sat down next to Constantine in the back seat.

“Exactly. I’m sorry that you have to endure listening to such rude language,” Constantine said sorrowfully. “I suppose they’re angry and tired after a long day.”

January regarded the man next to her and found herself agreeing with the lady who helped them out of the bus. Constantine was one of a kind. “All right. Let’s drop you off first. I can tell you’re cold.” And she wanted to make sure there was someone to take care of him when he arrived at his granddaughter’s.

“All right. And please, January, let me pay for the cab fare. You’ve saved my life today, after all.” He patted her hand.

“No, no. We’ll share—” January cringed. “I never meant—”

“Please.” Constantine opened his briefcase and pulled out a business card. “My granddaughter’s private address and cell phone number is on the back.”

January took the card but was still trying to argue with Constantine and didn’t look at it. “But it’s not fair that—”

“Humor an old man.” Constantine closed his eyes hard for a moment, and this made January stop protesting.

“All right. Thank you for making sure I get home at a decent hour.” She turned the card over as she took his left hand in hers. “Let’s see.” And then all she could do was stare at the business card as if she had never seen one before.

Chapter Three

Rolling the snifter in her hand, Mallory inhaled the aroma of the Rémy Martin cognac with a feeling of sudden calm. She didn't often indulge, but when she did, this brand made all the difference. After today's showdown—not one of the worst with Peter, but bad enough—she could use the comfort of the familiar scent. Her father had been a cognac afficionado, and Mallory had often sat on his lap as a little girl while he was going through papers, a glass of cognac by his side.

Mallory was not eager to rehash today's argument, but the fact that January had been a witness to the way Peter behaved made it hard for her to let it go. It had been refreshing how January had stood her ground against Peter, and it had been quite educational to see her ex backpedal when HR's policies came up. The last thing he wanted was for old and new clients to catch wind of anything untoward going on at his law firm. Unfortunately, this didn't extend to how he had treated his wife the last few years.

Sipping the cognac, Mallory walked along the panoramic window and studied the falling snow that only moments ago had presented as a torrential rain. Christmas had been three weeks ago, and it had been a sad affair weatherwise, not unusual for Seattle. It hadn't bothered Mallory, who had let the holidays pass her by without doing much about it on a personal level. She had spent all her time with her foundation making sure that as many people as possible had some sort of festivities. The only time she had felt the holiday spirit coming on was when she and her employees were able to have Santa show up in shelters and soup kitchens.

The road that wound itself up to her house, which was located at the top of a hill, was almost snowed over, but a car still made its way up. Frowning, as she wasn't expecting anyone, Mallory followed its progress. She shared the hill with two other properties. One neighbor was away for the weekend, but it could be a delivery or visitor to the bachelor living on the other side of the cul-de-sac.

To Mallory's surprise, the car, a cab, turned toward her driveway. It stopped and the driver jumped out and rounded it and opened the door. A woman dressed in a long, black coat with a hood and knee-high boots more made for the city than plodding through the snow got out. She wasn't very tall, and the pulled-up hood made it impossible to identify her.

A man, tall, gangly, and all too familiar, got out of the cab after the woman. He was dressed in his blue trench coat, which wasn't warm enough in this weather. A hat covered his white hair, and he held the briefcase she gave him for Christmas more than ten years ago.

"What the hell?" Mallory put the snifter down on the baby grand piano and hurried through the house to the front door. She flung it open just as her grandfather walked along her driveway with the cab driver and the woman flanking him.

"Granddad? What are you doing here? In this weather—and at this hour?" Mallory heard her voice being too shrill, but she was stunned to see him.

"Surprising you, sweet girl," her grandfather said, his beautiful baritone voice warming her, despite her shock to see him. "I had help getting here, thank God. The bus broke down and this girl saved my life." Granddad smiled a little too broadly, and Mallory could see he was shivering.

"Come inside." She held the door open and let Granddad pass. The woman hesitated at the threshold but stepped into the foyer when Mallory motioned for her to do so.

"Hey, I got to keep going while I can still make my way down the hill. If you're going to make it home, lady, you need to come now." The cab driver spoke up.

"I should, yes. You'll be okay now, Constantine," the woman said, keeping her face turned toward him.

"I'll be fine, but you should meet my granddaughter. I'm sure she can drive you home later. It's not far, right?" Granddad took off his trench coat, and Mallory took it when he looked confused at what to do with it.

"I need an explanation regarding what's going on. I would appreciate if you could stay a while and help me sort this 'surprise' out." Mallory turned to the young woman. "Please."

"All right," the woman murmured, turning to the cab driver. "Thanks for coming so quickly. Let me get my card—"

"I won't hear of it." Her grandfather's voice still had the resounding tone from the days when he commanded every room without really trying. "Here you go, young man. You were most helpful." He walked over to the doorway and handed over a set of bills. "Keep the change, please."

"Thank you, sir. Stay safe now." The cab driver nodded to them and walked back to his car.

"Let's get you warm and comfortable before we call your staff." Mallory hung the trench coat on the handle on the outside of the foyer wardrobe. She turned to the woman and said, "Your coat—" only to stare in disbelief. The woman had removed the coat and held it folded over her right arm.

"Good evening, Ms. Davigne," January Wild said, as she smoothed down her straight blond hair. "What a coincidence, huh?"

That was putting it mildly. January looked concerned, which was hardly surprising. She had some explaining to do, but not here in the foyer.

"Why don't you go to the living room and sit down, Granddad?" Mallory motioned toward the spacious room with the panoramic window she just left. "I'll bring you something hot to drink."

"Let me help you, Constantine," January said and offered her arm. "You seem a little unsteady."

"I'm fine, my dear. Just a little cold. I seem to have forgotten to put on my cardigan." Granddad still took January's proffered arm and allowed her to guide him into the living room. Mallory followed just behind them, not comfortable with how January took over the care of her grandfather in her own home with such ease.

Her grandfather sat in one of the recliners, and another big grin spread over his face. "Now, this is the ticket," he said and patted the armrests. He found the button that maneuvered the footrest and chuckled as he got comfortable.

Mallory took one of the cashmere blankets and draped it over his legs. “There you go. I’ll be back with some hot tea if that’s all right?”

Granddad nodded. “Think you can scare up a cookie too, perhaps?” He winked at her.

“I’m sure I can. Chocolate chip?” Mallory smoothed down his thick, white hair.

“You know me well, darling girl.” Granddad closed his eyes, still smiling. “I’ll just rest my eyes in the meantime.”

Mallory regarded him for a few moments before turning to January. “Join me in the kitchen, please. I need to know what happened.”

In the kitchen, Mallory pointed to one of the island stools. “Please, have a seat.”

January climbed the tall stool and then rubbed her face with both hands. “This wasn’t the Friday evening I had in mind.” She sighed. “The most important thing is that your grandfather is all right.”

“He said you saved his life. What did he mean by that?” Mallory set the electric kettle to boil water.

“He means he came close to sliding off the seat and down into the aisle. The floor was lower along the center of the bus, and it would have been quite the fall. He was sure he might have broken something if he’d fallen.”

“Why were you on that particular bus?” Mallory wasn’t going to comment on such a dramatic deduction.

“It’s my bus. I mean, it’s the bus I always ride home from work. I get off where you would normally switch buses to get to this part of town.” January shrugged. “It was just happenstance that I ended up sitting across the aisle from Constantine.”

Mallory forced her tense shoulders to lower themselves as she pulled three mugs from a cabinet. “Do you drink tea?”

“Sometimes. Thank you.” January traced the pattern of the marble countertop with her index finger. “I really should get home now that your grandfather is safe. This, my being here, isn’t a good idea at all.” She looked up at Mallory with a frown. “If Peter finds out, God knows what he’ll think.”

“You think he’ll suspect you of colluding with the enemy?” Mallory placed tea bags in the mugs. She knew Peter was quick to anger even when his life was going smoothly. January was correct in her assumption that her presence in Mallory's home would not go down well with Peter.

"What's that sound?" January asked, tilting her head. "Is that the dogs?"

Mallory was just about to pour the steaming hot water into the mugs. "Damn it. That's Corma and Hera. I forgot I let them out a little while ago. They want to come in."

"Let me get them while you finish the tea." January slid off the stool. "Where…?"

"Through that door and to your left. Use my boots." Mallory watched with reluctant fascination how January hurried across the kitchen and pushed her feet into the lined rubber boots that Mallory used for the backyard during the winter season.

January went outside in just her trouser suit, and Mallory wanted to kick herself for not remembering to tell her about the Canada Goose jacket that hung on a hook just beside the kitchen door. She could hear her call out the dogs' names.

It only took January a couple of minutes to return with Corma and Hera. The two retrievers acted as if they hadn't seen Mallory in weeks, but only until Corma stuck her nose up in the air and sniffed intently. She gave a low woof and took off toward the living room.

"Bring your mug. I have to make sure they don't try to sit on Granddad's lap, both of them." Mallory grabbed two of the mugs and hurried after the dogs. To her relief, they were flanking her grandfather on both sides, licking his fingertips and wagging their tail in utter bliss at the sight of him.

"These are my other sweet girls," Granddad said, and Mallory was relieved to see that he had rosy cheeks and appeared a little less out of it.

"They adore you." Mallory made sure the dogs lay down and handed Granddad his tea. "Careful. It's—"

"Hot. I can tell." Granddad looked just behind Mallory. "And there's my guardian angel. Come sit down, girl. Are you still cold? You're shivering."

Looking over her shoulder, Mallory saw that January was clinging to her mug with both hands and trembling. Cursing under her breath, Mallory pointed to the corner of the couch closest to her grandfather.

"There. Have a seat. And for God's sake, use one of the blankets." Mallory pulled her phone from her back pocket and dialed the home care staff that normally took care of Granddad's needs. After talking to an infuriatingly indifferent young person, she harnessed the impulse to send the innocent phone through the closest window. Instead, she placed it on the coffee table and sat on the opposite end of the couch from January.

"First of all, thank you for helping Granddad," Mallory said slowly. "A strange fluke, but I am truly appreciative that you came to his aid now that he got it into his head to visit with me." She shot her grandfather a firm look. "Next time, you call me. That's non-negotiable. What if I hadn't been home?"

"You're right." Granddad sighed. "I didn't think of that."

"I would have taken him home with me and then located his address and made sure he got back in one piece. Still, Constantine, you took a big risk. Just look at the weather. It's coming down even worse now. Huge snowflakes. I was just out for a minute, and I'm soaked."

Mallory winced. Of course. "I didn't realize. Do you need to borrow a shirt, or a sweater? At the very least, you need a towel."

January colored faintly. "I…no…I mean, it's not that bad." She pulled the blanket up under her chin.

"You just said you're soaked." Mallory couldn't take her eyes off January. Her damp hair was becoming wavy as it dried. This meant she straightened it in the mornings. Was her natural hair curly? Mallory had only seen her with shiny, straight hair, parted in the middle in a perfect shoulder-length hairdo. "Come with me." She waved to January to follow her. Before she stepped out of sight of her grandfather, she shot him a firm glance. "You remain where you are and I'll fetch you something dry as well, all right?"

"Certainly, sweetheart. You're always so considerate." He waved at her and then closed his eyes.

"He's truly exhausted. Not sure how long he's been on different buses," January said where she padded on sock-clad feet behind Mallory.

"I'd guess at least four. Not that I ever use public transport." Mallory opened the linen closet in the closest bathroom. "Here. Use whatever you need. I'll go help my grandfather and then I'll find something for you to wear."

January colored and studied her clothes. "The downpour turned into snowflakes nearly the size of mittens, and that did a number on my best office suit." She sighed but then grabbed a towel. "Thanks, though."

"You're welcome. I'll be back." Mallory took two towels and then stopped by the guest room across the hall and pulled a terrycloth guest robe from the closet. She checked on her grandfather and saw that he was asleep. Loath to wake him, Mallory knew she had to since he was sensitive to the cold. He would suffer badly from sitting in damp clothes.

"Grandad?" She gently shook his shoulder, and he slowly opened his eyes. "Your trousers are all right, but we need to get you out of that shirt. I have a nice robe you can borrow." Mallory held up the garment.

"That's very stylish. Forest green is a favorite color of mine." Granddad sighed. "And you're correct as always, dear girl, I seem to be a bit damp. I hope I haven't ruined your chair."

Mallory helped her grandfather out of his shirt and tie. "Never mind the chair. Here we go." She steadied him as he stood and pulled on the robe. "There. Better?"

"I'm quite comfortable, thank you." Granddad looked at the couch. "Would you mind if I tried out your guest bed for a spell? The couch is really not the place to have a nap, not when you're entertaining another guest." He began to move toward the bedroom wing of her house. "It's over here unless I'm mistaken."

"It is. And you can stay in my guest room for as long as you like." Mallory knew she was promising way too much, but right now, all she wanted was for him to be safe. She guided him into the guestroom and up on the bed. Covering him with a wool blanket, she made sure he had bottles of water on the nightstand and left the door slightly ajar.

Sighing, she walked toward the bathroom to put his shirt in the hamper. As she opened the door, she cursed under her breath, having forgotten that January was still in there, waiting for something dry to wear.

Chapter Four

January pivoted and pulled the towel closer around her when the door swung open. Mallory stood there, looking as stunned as January felt.

"For heaven's sake," Mallory said and pressed her lips together. "I apologize. Unbelievably, I lost track of what I was doing." She tossed what looked like Constantine's shirt and tie into a hamper. "I'll find you something to wear while we dry your clothes."

"Thanks." January tried to sound casual but found it difficult to take her eyes off this unfamiliar version of Mallory Davigne. Where January had mostly seen the stern—even outraged—Mallory, she had occasionally also glimpsed other sides to her. Humor, regret, and even sadness. Now she knew what bewildered embarrassment looked like on those classic features. No matter what expression Mallory displayed, it was only adding to the passion January felt for her.

"Come with me. That way you can pick something out yourself. Saves time." Mallory was already walking down the hallway when she turned her head over her shoulder. "Bring your clothes."

January scooped up her outfit, acutely aware that the only garment not soaked through was her blue lace panties. Everything else needed to go in the tumble dryer.

They entered a large room that turned out to be a huge walk-in-closet. Walnut shelves and open cabinets displayed Mallory's impressive wardrobe. In the center of the room sat a large counter that held drawers on both sides. The glass top showed off watches and jewelry that made the ceiling above it sparkle.

"The washer-dryer unit is over in that corner." Mallory pointed it out. "Let me know if you need help with the settings."

"All right. Thanks again." January stepped into the room and her bare feet sank into the lush, off-white rug. She did her best to keep the towel in place while maneuvering her pile of clothes. Thankfully, they were all able to go in the dryer. Just as she opened the hatch to the dryer and pushed her clothes inside, everything went dark.

A stunned silence, and then Mallory's sharp voice reached her. "What happened? What did you do?"

What did *she* do? January held on tight to the towel. "Nothing. I just opened the dryer and put my clothes in. I haven't even touched the controls." Annoyed now, and a bit freaked out at finding herself in a pitch-black, unfamiliar house. Wait, pitch-black… "It's the entire house. We should look outside to see if it's the entire neighborhood. And check on your grandfather."

"Right."

January heard shuffling of fabric, a muttered curse, and an exasperated sigh. All was quiet for a few moments and then Mallory spoke again, sounding much closer. "Here you go. A leisure suit. It'll be big on you, but it's something, at least."

January held out one hand to receive the clothes, but misjudged where Mallory was standing. Her hand touched something soft and firm, eliciting a clipped gasp. Realizing she had just brushed along Mallory's entire left breast, nipple and all, January pressed her lips tightly around a panicked whimper before she was ready to speak.

"I'm so sor—"

"Get dressed. I'll find the flashlights and candles and check on Granddad." And then Mallory was gone. Of course, she knew the layout of her own house and was able to move much faster. January felt around the hems and linings of the clothes, hoping not to put them on backward.

She put on the amazingly soft leisure suit, and she didn't care that she imagined the garments carrying Mallory's scent—in her mind they were. This made her inhale in a half-guilty sort of way, which was of course absurd. Turning toward the barely closed door, she could see a soft light flicker, like from a candle, around the doorframe. This lit up the walk-in closet enough for her to spot a pair of white socks that had fallen to the floor next to her. After putting them on, she went in search of Mallory and found her coming out from what had to be the guest room.

"He's asleep. I'll just leave the door open. I don't dare leave him with an open flame in there, even if it's only a candle." Mallory sighed. "And I looked outside. It's affecting the whole neighborhood."

"I hope they'll have it fixed soon. I need to dry my clothes and call for another car." January pushed her fingers through her hair. As she suspected, large ringlets of curls were forming around her face. "Or an Uber. That might be quicker."

"It's not safe to venture out in this," Mallory said firmly. "Why don't you take a seat and I'll get you something to drink? I wish I could get you something hot. You're still shivering." Mallory indicated January's hands.

She looked down at her fingers and was about to object and say she wasn't cold at all any longer when she saw the obvious tremors. January couldn't very well tell Mallory that it was her presence that made her tremble. "Just a little. I'm much warmer now, thanks."

"Still. You can take the couch and choose a blanket from that basket." Mallory pointed at a wicker basket to the left of the couch.

"Thanks." January knew when it was time to relent. As much as she would rather have placed the entire city of Seattle between her and Mallory, she had to be practical. The snowflakes were even bigger now, and it was coming down faster. She hugged the dark blue blanket to her and groaned. "This isn't going to melt in a few hours, is it?"

"I doubt it. If it were just a matter of snow, a cab could make its way up here, but in this storm, it'd be suicide." Mallory didn't wait for a reply but left the room.

January sat on the couch and pulled her legs up. Her still-damp hair clung to her shoulders, and it was a relief to place the blanket around her and lift her hair up and over it. The situation was surreal, no, unrealistic, even. Weeks away from getting her hands on her much-coveted letter of recommendation that would open a lot of doors for her, she was in the presence of the one person who could screw everything up for her. If Peter found out that she was at Mallory's house, and might have to spend the night, he would dissolve into one of his tantrums. He was infamous for his bad temper these days, and fraternizing with the cause of his lack of self-control was asking for trouble.

Mallory returned with a tray of two steaming mugs and what looked like cheese sandwiches. "I have two propane burners on my stove, thank God, but I still hope the blackout will be done with before I actually have to use them for cooking." She eyed January as she placed the mug in front of her. "I hope sandwiches are enough for now."

"It's great. Thank you." January knew she sounded short, but her situation was far from ideal, and all she could do was pray that Peter wouldn't find out about it. At least not until after her notice was up. To avoid talking, she grabbed one of the sandwiches and bit into fresh bread with luxurious cheese. Rumor had it that Mallory Davigne came from old money and Peter Sundh wouldn't be as successful as he was if it weren't for her connections and wealth. And the stupid idiot couldn't appreciate what he had. January chewed miserably on the sandwich. She would have given all her limbs for a chance to get to know Mallory the right way. How many times had she daydreamed about Mallory turning out to be a lesbian, or bi, and that they met under different circumstances where January hadn't been employed by her ex? Too many to count.

Mallory wasn't eating, but cupped her mug with both hands and sipped from it while she sat in one of the armchairs, her legs pulled up. She had pulled one of the blankets over her legs, and now she studied January over the rim of the mug.

"An interesting coincidence, this." Mallory placed her blue mug on the side table to her left. "My grandfather hasn't been on one of his excursions in a while, and when he used to leave home unattended before, it was always to go to the cemetery, to the family grave. Today, he came to visit with me, completely unexpected as far as I can understand, and *you* are on the bus." She tilted her head and her glossy, light brown hair with meticulous golden highlights feathered out against her shoulder. "I know it's pure happenstance, but I have a healthy suspicion against coincidences, generally speaking." She still had her left hand around the mug and now pulled her index finger in a slow circle around its rim.

January swallowed. That looked far too much like a caress, and she wasn't prepared for how the muscles in her abdomen clenched at the sight. "If you think that I had someone follow your granddad and made sure I got on the same bus—"

"No." Mallory let go of the mug and interrupted January with a quick, dismissive gesture. "That never entered my mind. Despite the circumstances of how we know each other, I find that a ridiculous notion. If it were Peter, though—" She shrugged, and then appeared to study the ceiling. January suspected Mallory wanted to hide her face to not give too much away. She could have told her it was too late for that. January had furtively studied Mallory for months, until she feared she was becoming stalker-adjacent. All she had to do was close her eyes and images of how Mallory moved appeared. Certain and with purpose, the cadence of her heels—usually at least three inches, if not four—made January's heart pick up the same rhythm. Mallory's hair moved half a beat later, dancing around her shoulders if she kept it loose, its highlights sending sparkles like tiny fireflies.

As if to contradict Mallory's strong gait, the gentle sway of her hips had been known to enter January's dreams, awake and asleep. She had pictured them dancing, swaying slowly, her hands on Mallory's hips, or waist, to a slow, sultry song. Not above torturing herself, January had pictured Mallory burying her face against her neck, humming the melody, as she cupped January's ass.

"No matter," Mallory said and sighed. "It is what it is. The most important thing to focus on, to mitigate potential fallout, is to strategize."

Blinking, January tried to push the idea of dancing with Mallory from her mind. "Fallout?" She fumbled for the mug Mallory brought her and nearly knocked it over, only rescuing it at the last second. "Whoops."

"Unless I'm misinformed of your situation, you're not too keen on having Peter know you're fraternizing with the enemy, correct?" Mallory remained still, but the way the cushion behind her folded around her, she seemed to press her back harder against it. "As for me, that should be obvious. If Peter finds out that you're here, no matter the circumstances, he'll use it to challenge our prenup in a heartbeat."

"What could possibly be in the prenup that would give him that chance?" January took one more sip of the tea, and then replaced the mug on the coffee table with great care.

Mallory's shoulders rose, but then she lowered them, and January could see the effort that took. "It's hardly a secret that I'm bisexual. He would argue that not only were you giving me confidential information, but you did so as part of intense pillow talk." Her chin set in a clear challenge, Mallory turned her head and looked out the window at the snow.

January tried to get her dervish-like thoughts to calm down and sort themselves into their respective compartments. The one squealing "She's bi!" was particularly difficult to harness, right after the one about fraternization. Both sucked the oxygen out of the space around her.

"January?" Mallory slowly raised a very deliberate eyebrow. The way she did it shouldn't have been all it took to kick January's arousal into high gear, but it did.

"Um. Well. He won't hear it from me, if that's what you fear. As you said, I have a lot to lose as well."

"Worth fifty percent of eight hundred million dollars?" Mallory's upper lip pulled up in a low growl.

"Worth two years of my life where I have worked twelve-hour days and tons of overtime to not risk the letter of recommendation I need to stay on track and not screw up my career. Not everything is dollars and cents." She put her sock-clad feet on the thick rug, ready to walk out of there, even if it meant hoofing it through the snow to the closest public transport.

"Point taken," Mallory said, and to January's surprise, she seemed less on edge. "It proves my point, though. We both have a lot to risk, or lose, and we've got to be smart about this."

"Your granddad would be able to state how he and I ran into each other and that I only wanted to make sure he got here in one piece." As soon as she spoke the words, January realized they might not be enough.

"He's often quite clear of mind, but there are days when he's utterly confused. He might just as well agree with an arbiter suggesting that we're in a relationship." Mallory colored faintly. "No good deed goes unpunished. Obviously." She checked the time. "Speaking of Granddad…I better check on him."

"And I should go," January said and stood. The blanket fell off her legs and she began to shiver.

"Don't be ridiculous. That'd be insane in this weather. Wait until daylight and then make an informed decision." Mallory gave her such a stern glance, January promptly sat back down. She tugged the blanket off the floor and curled up under it in the corner of the couch.

"All right. Let me know if I can help with anything." Inwardly chastising herself for always being the goody-two-shoes assistant, January grabbed a coffee table book, knowing full well it was too dark to read. Mallory's still slightly flushed face was too much to handle right now. All January could think of was kissing Mallory's lips. How the hell did she have this push-pull effect on her?

"Thanks. I've got it." Mallory left the room on quick feet. As she was wearing soft indoor shoes, her steps were close to inaudible, which January found oddly jarring. She looked around the room, hoping to see a fireplace. She wouldn't mind throwing a log on a roaring fire, but all she spotted was something resembling a gas-driven fireplace. She had no idea how to operate one of those and was not about to risk blowing up Mallory's house.

She heard murmuring voices from the other end of the house but couldn't make out what they were saying. Hopefully, Constantine had not become ill from his adventure on public transportation and getting soaked. He seemed like a sweet older gentleman, and January loved the soft timbre of Mallory's voice when she spoke to and about her grandfather. It was so different from her normal clipped tone. Then she realized that Mallory hadn't sounded that short since she'd come upon January in the bathroom and slowly perused her where she stood wearing just a towel. It was probably an exaggeration to label that a pivotal moment, but it wasn't entirely untrue. Something had changed, but January was not going to sit and guess about the exact nature of it. She was prone to wishful daydreaming, but that wouldn't lead to anything but heartache.

January grew still inside. Heartache? Why had her brain gone down that route? Sure, she found Mallory immensely attractive and that had been the case for months, and she could even concede to being infatuated, but to think that her heart was in danger was a bit of a stretch, surely? And yet, was it? Crushes and physical attraction didn't run that deep. So what was going on? Was she truly falling for a woman who was the ultimate forbidden fruit, and thus, a surefire way to heartbreak?

Chapter Five

After helping her grandfather to settle properly under the covers after he had some soup and warm milk, Mallory stood in the doorway and regarded the lovely old man who had suffered tremendous heartbreak in his life. Losing his son when Mallory was only three, and then his wife a decade later, had shaped him, but not hardened him. He had always been there for her, and when his memory began to fail him, she tried to return his love the same way. If it hadn't been for the exhausting war with Peter, she could have been there for her grandfather so much more. She had tried to discuss the topic of her grandfather moving in with them while they were still married, but she had the notion this was the last straw for Peter, and certainly for her. The tirades Peter had gone on, and his offensive words regarding her grandfather, had certainly hindered her struggle to keep up appearances.

Mallory returned to the candlelit kitchen with the dirty dishes and placed them in the sink. She looked at the dishwasher, which had run its cycle, and contemplated emptying it, but confessed to herself that she was only stalling. Going back to the living room seemed, as ridiculous as it sounded, dangerous. January had witnessed every stage of Peter's and her divorce journey from the front row. Sometimes, Mallory had detected sympathy in January's expression, but mostly, she had kept an impassive demeanor.

Mallory was close to the final signatures being handled at her divorce attorney's office if Peter could just refrain from his innate pettiness.

Straightening her sleeves and then the hem of her top, she detoured to her bedroom to fetch two duvets and proper pillows, and then returned to the living room. As it turned out, she needn't have worried. Covered with three cashmere blankets, January appeared fast asleep.

Mallory still covered her with a duvet before taking the second duvet and returned to an armchair. She curled up and covered her now shivering body. Using two small decorative pillows, she found a position that hopefully wouldn't give her any serious kinks in her back or neck. Sighing deeply, she closed her eyes, certain that she wouldn't sleep, but she would at least rest a bit.

Mallory jerked awake and then looked around the dark room. Disoriented, she noticed the tip of her nose was cold, and so were her fingertips, which gripped the corner of the duvet. She blinked hard as if that would help her see better, but the darkness was still as impenetrable. Remembering her circumstances with the blackout and snowstorm, she could now tell that the candles had burned out. How long had she been asleep? She checked her phone that sat on the coffee table. Gah…it was 4:35 a.m. Which was the same as the middle of the night.

A whimper originated from the couch and Mallory realized it was the same sound as the one that woke her up. She sat up and turned on the flashlight on her cell, directing it toward January. To her dismay, it was obvious that she was in the claws of a bad dream. Her normally so pretty face was distorted into a mask of horror, and she seemed to push at something in front of her. Her flailing sent the duvet and the blankets off her and slipping down onto the floor.

Sighing, but more from jitters than exasperation, Mallory rounded the coffee table and picked up the duvet. She draped it carefully around January but had to adjust it right away again since she pushed at it, muttering, "No, you can't. S'not fair."

"Hey." Mallory crouched next to the couch and gently gripped January's shoulder. "You're having a bad dream."

"Not my fault." January opened her eyes and stared dazedly up at the ceiling. "What?"

"You're in my living room having a bad dream." Mallory pushed the duvet firmer around January. "Are you all right?"

January blinked repeatedly, but then appeared to wake up more and shifted her focus to Mallory. "Damn. Yes. I did dream. Was I loud?" She rubbed her cheeks.

"No. You kicked off the covers. I was afraid you'd get cold. Power's still out."

"Oh. Okay. I see." January sat up and pushed wild strands of hair from her face. "How's your granddad?"

"Asleep and doing well." Mallory slid onto the couch next to January. "You seemed tortured by something. In your dream."

Avoiding her gaze, January laced her fingers together. "I—I can't remember. Dreams. Thankfully, they leave us fast enough. Mostly." A fast, broad smile made her seem uneasy rather than casual.

"That's true." Not sure why she pried, as January's dreams were none of her business, Mallory persisted. "You said something like 'no, you can't, it's not fair.'"

January raised her hands, palms up. "No clue."

Mallory couldn't very well force her to share what had made her sleep so fitfully, but something told her it had something to do with their current situation. "No matter. Well, I'm going to try to go back to sleep in the armchair. I've closed off all the other rooms, except where Granddad sleeps, which will help this room remain reasonably warm." She moved to get up, but stopped when January's slender hand gripped her wrist. "What?"

"You can't sleep in the chair. It looks comfy enough to sit in, but sleeping an entire night—"

"A few hours are all I need." Mallory looked down at January's hand. The touch was firm, but not hard. And it was scorching her skin. Was January aware that her thumb was caressing her? She certainly was, and it was making her tremble, which of course was absurd.

"Even that will be enough to hurt you," January whispered.

"Where do you suggest I sleep? The rest of the rooms are too cold." Mallory shook her head.

"The couch. It's huge. And long. There's room right here." January's voice was barely audible, and yet every word sent tremors through Mallory's body.

"If you're sure," she said slowly.

"It's the smart thing. To stay warm. To be comfortable. We can sleep head to toe if you like." Shifting closer to the backrest, January gestured at the space she created.

Mallory swallowed hard. "If you would have seen how you kick your legs when you dream, you wouldn't suggest that."

January lay down with her head against the stack of small pillows by the armrest again and held up the duvet. "By all means. You've persuaded me. This way, then."

Mallory's throat sent a groan forward before she resumed control. She collected her duvet and the proper pillows from the recliner and returned to the couch. She gave January one of the pillows, which January promptly placed under her head instead of the decorative pillows, and then hesitated briefly.

Nobody would know. Least of all Peter. It would make it easier to function the next day when she would have to figure out the whole situation properly. She had all kinds of reasons to take January up on her wild offer. And yet she knew she was making up excuses while trying to hide the true reason she was now lying down with her back to January. There would only be this one chance for this, with her. Once January's two-year tenure was over, she would move on to her much brighter future—perhaps in another city, and even another state. January would be gone, and if Mallory insisted on being prudent and sleeping curled up in a chair, there would not even be the memory of feeling the warmth of January's body next to hers.

"You're balancing on the edge." January placed a gentle hand on Mallory's hip, making her jump.

At first, Mallory thought January meant figuratively speaking—because wasn't that the truth—but then she realized that she was holding on to the edge of the pillow with a painful grip. Not for fear of falling onto the floor, but to not lean closer against January. She forced her hands to relax and maneuvered back a few inches. Utter shock made her gasp when January's arm slipped around her waist and pulled her closer, virtually spooning her. Apart from the audacity, this would never work. Mallory had always hated having anyone crowd her space in bed. The mere touch of someone else's breath could be enough for her to switch rooms or leave their home entirely. Hardly an option now when the house was hers and getting colder by the minute.

"Better? Can't have you fall off and risk hitting your beautiful face on the coffee table." January was so close that Mallory could feel every word she spoke move the hair at the back of her head.

"I'm fine," she said after clearing her throat. It was ridiculous. Her onset of nerves was driving her crazy, and her gut reaction to push back further into January's arms was unfathomable. When had she ever felt like this? Certainly way before she met Peter, if ever.

"Good." January sighed and grew even softer against Mallory's back. "Mmm."

Did she just hum? Mallory reached out her hand for her phone that still lit up part of the living room. She turned off the flashlight and put it back down, grateful they were now in darkness, even if she was facing away from January. She tried to disregard the fact that January still had her arm around her waist. Not that she didn't want it there—the opposite, in fact—but she had no idea if January was this free-spirited with most people, or if this was, well, personal. Was she just being conceited when she remembered seeing desire and confusion in January's expression on a few occasions? Mallory didn't think so. Which made this situation even worse. More dangerous. If Peter got even a hint that Mallory had as much as looked at another, well, love interest, she would lose half her inherited and earned fortune. Her foundation would suffer, and that meant the people who depended on its aid would hurt as well.

"Think you can sleep?" January shifted her hand back onto Mallory's hip.

"Of course," Mallory lied. "You comfortable?" Why the hell did she ask that? Why keep any sort of conversation going and risk saying something she would truly regret?

"Very." January shuddered as if to belie her own words. "Just a little, eh, nervous."

This made Mallory snap her eyes open. "Nervous?" She half turned back to try to see January despite the darkness.

"I'm being too forward, maybe? I mean, I'm usually not this brazen. Not sure where it comes from." January chuckled and there was something, an undertone of sadness, in her voice. "Perhaps it's because this situation happened even though it shouldn't have."

"How do you mean?" Mallory held her breath to not miss a word, or cue, from January.

"My being in your house. During a blackout. I mean, in a couple of weeks, you won't have a reason to stop by the office, and even if you did, I won't be there. That would make running into you incredibly unlikely. Perhaps that's why I'm acting a bit out of character. You know, making the most of this last chance of finding out…" January's voice became husky. "Damn it."

"What—what's wrong?" Mallory managed to turn around to face January and not slip off the couch while pivoting. "Are you crying?" Now she was genuinely concerned.

"No. Eh…a little? Just from being tired, I'm sure." January drew a trembling breath and Mallory felt rather than saw her wipe at her cheeks. "It's been a day."

"Yes. It has. Tell me. What did you want to find out?" Mallory asked. She meant to sound careful but heard how fast she spoke.

"You're relentless." January pressed her forehead against Mallory's shoulder. "This. You. Obviously."

Obviously? Nothing was obvious, but some things began to make a little bit more sense. Dread mixed with desire as Mallory debated what to say. It was one thing to suffer alone and in silence when pining for a much younger woman who could never be hers. As things stood, it was a completely other matter if there was even the slightest, remotest chance any of her feelings were reciprocated.

Chapter Six

January could barely make out Mallory's classic features in the dark. Being a mere few inches apart, she smelled the expensive, warm, and spicy perfume she associated with Mallory.

"There's nothing obvious." Mallory spoke as if through clenched teeth.

"You mean, we can never acknowledge that there is something since we both stand to lose so much." Annoyance mixed with empathy as January tried to decipher Mallory's words. How the hell was she supposed to be able to read between the lines when the woman spoke in such short sentences most of the time? Granted, Mallory's tone was easier to interpret, but there were still too many ways to misconstrue.

Mallory seemed to mull over January's words. "That about sums it up, I suppose. It's absurd to not acknowledge that there is a certain, I guess, attraction, which as you so astutely pointed out, is enough to toss us both into positions where we can lose everything."

Having just assumed that Mallory had decided on brevity being her way of dealing with this situation, January now had to try to decipher what was essentially a confessional speech from Mallory.

"Hey. Let me wrap my brain around this." January still kept her hand just above Mallory's hip. She gently squeezed her while trying to figure things out. "You don't deny that we have a mutual attraction going on?"

A brief shudder gave the palm January rested against Mallory a buzz. "No. As ill-timed and risky as it is, denying it is…" Mallory shrugged. "And with risky, of course I mean potentially disastrous."

"For both of us." January wished with every cell in her body that she could just shrug the ramifications away—for both of them. To hold Mallory this close, making sure she wasn't cold…the fact that it was equally heartbreaking as it was miraculous didn't escape her.

The sound of paws against the hardwood floor made January flinch. She had all but forgotten about Mallory's dogs.

"They've been checking on Granddad. They're bound to settle down." Mallory patted January's hand.

The dogs reappearing made January lose track of her thoughts, but that didn't help the situation. Mallory was still in her arms, and January's senses were still filled with her scent.

"He tried to get custody of them," Mallory said quietly. "The dogs."

January knew this. "A dick move."

Mallory chuckled, but it wasn't a happy sound. "Agreed."

"I hope you realize that the only reason I'm appearing as if I'm loyal to your ex is because he owes me that letter of recommendation after two years of, well, not hell, maybe, but it's been a lot." January hoped she hadn't been too open. At some point she would have to decide if she trusted Mallory not to use her words against her in the future. It seemed that their situations were on an even keel, but perhaps that was just the way it appeared.

"You have been very loyal from a business point of view. I would have thought that'd be enough for me to be able to harness this…this *attraction*." Mallory's exasperation was evident in her voice.

January didn't know what to do to reassure her. Without thinking, she stroked up and down Mallory's hip in an attempt to soothe. The way it made Mallory tremble and hold her breath proved it wasn't having the desired effect.

"What are you doing? Are you trying to prove just how thin my resilience is?" Mallory hissed.

"No. Not at all. I'm…damn, I don't know what I'm doing, or thinking." January slipped her arm around Mallory's waist. "What I do know is that this opportunity to at least hold you will never come again. Nobody knows that I'm here. Nobody ever will. It may be selfish, but I can't help how I feel."

Mallory grew still for a few long moments, and then she placed a hand on top of January's. "You're not playing fair." Her voice had grown stark. "You show up at my house and prove to be just as dangerous as I feared. It isn't fair that I must be the strong one."

"I know. But you don't have to. Just this once, this night, we're in a sort of limbo." January pressed against the backrest of the couch and tugged Mallory closer. She made sure the duvet was covering them as the tip of her nose proved the room was steadily growing colder. "Just holding on. That's all."

Mallory shifted and let out a sigh. Her breath was sweet and minty. "You're not thinking straight at all. If you think it'll be possible to just carry on as if nothing happened after this night, even if we weren't together here on the couch, you're delusional. Just being this close, will change everything." She pushed a hand into January's hair and tugged gently at it. "This suggests to me that you haven't quite grasped just how much I have fantasized about this. About having you this close. It's insane."

January gaped. Mallory's words were unfathomable. Impossible. And they sent all kinds of sensations through her system, and every single muscle in her abdomen and her thighs clenched. She whimpered, unable to keep the noise from leaving her lips. "Mallory."

"See? That just proves my point." Sounding almost angry, Mallory pressed her lips against January's, not painfully hard, but firm enough to convey her torment. January pulled Mallory even closer, their stomachs and breasts pressed together.

❖

Mallory's body went soft and pliable against January's as soon as she felt January's curves press against hers. Her lips eased up on the pressure and so did January's, even parting a little. She wasn't aware that she was holding her breath until pain began to spread along her chest and the urge to exhale made her pull back. She drew a couple of deep breaths, her hand still in January's hair, holding her in place.

"Kiss me again?" January whispered, her hand stroking up and down Mallory's back, over and over. "Please."

Mallory knew she would never be able to resist January when they were near each other. She slowly closed the distance between their mouths and claimed January's lips again. This time, she took the time to explore and sample the taste of her. She knew it was going to turn out to be the worst emotional mistake of her life, but January had a point. This was the only night they'd ever have. Even if they did run into each other again, perhaps even years from now, their lives would have moved on. The pain erupting in her chest at the thought of this being it, this being all she could have when it came to January Wild, made her sob.

January returned the kiss with so much tenderness, it almost soothed some of the emotional agony. When she carefully ran her tongue along Mallory's lower lip, it started a completely different torture. Mallory rolled on top of January and returned the caress, slipping her tongue between her lips, eager to taste her even deeper.

Moaning into January's mouth, Mallory explored it, over and over. Only when January wrapped a leg around her hip, effectively making room for her between her legs, did she raise her head.

January was staring up at her with hooded eyes. Her hands had moved under Mallory's shirt and now lay still against the bare skin of her waist.

Mallory's arms grew weak, and she could no longer support her weight. Instead, she grew heavy and pressed even closer to January. Every single curve of her body ignited where it met January's—even through layers of clothing. Bellies trembled against each other while breasts tried to find room by pressing together. Mallory pushed at the couch with her elbows, but it was a feeble attempt as all her brain could think was to kiss January again.

January's leg around Mallory's hip didn't exactly help cool things down. Instead, she held Mallory closer. Mallory didn't know when the undulation in her hips began. From one moment to the next, her aching core rubbed into January's, making them both gasp.

"Hot." Mallory tried to speak. "Too hot."

January's leg stilled. "Too much?"

Mallory's chest clenched as she found she couldn't lie. "Too hot for me to ever want to stop, but we must. You know why." She wanted to take the words back instantly, but no matter how she wished for things to be different, they weren't.

"Then you need to move," January said, her tone tender. "Mallory?"

Sliding back to the outer edge of the couch, Mallory felt as if she lost something precious, when their bodies disconnected. "There." That was all she managed at this point. One word.

January still had her fingertips on Mallory's hip, as if making sure that she wouldn't fall off. Like embers, they created fiery circles on the skin of her belly.

"Seems I don't have the same clear-minded sense of restraint as you do." January shook her head. "I'm starting to realize that braving the elements and going home might be my only chance to do the right thing."

"You can't. It's a blizzard out there. I won't allow it." Mallory clamped her mouth shut around her sentences.

"You won't allow it?" Predictably, January repeated her words in an "excuse me?" kind of voice.

"That came out wrong. I meant it's not advisable. The snowstorm. The cold. You would be taking your life in your hands." Mallory tried to think of more reasons, preferably reasons that didn't make her sound entirely unhinged. "I'd never forgive myself if something happened to you." Damn. That sounded too dramatic and over-the-top, no matter how true it was.

January pressed her face against Mallory's shoulder. "Turn your back against me again. I promise I won't rush out into the blizzard and get myself killed. Unless you'd rather move to one of your beds, you need to turn your back to me." January drew a trembling breath.

As if that would make things easier. Feeling January's breasts against her back and her thighs aligned with hers wasn't going to settle Mallory's arousal, but January was right. Being face-to-face with her lips within reach was more dangerous.

A confronting part of her questioned why it would be so bad if they did make love. January was here. It wasn't as if they'd be risking detection anymore if they had sex—or if they didn't. They could enjoy each other throughout the night, and since nobody knew January was here, no one would be the wiser about anything at all.

Furious at herself for allowing the destructive voice so much room, Mallory clenched her teeth. January settled in behind her, soft and, oddly enough, reassuring, in the way she aligned herself against Mallory's back. This feeling was enough to know the answer to the questions posed by the devil-may-care voice. What she felt for January wasn't just sex. Granted, she would have made love with her all night, if the circumstances weren't so against them. If their stars had aligned more favorably, nothing could have kept Mallory away from January.

And then, once she'd quenched the initial thirst for January, she would have done what she was doing now.

Reveling in the bittersweet sensation of what spending every single night in January's arms could have been like, Mallory had to settle for this night only, and knowing this prickled her heart with a thousand icicles.

"If this is all we'll ever have, it's at least something," January murmured into Mallory's hair. "I wish for a lot to be different, but as it isn't, this will be what I take away from the last two years."

Mallory swallowed several times before she could speak. She wasn't crying but knew there were tears evident in her voice when she said, "I hear you. And yes. At least it's something." She vowed not to waste a single moment sleeping. The gentle arms around her and January's breaths moving her hair were worth staying awake for.

And yet, Mallory fell asleep and when she woke up to sunshine, restored power, and tail-wagging dogs, she was alone on the couch. Rigid, but unsurprised, she rose and went looking for her grandfather. The house was quiet and getting warmer, and she was relieved to find him in the kitchen, having toast and coffee.

"You found your way around, Granddad. That's good." Mallory looked over at the coffee machine that was almost full. "Did you do all this?"

"Not at all, darling girl. That nice young woman from last night made this for me." Granddad bit into another piece of toast. "She seems like such a sweet girl."

"Yes, she does. She is." Mallory busied herself by pouring coffee into her mug. She had known it from the moment she woke up. January was gone.

Chapter Seven

January closed the long drawer where Peter kept hard copies of important documents. Everything was normally digitalized, but Peter insisted on current cases having hard copy backups. Another large cabinet held hard copies of wills. The cabinets in turn were kept in a room that was literally a fireproof safe.

"Glad you're better," one of her coworkers, Nina, said from behind. She was the likely replacement for January once she had moved on to her new job. She had applied for a position with a company across the city, where she would be the office manager for a nonprofit law firm. Turning her head over her shoulder as she reset the alarm for the document drawer, she smiled at Nina. "Thanks. Yeah, me too." January had called in sick yesterday and spent the day interviewing one more time for the law firm—and later in the evening—aching for Mallory's touch.

It had not been very courageous to leave Mallory's house before she woke on Saturday morning. Constantine had milled around the house, looking for the kitchen, and when she saw the old man, she'd been unable to just leave him to his own devices—even if that meant risking Mallory waking up. If she had been forced to face Mallory after their night on the couch, she wouldn't have been able to resist her—or mask her emotions. So, she made breakfast for Constantine, downed a quick coffee, and made her way down the hill in the snow that had already begun turning into slush. When she managed to raise an Uber, she went home and then hibernated all weekend as she tried to make plans for how to leave her job with her CV intact—and with her coveted letter of recommendation in hand.

The answer had been rather simple. She had a good rapport with the guy running HR, especially after keeping Peter from abusing the HR department, something he'd been infamous for before hiring her. This made her popular enough for the HR manager to assist her with general recommendations from Peter's firm. If she lucked out, she might stand a chance even without Peter's recommendation—but perhaps that was a naïve thought. She couldn't risk him going back on his word, as she had worked her ass off and lost all connection with friends and family in the process.

Not to mention being subjected to the amazing Mallory, who was now breaking January's heart even though she didn't have a clue about it. Walking out of Mallory's house, escorted by sleepy golden retrievers, was the hardest thing January had ever done on a personal level. She knew she had left something important behind her, and replacing that missing piece of her heart would take some doing, and time.

"A stomach bug?" Nina asked as she unlocked another drawer in the cabinet.

"Just a bad headache. All better." January shot Nina a broad smile and left the room. She headed back to her desk, which was located just outside Peter's office.

Obviously, he heard her as he bellowed her name. "January! Where were you? I need you in here now."

January gripped her tablet and hugged it against her chest as she entered his office. He was pacing over by the window, having tossed his jacket haphazardly across his desk, half covering his laptop. His hair stood on end, and if eyes could make something self-combust, he would have set her on fire.

"What can I do, Peter?" she asked calmly, even if she came close to creating a permanent indentation in the tablet. She wasn't afraid of him per se, but the way he had become unhinged so easily lately was unnerving.

"Grab your magic wand and make my fucking ex move to the other side of the world and take her crook of an attorney with her!" Peter pushed at his office chair, which only made it bounce against the desk and hit him in the shins. He cursed again and raised his hand as if to slam his fist against the window, but fortunately he thought better of it and stopped himself.

"These are private matters that don't concern me, Peter." Struggling to make her voice sound calm and cool, January stood straight with her shoulders pushed back. "If there is anything I can do that's purely practical, I'm ready to do so, of course."

Peter had resumed pacing but stopped at her words and glowered at her. "How the hell can you be this matter-of-fact when I'm being thoroughly screwed over by that bit—woman," he corrected himself at the last second. "This divorce was her idea, and that should have made the prenup invalid. Her attorney, who is a well-known weasel of the female persuasion, managed to find a loophole that made it possible for Mallory to claim 'unresolvable differences' on a very loose basis. And now, just as I was getting close to finding evidence of her not heeding the prenup in another way, she has the nerve to accuse me of, well, misconduct."

January gaped. She tried to smooth out her expression of utter shock, but it was damn near impossible. First, Peter insinuated that he knew something about Mallory's life after the separation, and now he was frothing at the mouth about Mallory's lawyer having similar evidence. Her stomach trembled and she wished more than anything that she'd taken another sick day.

"What can I do?" she asked again. She couldn't get out of the room fast enough where Peter's frustration and wrath seemed to make the air thicker.

Peter was still seething but seemed to be in control again. This made him lethal—she had seen him go cold before. It wasn't pretty. "I seem to remember you exchanging small talk with Mallory in the beginning of your employment here. Granted, that was when she and I were still okay." He tapped his nose a few times, something he often did when he was hashing out a plan. Brightening in a discouraging way, he pointed at her with his right index finger. "I'm going to a charity function on Friday evening. I happen to know Mallory will be there too. You'll be my plus-one—"

"Sir. Peter." Aghast, January held up her free hand, palm toward him. "That's not appropriate, I can't be seen with my superior—"

"You'd be there as my assistant, nothing else. I'll make that clear to HR if you are concerned. What I want from you is to chat her up, get her to talk about her future, professional—and private."

This was a crazy, terrible idea. Even if January hadn't been utterly in love with Mallory, it was skidding along so many rule-breakings, it was insane.

"I would rather not get involved in your marital issues. You know a lot of people. I'm sure any of your friends will be able to accompany you." January eased one step backward.

"That won't work. Our friends, they're all loyal to her. Goes to show what they don't know about her, which is a lot. She agreed to invest in my career, in *me*. It wouldn't even make a thimble-sized dent in her fortune. And yet she's acting as if I'm robbing her blind." Peter sat in his enormous leather chair.

"I'm sorry to hear that, but it's not something I can involve myself in. If such an action on my part reached a future employer, it could ruin everything for me. You need to look out for your future, but so do I." Hoping she sounded reasonable, because a person like Peter would notice someone coming off as pleading. He saw such things as pure weaknesses.

"Actually, the opposite," Peter said. There was something ugly in the way he laced his fingers and rested his chin on top of his joined hands. "I have drafted a glowing letter of recommendation for you. It'll assure future employers of your complete loyalty."

The fuck? Was he blackmailing her? Fury rose within her like an overflowing well. Every vein in her body went cold after being flooded by the icy water, and she took two steps forward, her free hand balled into a hard fist. "Is that an ultimatum?" January hissed. "I'm sure HR will find it most interesting if that's the case." She wasn't going to let Peter bully her. Her anger mixed with sadness. She had worked for Peter for almost twenty-four months, and it had catapulted her into this world. Was he truly going to ruin everything now?

"Hey, no need for that. I'm not suggesting anything untoward—"

"You weren't suggesting anything. You were setting ultimatums for something you'd already promised me months ago. I was going to hand in my formal letter of resignation on Friday, but I might as well do it right away…"

Peter sat back in his chair. "All right, all right. Forget it." He glanced at her tablet. "Are you recording me?"

"No." January wished she had. "Can I assume that this matter is closed?" She raised her chin.

"Damn. No matter where you end up, you're going to be formidable," Peter muttered. "I suppose I'll have to deal with the old ex on my own. I may not get more money for my trouble, but I'll find a way to show her that I *know*."

January regarded Peter's flushed face. "And what about your promise to me about that recommendation?"

He rolled his eyes, looking bored now—another approach on his list of manipulative tricks. "Since you're being stingy about joining me at the party, you'll get that letter on your last day, not a minute before."

Oh, wonderful. She hoped her potential new employer was patient.

On her way home on the bus, January found herself thinking of, and looking for, Constantine, which was silly. He was in Mallory's care and wouldn't be out gallivanting around the city on buses. He had stolen a piece of her heart with his cordial, warm ways, and she had wistfully observed how he had regarded Mallory—his darling girl—with such tenderness and affection. January's own family was scattered over at least eight states, and some in Canada, which sometimes made her feel displaced even if it was them who moved away, one by one. When her work at Peter's firm had demanded her every waking hour some weeks, her family had still managed to claim that she was the one ignoring them. The fact that they had left her behind didn't seem to occur to them.

Walking from the bus station, January thought of the heated argument in Peter's office. He had seemed genuinely frazzled behind his bad, inappropriate behavior. He often became flustered these days and gave a frantic impression. In court, he was still the savvy, brilliant attorney, but as soon as he stepped out of that role, it was easy to see the tension growing within him.

After ducking into the local grocery store to buy some frozen dinners, January was relieved to climb the two stairs to her one-bedroom apartment. When—she would not stoop to thinking in the terms of *if*—she was secure in a new and better paid position, she would look for a two-bedroom apartment closer to work. She had browsed the neighborhoods online and found several where she could see herself creating a home. There were several parks with ponds, and one even had a small lake with a beach. This felt luxurious compared to the small place she resided in at the moment. It was all right, but that was the best you could say about it.

She placed one of the meals in the microwave and headed for the bedroom. Undressing, she was filled with relief to peel off her office persona and step into her favorite lounge wear: leggings and an oversized T-shirt. The T-shirt reminded her of what she wore at Mallory's house, and this created a strange sensation of Mallory pressing against her entire body.

Shaking her head, January sauntered into the kitchen and plated her lasagna. She refused to eat from a cardboard plate. It was bad enough how seldom she made the time to cook from scratch. Her repertoire at the stove was limited, but the dishes she knew how to make always turned out delicious. Another reward with the new job was the set work hours. She wouldn't be expected to be at anyone's disposal after hours. Not only that, if she did stay longer, the overtime paid double.

Sitting on the worn couch that came with the apartment—another thing she wouldn't be sad to say good-bye to—she opened her laptop, which doubled as her entertainment set. Just as she found there was a new episode available of her favorite crime show, her phone rang.

Groaning, she looked at the screen. An unknown, local number. Landline? Who used landlines these days? Reluctantly, she answered. "January."

"Dear girl, how lovely to hear your voice," a man said and chuckled. "I bet you're surprised to hear from me already."

January blinked. What the…? "Constantine? What—are you all right?" She pictured him on a bus, perhaps a Greyhound this time, heading for Vegas or something. "Where are you?"

"I'm at Mallory's house, of course. Where else would I be? I suppose I could be home, but then I wouldn't find your phone number so easily. You're not listed for some reason." Constantine sounded genuinely puzzled.

"I'm a single woman living alone. Listing my phone number and address would not be safe." She assumed that in Constantine's youth, being listed in a phone book was just how it was done. "Can I help you with anything, Constantine?"

"Absolutely. That's why I'm calling. You see, I'm worried for Mallory." He sounded somber now.

"Why? What's wrong?" January put down her fork and pushed the cooling lasagna aside.

"That's just it, dear girl. I'm not entirely sure. I overheard her talking to someone at the foundation, and she was clearly concerned. She had the feeling someone was following her." Constantine sighed. "Why anyone would do that is beyond me."

"What? Are you sure? Is she afraid?" Not realizing she had gotten on her feet in a rush, January swayed before she regained her balance and could avoid slamming into the coffee table.

"She seemed annoyed more than anything—at first. This morning, when she was getting ready for work, she grabbed her phone and left the room in a flash, after glancing out the window. I'm not sure, though. I could be wrong."

January closed her eyes. "Is it possible that you're reading too much into this?" She covered her eyes as she truly didn't want to insinuate that he might be imagining things.

"I understand why you might think so, but no. I know Mallory better than I know anyone else, and even if she's been stressed no end regarding her divorce, she hasn't had this particular look on her face." Suddenly, Constantine sounded less sweet and polite, and instead his voice showed a firm resolve. January understood that he had been as formidable a person as Mallory was, once. Obviously, these traits remained under the surface, despite the onslaught of potential dementia.

"All right. I believe you. What can I do?" January asked.

"Find out if that soon-to-be ex-husband of hers is behind this. You work for him, right? You must know if he's hired someone—"

"Damn," January whispered. Peter had said something about trying to prove any infraction against the prenup on Mallory's part. If he found out that she and Mallory had been, well, spending the night together at Mallory's house, that could be it for both of them. One prenup and one vital letter of recommendation down the drain.

"You know something, don't you, dear?" Constantine's voice was back to being sweet. "I can tell."

"Perhaps." January pinched the bridge of her nose. It didn't alleviate her budding headache, but it made it easier to focus. "But even so, I'm not sure what I can do."

"I know you care for Mallory," Constantine said, his tone warm.

January flinched. "Excuse me?" How could he possibly know?

"Don't worry. I would never be indiscreet regarding other people's privacy. I got up in the early hours and saw you and Mallory on the couch. It was a sweet sight to observe the serenity on both your faces, that's a fact. I haven't seen my favorite granddaughter look like that in a very long time. Young and at ease. And you, January Wild, held her so tenderly, it brought tears to an old man's eyes."

Dear God. She was screwed. If Constantine in his innocence spoke about this to anyone who could report it to Peter, she and Mallory could kiss the futures they coveted good-bye.

"I see," she managed to say, even if it wasn't true. She couldn't begin to understand how to deal with this situation. "Yes, I do like Mallory, but we were trying to stay warm, that's all."

"Of course." Constantine's polite tone clearly stated that he was agreeing because he was a gentleman.

"You understand that you can't let anyone else know what you saw, right? It could hurt Mallory before the divorce is finalized." January crossed two fingers on her free hand.

"Of this, I'm well aware. The family fortune is in her hands, and the foundation would be in jeopardy. The money in itself means very little, but all the good she can do with it…it would be disastrous if Peter had a reason to claim she broke the prenup agreement." Constantine was quiet for so long, January feared he might have zoned out completely, but then he continued, his voice back to its sharp tone. "I wish there was something we could do to fix it all."

January thought fast. "There is a function on Friday that Peter and Mallory will attend."

"Yes, yes. Mallory asked me to be her plus-one, as they say." Constantine chuckled, but then showed signs of his old persona. "Can you be part of this cocktail party without arousing suspicions?"

Damned if she knew. "I worry my presence will arouse suspicions, but I can attend. What I can do is keep my eyes open for any signs of surveillance directed against her. And keep my ear to the ground about anything Peter says or does." The more she thought about it, the more she felt certain her boss was up to something despicable.

"He's not the first to cause trouble. Mallory's money has caused issues before. Unworthy individuals, scammers, and gold diggers have homed in on her ever since her status as the heir to it all became common knowledge." Constantine huffed. "Let's put it this way. If I don't hear from you, I'll assume you'll be there."

"Sounds like something out of a secret agent film," January muttered. "All right. I'll see you there on Friday." Unless she strangled her boss first. Then it would all be a moot point.

Chapter Eight

Mallory stepped out of the elevator that brought her to the penthouse restaurant overlooking the city she had called home all her life. She had lived in many other places over time but always returned to Seattle, where all her childhood memories were made.

She felt Granddad's hand at the small of her back. His warmth and obvious affection helped her feel safe and focused. The charity event was partly sponsored by her foundation as a means to bring in more money for people in need. Tonight, the demographic that would benefit from the gathering of the rich and slightly famous was disenfranchised young people who otherwise could not afford bills from the healthcare industry.

"Mallory. Constantine. This is a welcome sight." A man dressed in a tailored tuxedo approached them with outstretched hands.

Granddad looked uncertain. "Likewise…eh…"

"You remember Benjamin, don't you, Granddad?" Mallory hurried to interject. She shot Benjamin Gold a smile. "It has been a long time."

"It has." Benjamin, the chair of another major foundation, shook Granddad's hand. "Old friend, we must get together more often. I miss how we used to play backgammon every other Friday evening."

Her grandfather brightened. "The winner could pick and choose from the loser's wine rack."

"That's why you had a second one installed and I had to restock." Benjamin laughed.

Relaxed now and stepping into his completely lucid frame of mind, Constantine looked taller, and his eyes were brighter. "That's the God's honest truth."

While the men discussed old times, something her grandfather did with much more ease, Mallory snagged a glass of champagne from a waiter passing with a freshly stocked tray. Sipping it, she held back a grimace. This wasn't champagne. It was something sparkly that had a sour aftertaste.

"Mallory." Peter's voice made Mallory want to down the rest of the wine, but instead she turned around, making sure her smile was as cold as it could get. When she met her soon-to-be former husband's smirk, she debated using the horrible wine to toss in his face, but her thoughts came to a complete halt. Next to Peter stood January, looking amazing in a short, black cocktail dress. A silver slider in the shape of a fairy rested in the indentation just below her neck and was kept in place with a thin chain. She wore a small watch but no other jewelry. Her hair was pulled up on the top of her head, and small tresses curved in gentle locks around her temples.

Why was she here—and with Peter? Had she decided the perfect way to secure the letter of recommendation of a lifetime was by telling Peter about their night on the couch? The smug look on Peter's face suggested as much, but there was something tense around January's eyes that appeared to belie it.

"You know January, of course. She's my plus-one tonight. Working overtime as my assistant, of course." Peter winked at January and then fired off a broad grin toward Mallory. "I see you're here with the old goat."

"Excuse me?" Mallory meant to whisper, but it turned into a vicious hiss.

"Aw, come on. It's no secret that there's no love lost between Constantine and me. He's always made it clear that he never liked me. He should be ecstatic that the divorce is only days away."

"He is." Mallory forced her shoulders to relax. Getting her expression under control, she turned to January. "Ms. Wild. You look lovely tonight." Did January realize her words were meant as a test of sorts?

January motioned at Mallory. "Ms. Davigne. A stunning dress. You outdo us all." When she lowered her hand, she made a quick okay sign before hiding it behind her clutch.

Something inside Mallory melted. Whatever had possessed January to show up at this fundraiser, it didn't appear that her motive was betrayal. Hearing her grandfather's voice in the background, Mallory tensed. What if Granddad was clear-minded enough to recognize January, but not aware enough to realize it needed to be a secret?

"Enjoy your evening," Mallory said dismissively. "The secret auction starts in a moment, and I need to find Granddad."

"Good luck," Peter said, and it wasn't obvious if he meant finding Granddad or winning her bids. Probably neither. If anything, Peter was always the type that put in bids all over the place at these functions, whether he wanted the object or not, just to show off.

Weaving through people, Mallory eventually found her grandfather on a couch between Benjamin and his wife. Despite her elevated stress level, it was a delight to see her grandfather enjoy himself among friends.

"Granddad, I'm going to place our bids, all right?" Mallory bent to kiss him.

"Excellent, my girl. Let me know what we win. I'll be right here with my brandy and my good friends."

Benjamin nodded. "Enjoy yourself, Mallory. Take your time. Constantine is safe with us." His kind eyes showed he understood the situation well.

"Thank you. I'll be right back." After getting rid of the wine, Mallory made her way over to the long tables where the listings were placed. She had read up on what was available and knew what she would want for Granddad and for herself. She shuddered at the last thought. There was no way she would ever be given the gift she desired the most. Behind her, among the throngs of the rich and powerful, January Wild stood by Peter's side, whether she sided with him or not.

Forever out of reach.

❖

January regarded the people around her much like she would regard animals in a zoo—if she ever visited one. It was not hard to judge who had come into money recently. Some of them, at least, seemed to want to parade their clothes and jewelry around. She could imagine they would regard her simple items and the dress from an outlet mall with newly acquired disdain for the middle-class individual before them.

Peter ushered her over to the table holding the hors d'oeuvres by the panoramic window overlooking the valley below them. It was dark out, and the houses below looked as if some giant had tossed diamonds around. Cars drove among the houses, and it was a fascinating view for someone like her who lived without much of a view at all in an apartment.

She turned her focus on Peter. "So, I'm here. We're making the rounds on the floor. You made a point to talk to your wife." Just calling Mallory his wife hurt. "I want the letter of recommendation—now. This minute, or I'm leaving."

"Geez, it's not like I'm going to back out of our agreement." Peter raised his eyebrows. "I'm a man of my word, after all."

January doubted it but accepted the letter he produced from inside his tuxedo. She had to force herself not to yank it from his hands, but merely took it and opened it right away. Trust wasn't high on her list right now. She glanced through the text and made sure it was signed. It was a fair description of her duties, strengths, and abilities, and once she had tucked it in her clutch and snapped it closed, she managed to offer a faint smile. "Thank you."

"You earned it." Peter shrugged. "I'm going to look over the items in the secret auction. You can entertain yourself for a bit, right?" The way Peter straightened his cuffs and jacket made the fine hairs on January's arm prickle and stand up.

"Sure. Plenty of food." She snagged a toothpick with cucumber, a sundried tomato, and gravlax.

"Excellent." Peter turned and made his way through the crowd. He wasn't heading toward the auction tables. Instead, he looked around several times and made a beeline for a door next to the large opening to the foyer.

Putting the hors d'oeuvre in her mouth and then tossing the toothpick into a bin, she followed Peter, making sure to keep several people between them. In the foyer, he turned left and headed up the impressive staircase leading to the next floor. After waiting until Peter was just at the top, January hurried up the red carpeted steps, hoping her four-inch heels wouldn't snag.

Just as she rounded the pillar on the left side of the stairs and ended up on the landing, she saw Peter enter a room three doors down. She didn't hesitate. Half running, she pulled out her phone from her clutch. If Peter was meeting with whoever he might have hired to spy on Mallory, she was going to snap a photo of them. At least Mallory would be able to recognize that particular person if they followed her around.

Reaching the door, January found it closed. She could hear murmurs but couldn't make out any words. After a quick look around, she tried the doorknob. She nearly stumbled backward when it turned out to be unlocked. Peter Sundh, the demonic lawyer, could be careless after all? She tapped the screen of her phone and pulled up the camera, making sure it was set to not use a flash. All she had to do was crack the door open and—

An unexpected sound from inside the room made her jump. Clutching the phone in her hand, January held her breath and opened the door with trembling fingers. And then she began to film.

Chapter Nine

"Granddad, you look like you're as ready to get out of here as I am." Mallory had joined her grandfather on the couch after the silent auction was over. "I won three of the auctions and made sure it was something we could use at the foundation to enrich the lives of those we help. How about that?"

"An example?" Granddad patted Mallory's arm gently. His eyes glittered and he seemed more himself than he should as it was close to ten p.m.

"All-expense paid trip to Colorado Springs. Hiking the trails, enjoying the scenery, spa days, fancy dinners, the works—for four people. I scored four such tickets. I can think of several who would benefit greatly to have something like this to look forward to." Mallory took Granddad's hand. "What have you been up to while I was rubbing elbows with the tuxes and cocktail dresses at the other end of this room?"

"Oh, I was entertaining myself with people spotting." Constantin winked. "I saw our little calendar girl."

Mallory blinked. "What? Who—oh. You mean January." She lowered her voice. "Was she with Peter?"

"Not per se. And don't look so worried, I didn't acknowledge her, nor did she me. She just passed me by like we were strangers. Smart girl." Granddad rose to his feet. "My friends left just ten minutes ago, so that means I'm truly ready to ditch these people until next year, God willing."

Mallory's chest created a series of pings at the thought of her grandfather perhaps not being around next year, but she pushed the thought away. Nothing was wrong with him physically. He was just in the first throes of dementia. With the top-of-the-line medication he was on, he could have several more wonderful years in front of him. She took him by the arm and guided him toward the wardrobe area. "Let's get you home, Granddad."

In the town car, Mallory gave the instructions for her driver to take her grandfather home first. He nodded and pulled out from the congested parking lot and into traffic.

"I was not entirely truthful, my sweet girl." Granddad shifted in the seat and looked at Mallory with a slight frown.

"Excuse me? What are you talking about?" Mallory had just reached for her phone in her tiny handbag but stopped in mid-motion. She studied her granddad closely to see if he was all right.

"I did communicate with January, but not verbally. She merely gave me a discreet thumbs-up." He smiled wistfully now. "I hope that means she found out something that can take the pressure off you—and her."

Mallory's thoughts raced. "I admit that I'm at a loss. Why don't you tell me exactly what you mean?"

"January and I suspect that Peter has you followed and perhaps for some time. January was going to keep an eye on her boss tonight, and the way she looked at me makes me think she may have found something out. Something useful. I really have no idea." Granddad stuck his hand in his inner pocket and pulled out his phone. "My phone vibrated only moments after she gave me a thumbs-up. Perhaps she sent something."

"Cloak-and-dagger tactics? What are you two up to? Having me followed? That sounds insane." Still, she remembered earlier in the week, when she had spotted a car idling across the cul-de-sac by her house for too long. Mallory watched her grandfather unlock his phone and then he gave it to her. "There's a new text message. It's from her."

Mallory looked at the screen. How could her grandfather and January be collaborating like this—and she not know anything about it? The row of texts was mostly from Mallory, checking on him, but at the top there was a recent text from a "J." January. It had an attachment, and after hesitating briefly, Mallory clicked on it and leaned closer to her granddad so he could see. He already had his reading glasses on and stared intently at the screen.

It was a film clip. At first there was only darkness, then a flicker of a red carpet and pretty feet in sandals. A shuffling sound, more darkness and then a dimly lit room. It took the person, most likely January, a moment to steady the image, but then the camera compensated for the muted light in the room.

In the center, at the foot of a large bed, Peter stood with his arms around a person. A woman. When he pulled back after kissing her, Mallory saw that it was a much younger woman who clung to him. Gaping, Mallory let the clip play. A quick glance to the corner showed that it was four minutes long.

Peter murmured something inaudible as he pressed his lips against the woman's neck, but then his words came out more clearly. "I can't believe I've had to stay away from you for two days."

"It won't be long now. The divorce will be finalized in a few days, right?" The woman pushed at Peter's unruly hair. "Our plans will work. Mallory will be found in a compromising situation tomorrow evening, and your people will be there to make sure you get it on film. It was an easy enough plan to figure out. You just got to have faith in me. In us. In all that Davigne money."

"I never should have agreed to such a cut-and-dry prenup, but as it turns out, it's working out anyway. It's amazing that I used to love her once. These days she is nothing more than a four-star bitch."

"I don't like to hear about you loving her. Ever." Peter's young girlfriend pouted. "You love *me*. You will share everything with *me*."

Peter's smile waned. "Of course, sweetheart." He looked uneasy. Perhaps he realized right then that this woman had a hold on him, simply by being his lover—proof that he broke the prenup rules way before they meant to set Mallory up.

January had kept filming a little longer but thankfully stopped when it looked like the woman was going to make Peter prove his undying love literally.

Mallory leaned back. "I'm supposed to have dinner with friends tomorrow. They must have found out…I can think of how, but that doesn't matter. I'm going to postpone."

"How do you plan to use this clip?" Granddad weighed the phone in his hand.

Mallory gave a lopsided smile while she checked her own cell. "January sent it to me as well. You can just hang on to your copy as a precaution. I'm going to send Peter a text where I inform him that his plans have been foiled and that I have irrefutable proof that he has not only had an affair but has been trying to frame me. He'll get it. He's a clever lawyer, after all."

"And January?" Granddad smiled gently.

"I'll text her tonight, and if she wants to see me, I will ask her out to dinner on Wednesday." Mallory pressed her cell to her chest.

"She could be the one. She is." Granddad tugged gently at a lock of Mallory's hair.

"You romantic old fool," Mallory said and kissed his cheek. "Don't think I don't know that I owe you everything—as always."

"Nonsense." Her grandfather looked out the window as the car came to a halt. "Ah, this is me. I better hurry. Eloise is probably heating the milk for the cocoa as we speak." His bright eyes radiated such love and affection for Mallory's dead grandma, it broke her heart.

"Granddad…" Mallory put a hand on his arm. "Grandma isn't there. She died, remember?"

Granddad's eyes lost their sparkle, but the clarity was back. "Of course, I know, sweet girl. She's been gone a while." He stepped out of the car where their driver assisted him up to his front door. The driver waited until he heard the door lock and saw the light come on before returning to the car.

"Thank you," Mallory said. "You always take such good care of my grandfather."

"My pleasure, Ms. Davigne. Home?"

"Yes. Home."

It was a blatantly luxurious feeling to sleep in on a Wednesday. January stretched and then slid out of bed in need of coffee. She pulled on a robe and combed through her tousled hair with her fingers and put it up in a messy bun using a scrunchy. After pushing her feet into fuzzy slippers, she padded to the kitchen where she started her coffee machine, making half a pot.

After using the bathroom, she sat on her couch with her phone, browsing her messages. She had heard from several potential employers, which was great in case the one she wanted the most should fall through somehow.

She clicked on the message she had received last Saturday just before midnight. It only showed a thumbs-up emoji, but it was from Mallory, which was huge. Or it had been huge then—she hadn't heard a word from Mallory since.

Her doorbell rang, making her almost drop her mug. She placed it on the coffee table and hurried to the door, wondering which one of her neighbors had forgotten to buy something essential this time. She glanced into the door-eye, having decided to not open at all if it was the young guy further down the corridor. She gasped. Mallory.

She flung the door open so fast it rebounded on the wall and nearly closed again. January stared at the unexpected sight of Mallory Davigne. Dressed in a trench coat, black slacks, and pumps, she looked the epitome of elegance as always. Her hair hung loose, styled into gentle waves framing her face.

"Hello, January. May I come in?" Mallory sent January's front door a look under raised eyebrows.

"Oh. Sure. Absolutely." January cast a glance behind her, trying to remember what shape her apartment was in. Not too shabby, she hoped. She helped Mallory by hanging the immaculate trench coat on the only hanger in the small hallway. "Come in. I just made coffee. Would you like to—"

Mallory pulled January into her arms and hugged her close. "Is this all right? I have thought of this for days. Holding you."

All of January's senses went into overload. "Wow. You're not the only one. So yes. Yes, it's all right." She ran her hands up and down Mallory's back, feeling the tremors travel through her cashmere sweater.

"Thank God." Mallory tipped her head back. "May I kiss you?"

"Yes. Anything. I give you carte blanche." January meant to smile, but Mallory captured her lips in a kiss filled with such longing and passion. Moaning against Mallory's mouth, January held on and let all the pent-up emotions since she saw Mallory last Friday roam free.

Mallory pushed her fingers into January's hair, as if she thought she needed to hold her in place. January willingly parted her lips and asked wordlessly for them to deepen the kiss before she self-combusted.

Tasting each other freely made little fires erupt along January's nerve endings. It was Mallory's turn to moan when their tongues met, over and over. When they eventually parted enough to draw breath through their mouths, she cupped Mallory's cheeks.

"Divorced?" January whispered.

Mallory nodded. "Yesterday. Without a hitch."

"Did I help?"

Mallory tilted her head and ran a thumb along January's lower lip. "You did. More than you can imagine."

"I'm glad." January took Mallory by the hand. "Coffee?"

Mallory's eyes darkened. "Yes. Later."

"Okay. Later." Tugging at Mallory's hand, she guided her across the living room and into the bedroom.

❖

Mallory had not expected to make love to January this way. Passionately, yes. Even with some urgency. But this… Her mouth couldn't get enough of January's hard, dusty rose nipples, and she had explored almost every inch of January's body. Now she hovered over her lover—dear God, *lover*—supported on one elbow, and her free hand was cupping the wet folds between January's legs.

"I know you said carte blanche, but I have to ask," Mallory murmured around the nipple. "Can I go inside? I want you so much."

January's slitted eyes glittered. "I want you. I want you to do everything with me."

The amazing words were all Mallory needed to hear. "By all means." She pushed two fingers between January's folds and found her opening. Using her thumb, she caressed around the clit, amazed at how swollen it was. When January gave a muted cry, Mallory pushed first one, then two fingers inside.

A hand pushed in between her own legs and Mallory nearly bit down on the sensitive nipple she was tonguing as a sharp pleasure pierced her abdomen. "Oh!"

"Good like this?" January entered Mallory's opening with several fingers and mimicked her movements. "Show me what you like by doing it to me."

The order was soft but made Mallory tremble. She rubbed January's clit with her thumb and fell into a slow, twisting movement with her other fingers. She shifted on her elbow to reach January's mouth with hers. "Open your mouth, darling." Their lips and tongues kept the same rhythm as their caressing hands. Mallory knew she wasn't going to last. She had wanted January long enough for it to feel like a perpetual foreplay.

❖

January rolled them over when she felt the first contractions start within Mallory. She wanted to see everything as Mallory came, and, oh God, was it a sight worth waiting for. Normally so cool and elegant, Mallory had dissolved into a bundle of glowing, sweaty skin, tousled hair, and swollen lips. She undulated against January's thrusting fingers, and when January curled her fingers up, Mallory went rigid and slapped her hand over her mouth as she cried out. Melting into the bed with a whimper, Mallory tugged January with her.

"You…you just…you…" Mallory shook her head. "Can't speak."

Straddling Mallory's thigh, January rocked against her as Mallory's fingers had slipped out when she came. "That's okay." She pressed into the slick skin, and after a few moments, Mallory raised her leg, adding to the pressure.

"Keep moving." Mallory found January's breasts and rolled the nipples between her fingers with perfect pressure.

"Like that. Yes." January couldn't get enough of the sight beneath her. Mallory Davigne naked in her bed. It was unbelievable, but yet so right. So perfect.

Flames began licking the inside of her thighs and gathered around January's clit. Another few strokes and she fell into Mallory's arms, still bucking against her slick thigh.

Minutes, or perhaps hours later, January could finally breathe. She was settled in the most comfortable of positions in Mallory's arms. Today was truly the first day of their freedom to be together on their terms. No threats regarding future careers or money belonging to important foundations. Just her and Mallory in this bed—in this world.

"I truly only came by to ask you out on a date." Mallory buried her face into January's hair. "I had planned to sort of be in the neighborhood."

"A very respectful approach." January smiled. "If a bit untrue. I'm not being conceited, but why would you be in this neighborhood unless you came to specifically see me?"

"It all backfired in the best of ways." Mallory chuckled. "I saw you in that cozy robe and your place smelled like coffee…My senses went on overload."

"You should talk. That trench coat is damn sexy." Nipping at Mallory's jawline, January was pleased when it made Mallory jump.

"January!" Mallory rolled on top of January, and her eyes sparkled dangerously. "You must realize just how much time I feel I need to make up for. Nipping at me…" She shook her head, and her broad smile made January's mouth go dry. "Dangerous. Makes me get all these ideas."

"I'm not stopping you." January wrapped her legs around Mallory's hips. "Take all the time in the world to explore them."

Mallory stopped in mid-motion. She held January's gaze firmly for several moments. "I want you to know that I'm falling in love. No, it's beyond falling. I'm in love with you."

Tears formed in January's eyes and ran down her temples and continued into her hair. "Mallory…"

"Don't cry." Mallory wiped at the slow tears. "Unless your tears are for all the right reason."

"They are. It's just…I never thought…you know?" January raised her head off the pillow and kissed Mallory. "You must know I feel the same way. I fell for you so long ago, and I'm very much in love."

As their voices became low murmurs and a different, slow lovemaking took place, January knew that every single caress, and every kiss, validated what they had just confessed to each other.

This was, in the end, all about love.

Her Therapist's Daughter

J.J. Hale

Chapter One

"So, you're telling me that my daddy issues have combined with my mommy issues to create my wonderful commitment issues? I feel like a cliché."

Freya Clarke gave herself an internal pat on the back as she caught the smile her therapist quickly smothered. Was this what winning at therapy felt like? She would keep that thought to herself before Moira pointed out that her need to succeed at everything, including therapy, also stemmed from her messed up childhood. That one she was fully aware of.

"That's not quite how I'd put it, but I'm not disagreeing. How does that thought make you feel?"

"*Now* who's the cliché, Moira?" Freya joked.

Nothing but a slight rise of the eyebrow from her therapist, who refused to take the bait. Freya was the one paying to be here, so she understood logically she shouldn't be trying to dodge questions or avoid the difficult topics. Understanding and doing were two very different things, however, and Freya had spent most of her thirty-five years avoiding. It was a lifetime's worth of habit that wasn't resolved in a few months' worth of therapy. Even the expensive kind.

"It makes me feel like I am no closer to understanding how I get past it. I know what I don't want for my life, but I have no clue how to figure out what I do want."

Freya fidgeted with the cushion that she had grown attached to on her biweekly visits. The edges were frayed and worn. Freya wondered how many other people had sat where she sat, with this cushion in their lap, playing with the edges of it to distract from the words they had come to share. Until the cushion, much like the people, became marred by those who used it for comfort.

"Where did you go just now?"

Freya snapped back to the room and her cheeks heated at the questioning eyes watching her closely.

"I was wondering how many people were comforted by this cushion. It's a little worse for wear, you know. Sorry, what did you say?"

Freya vaguely registered that Moira had said words that she hadn't processed while lost in her thoughts.

"I said that your answer wasn't about your feelings, it was about how to get past them. You need to take a few steps back first and figure out what the feelings you're trying to get past actually are."

"But if I can figure out getting past them, then I don't really need to figure out what they are. It feels like an unnecessary step."

Freya was partially kidding, but truth be told, she had never understood the whole feel your feelings thing. Surely if she were having feelings, that implied she was feeling them. The part that required her attention was getting past the ones she was sick of feeling.

"You're so focused on fixing them that you're not even sure what you're trying to fix. It might feel unnecessary, but there's a reason you're here. So maybe the way you've been doing things isn't quite working for you anymore?"

No shit.

"Touché. Okay, let's say I take those few steps back. Where does that leave me?"

Moira's pen taunted her as it darted along the page. To Freya's untrained eye, the pen often stayed still when Freya was saying things of actual worth. It hopped to attention when she was saying things that, to her, were unworthy of noting. She trusted that there was a method behind it all, but Freya didn't like not knowing how things worked.

"Let's go back to when you started coming here. What was the catalyst?"

Freya groaned internally. They had been through this, but if she had learned anything over her previous sessions, it was that Moira didn't ask something for no reason. Freya trying to rush to the point never worked.

"A woman who I had slept with got married to the person she

started dating not long after sleeping with me. Making her the second person to do that in a relatively short amount of time. Which may not seem like much, but apparently being the one before the one *twice* is enough to make me question myself a tad."

Moira nodded and the pen kept going despite the fact that nothing Freya had said was new information. Maybe Moira was doodling back there. The thought made Freya snort, and she followed it up with a cough as a cover.

"So, two women that you briefly dated married the people they dated after you, and it made you question why it wasn't you they chose to take that step with?"

"God no. I do *not* want to get married. And dated is a stretch. I slept with them, individually and not at the same time, and I guess they realized these other people were the loves of their lives shortly after."

Moira nodded and tapped the pen against her lips. Freya had come to learn that meant she was about to point out something that Freya had said to contradict herself.

"So, if you didn't want to date these women, let alone marry them, why do you feel them finding the loves of their lives, as you put it, affected you enough to seek therapy?"

Isn't that what I'm paying you to figure out?

"I guess it was another thing in a line of things that when strung together made me figure it was time I figured my shit out. I've spent most of my adult life avoiding relationships or getting attached to anyone, and I guess I just woke up one day and realized I'm, well, alone."

Freya shrugged as the word echoed around her mind.

"And you don't want to be alone?" Moira asked.

Freya considered the question carefully.

"I should be used to it by now. Only child, absent parents, alone has been my normal for a long time."

"You've spent a lot of weeks now telling me that you spent quite a lot of time with various women throughout the recent years, right?"

Freya chuckled lightly.

"Is that your way of telling me I've spent my therapy sessions talking about sleeping around? This is a no shaming zone, right?"

Moira tilted her head with a slight smile on her face and Freya added another point to her winning at therapy list.

"Do *you* feel ashamed of it?"

The classic answering a question with a question. Freya should have seen that one coming.

"No. I don't think so. Maybe? Logically, I know that there's nothing wrong with casual sex. Women get judged for it far too often, and I don't judge anyone else for it. Once it involves two consenting adults who both know it won't become anything more, then what's the problem?"

Moira tapped the pen against the paper for a moment as if waiting to see if Freya would continue or not.

"Are you asking me, or yourself? You've given a lot of valid reasons why there is nothing wrong with it from a logical point of view, but you're giving nothing about your actual feelings, Freya. What do you think is a problem?"

A bird landed on the windowsill outside the second-floor office, and Freya watched as it pecked at whatever it had dropped from its beak. It looked far too big to balance comfortably on the small ledge. Freya wondered what made the bird choose this landing spot, considering there must be dozens close by with far more suitable space for it to enjoy its meal.

"Freya?"

Crap, yes, therapy.

"Sorry. The bird distracted me."

Moira nodded in acknowledgement, and Freya was glad she didn't try to turn it into some metaphor for Freya's flighty existence. She replayed Moira's previous sentence in her head as she brought herself back on track.

"I honestly don't know. I guess I just know that I don't feel good about it right now, but I haven't quite figured out why yet. Probably my mommy issues," Freya said with a wry smile.

"My reason for bringing it up was because you said alone is your normal and it's what you're used to. But I think your actions are showing us otherwise. It sounds to me like you've spent quite a lot of your time trying not to be alone. You struggle with the idea of a relationship and depending on one person, so instead you've depended on many different people for the companionship you're seeking."

Freya opened her mouth to object and then shut it again as the words replayed in her head.

You've spent quite a lot of your time trying not to be alone.

Well, shit. It was obvious when stated like that, but somehow it wasn't something Freya had considered. She was aware that her proclivity for casual sex was filling some void within her, but she had missed the part where that void was simply loneliness. Freya prided herself on not needing anyone but herself. Except that wasn't true at all.

"You'd think I'd just, you know, make real friends or something. That would probably fill that void too, eh?"

Freya glanced at the clock on the wall. They were entering the last quarter of her session. She liked to stop with the deep topics around this time, so they weren't leaving it on a cliffhanger, so to speak.

"I imagine that friendship poses the same risk to you that a romantic relationship would. Casual encounters are a way to get companionship without the risk of loss or abandonment. Letting someone close enough to matter if you lost them is your real concern, whether that's romantic or platonic."

Freya knew that already, but hearing it from someone still made her squirm. She didn't love the idea of anyone seeing her so clearly, even if she was paying for that privilege.

"So, how do I change that? What should I do?"

Moira tapped the pen against her lips. Freya wondered if she was trying to decide whether to break the therapy laws and give her the answer or go the long way of making her find it herself. She crossed her fingers for the former.

"I think it would be helpful for you to consider taking a break from casual encounters for a while and see if that leads you to more clarity around what you really want. And let me be clear, I'm not saying this because I think there is anything wrong with casual sex. I'm saying it because I think that you do, and it's not benefitting you at the moment the way it has in the past."

Freya took a deep breath and pulled at the cushion as she considered the suggestion. No sex? Like, at all? The fact that the idea of it had Freya's stomach in knots was probably a sign that it was something she should consider.

"For how long?"

Moira crossed her legs and Freya braced herself for the response.

"That's up to you to decide, but how about you just focus on between now and our next session, and we can discuss your thoughts on it then? In the meantime, you could explore spending more time with friends, or those acquaintances that could become friends if you let them."

"Now you're pushing it," Freya joked as she set the cushion down beside her. "Okay, two weeks, that's not so bad. I can do that."

Freya sounded far more confident than she felt as she hopped up to grab her jacket from its hook.

"See you then. Maybe I'll have a friend to talk about."

Moira smiled as Freya waved goodbye. Another point for the list. Freya shrugged on her jacket and walked down the two flights of stairs. The session had been a long one, and she had a lot to consider from it. Freya was ready to take these steps toward the changes she wanted for her life, but concrete actions to actually do that were terrifying.

Freya was lost in her thoughts as she walked out the door and wandered straight into the path of someone walking toward the building. By the time Freya noticed, it was too late to veer fully out of the way. It was almost as if time slowed down as she observed herself awkwardly try to sidestep and still managed to knock the contents of the person's hands onto the floor.

"Fuck. Shit. What the hell?"

Freya winced as she glanced down at the victim of her clumsiness, a now empty takeaway coffee cup.

"Shit, sorry. I was away in my own world."

Freya glanced up and met deep brown eyes filled with obvious annoyance. Freya's heart thudded as she took in the rest of the stranger who was no more than a blur to her before their collision. The woman's shoulder-length, brown hair hung loose around her face. And what a face that was.

"You came out of nowhere."

The woman's words snapped Freya out of her probably obvious ogling and she smiled the smile that had gotten her out of more trouble than she cared to remember in the past.

"I could say the same about you," Freya said with a small shrug. "Make a habit of running into people in car parks?"

Freya's teasing had the desired effect as the woman's eyes flared in the way Freya had anticipated they would.

"I moved out of your way. You're the one who moved *into* my path again and knocked my coffee all over the ground. You're lucky there wasn't much left."

Freya smiled widely at that.

"Lucky, eh? What would have happened if it were full? Would you have given me an even worse death glare?"

The woman shook her head as if unsure whether to be amused or annoyed. Freya jumped in before the woman landed on annoyed.

"I am sorry about your coffee, though. Maybe I could replace it for you? A whole cup, so technically you'd end up better off overall."

Freya tilted her head and quirked an eyebrow at the end. It would be enough for anyone who was interested in women to catch her meaning, but not too much to scare away anyone who wasn't. She hoped. The woman had bent to pick up the empty cup and paused briefly on her way back up. She looked Freya up and down, so quickly it seemed almost involuntary, and her face tinged pink as she met Freya's eyes.

Bingo. Definitely queer.

"I…need to get going," the woman replied.

Freya nodded, but neither of them moved. She should accept the answer, walk away, and remember the goal she had agreed to only minutes before. No casual encounters. No flirtation disguised as coffee replacement. No hot brunette writhing naked as she lost countless hours between her legs.

The woman inhaled and turned to walk away. Freya was both disappointed and relieved at the same time. Something about the fiery look in this woman's eyes intrigued her. Following that intrigue would wind them up in one place and one place only. Her bed.

"Maybe another time."

Freya glanced up as the woman turned back around. She held the empty cup out in Freya's direction and Freya took it without even considering why. She watched the woman walk away and Freya's eyes fell to the mouth-watering curves perfectly moulded in tight jeans. What she wouldn't give to peel those…

Stop.

She halted the thought in its tracks as she shook herself. Two weeks suddenly seemed like a far longer time than it had in Moira's office. Freya glanced down at the cup still in her hands as she walked toward the street to find a bin. Her eyes landed on the number scrawled across the side of the cup in hurried scribbles.

Freya smiled and took out her phone to program in the digits before disposing of the cup. She should have thrown it away and left the number and the tempting brunette behind her as she focused on the future that seemed so important before their encounter. But old habits died hard, and one quick message couldn't hurt, right? Maybe, just maybe, this was nothing more than the friend Freya was supposed to look for.

Chapter Two

"What's put that smile on your face? Or is it a who?"

Blake Doyle glanced up from her phone at her mother's excited words and rolled her eyes.

"I swear that's all you care about, Mom. You'd have me married off tomorrow if you could."

Blake poured a fresh cup of coffee for herself from the small kitchenette in her mother's office. She had an hour to kill before her next class and was already regretting the decision to use the time to grab the bag she had left in her parents' house over the weekend.

"Yes, yes, your awful mother who wants you to pursue a healthy relationship so you can see the world isn't filled with people like Linda."

Blake bristled at the mention of her ex. She and Linda had broken up almost two years ago now, and nobody had been more thankful than her mom when Blake's rose-tinted glasses finally came off. Looking back, Blake could see the many reasons why her mom had never taken to Linda. It still baffled her how she had ignored so many glaring warning signs. The thought of how off her judgement had been had Blake terrified to try that again.

"The world mightn't be full of them, Mom, but how do you know that's not just the kind of people I attract? Look at my track record. Linda was by far my biggest lapse in judgement, but she wasn't the only walking red flag I fell for. Nina was hung up on her ex our whole relationship. Clo just used me whenever she needed to rebound. I'm a dumping ground for people who won't deal with their own shit."

Blake dropped into the couch and sipped her coffee as she thought about the reason she hadn't gotten to finish her last one. Her stomach flipped as she recalled the stunning blonde who had almost literally knocked her off her feet. Her anger at the spilled coffee had soon given way to intrigue as her eyes had met the woman's sparkling blue ones. The flirting had taken Blake by surprise, but she had surprised herself even more when she grabbed a pen and handed her number over to a stranger.

"The way other people chose to treat you was not your doing. You don't get to blame yourself for their actions. Besides, what about Sadie?"

Blake laughed and placed her coffee cup on the table in front of her.

"Sadie doesn't count. We were like twelve when we dated basically because we both figured out we liked girls. Thankfully, it didn't take long for us to figure out that didn't mean we had to date each other because we were not at all compatible. She's my best friend, so at least I have good taste in those."

Blake's mom sighed as she sat in the chair across from Blake.

"It would've been far easier if you'd fallen in love with Sadie. She's good for you."

Blake groaned at the statement she had heard far too many times before.

"She's also good for her wife, who I know you adore as much as I do. Love isn't the most important thing, Mom. I know you know that. I've got a great job teaching at the college, I have friends, and I have parents who frustrate me no end but who I know love me unconditionally. I'm happy. Isn't that good enough?"

Blake grabbed her favourite cushion from the couch and held it in her lap as her mom's face softened.

"My desire for you to date has nothing to do with you not being good enough, Blake. I am prouder of you than you'll ever know. If you are happy being single, then I can accept that. I just don't want you avoiding love because you think it looks like what your past relationships have shown you. I know there's more than that out there for you, and I don't want you to miss out because of people who took advantage of your caring nature."

Blake tugged at the frayed ends of the cushion and nodded.

"You need to let me figure it out by myself. As much as you say I can't blame myself, I also need to look at the reasons why I let things get to the point they did with Linda. I know you want to fix it, but I'm not one of your clients. If I need therapy, I will get it from someone who isn't my mother."

Blake glanced at the clock and hopped up from her seat.

"Crap, I need to go before I'm late for class. I didn't realize how much time I spent outside with..."

Blake's mom perked up as Blake trailed off with a wince. She hadn't wanted to open that can of worms. Her mom was good at her job, and Blake was an open book to her once she had enough information to prod.

"With?" Her mom prompted her.

"Nothing. I bumped into someone and spilled my coffee and gave them my number. That's all."

The words came tumbling out and Blake wanted to kick herself, but she figured it was like a Band-Aid. Better to rip it off all at once.

"Ah, so is this mystery person the reason you keep smiling in the direction of your phone?"

Blake's cheeks heated as she grabbed her bag and walked toward the door.

"Maybe. But look at the time, I've got to run."

"Just message her back, Blake. What can it hurt? If you do, I'll stop pestering you for at least a week."

Blake laughed as she waved goodbye and walked out of the office. Her mother was right about one thing, though: What could it hurt? If it came with the added bonus of getting her mom off her back for a week, then all the better. Blake pulled out her phone again as she walked down the stairs and clicked on the message that had arrived almost as soon as she walked into the office. This woman didn't waste any time.

Just making sure you know where to reach out when you feel like cashing in the coffee debt. Hope your day includes less collisions but can't say I'm sorry I ran into you. Pun intended.—Freya

Blake was grinning like a teenager. She chewed on her lip as she considered what to reply.

Risky move pulling out the puns so soon. They can be a deal breaker for some.—Blake

The three dots were up before Blake closed out of the message and she found herself waiting to see what would materialize. She had a class to get to and little time to get there, but if she put her phone away now, she'd be checking it again in a minute.

A woman who can't appreciate a good pun is not one I need in my life. Better to get the important stuff on the table at the start, saves everyone time.

Blake chastised her heart's reaction to the wink face emoji that ended the message.

Is that why you walk into women instead of more conventional methods of striking up a conversation? Time saving?

Blake walked through the corridor toward the classroom where she taught creative writing. She clicked the lock button on her phone, but the buzz of an incoming message had her hand stalling as she moved to place it in her pocket. She should continue placing the phone away. It was an hour class, and she could check it afterward. There was nothing pressing that would require her immediate attention. Logically, Blake knew all of that, and yet her phone was back in front of her face and her eyes were scanning the message before she could stop herself.

It was my first trial of this new method, but you can't deny the results. I'll need to conclude the study before I can report it a success though. So, coffee?

Blake walked into the classroom to smiles and waves from the students already awaiting her. She finally put her phone away and vowed to wait until after the class to reply. Clearly, Freya was good at this. Meaning she probably had a lot of experience with picking up strangers from the street. That should be enough to remind Blake to tread carefully and make sure she didn't fall too quickly for Freya's obvious charm. She would at the very least give Sadie a call first and get her opinion before accepting the coffee date.

She already knew what her best friend would say, though. Sadie and Blake's mom spent far too long conspiring about getting Blake out of her *romance rut*, as they put it. Blake was more into fantasy stories, but Sadie always had her head in a romance book. Blake liked to joke that those stories were far more unrealistic than the fantasy ones she read, but Sadie and her wife were living proof that sometimes real love stories did happen. Once Blake told Sadie about a beautiful stranger, who happened to be into women, randomly bumping into her and then asking her on a coffee date, Sadie would swoon.

Blake got the class started on their first writing prompt as she waited for her laptop to boot up. Her fingers twitched against her side until she gave in and pulled the phone back out. Her thoughts wouldn't settle until she did what her gut was screaming at her to do. She typed a quick response and clicked send before she could talk herself out of it.

Well, I can hardly stand in the way of research. I'm free Saturday if you are. Just tell me when and where.

Chapter Three

Freya glanced around the busy coffee shop and took in the various groups occupying the space. It was a place Freya had been coming to almost weekly for years, and some faces were familiar ones. People who played a supporting role in her life, as she remained a background character in theirs. The baristas always greeted her warmly, and her smile had gotten Freya more than one extra topping or a free chocolate treat in the past. Yet Freya was sure not one of the employees or regulars knew her name.

She had been ruminating since her last therapy session about the topics that had surfaced over the past few sessions. Freya had intentionally kept everyone in her life at arm's length, even within the most intimate of environments. She had refused to make connections beyond a night or two's comfort, and that extended to every aspect of her life. Even Freya's job as a contracted consultant offered the same barrier to developing relationships beyond the surface level.

Freya was never in one company for more than a few months, and in more recent years worked almost fully remote. Her role didn't align with making friends easily, either. She would come into a company with the understanding that most people knew she was there to point out where they had been going wrong. Years of learning from her parents had given Freya the skills to manipulate people into giving her the information she needed. When she coupled that with the charm that landed so many women in her bed, she never failed to dig through the corporate bullshit and get to the heart of most financial failings. It was often one of three things, and more often than not all three of them combined. Low morale, weak leadership, and big egos.

Freya would always make recommendations to fix the issues that often came with significant blows to the egos of the very people who gave her the information. Freya would present her report and then leave with her nice paycheck and any chance of potential connections snuffed out. Her work, much like her life, wasn't designed to make friends. Which left Freya with none.

"You got here early."

Freya startled out of her thoughts and smiled as Blake slid into the chair across from her.

"I actually worked from here for the morning, so I've been here for a while."

Blake shrugged off her jacket to reveal a casual linen top that dipped low enough to tease the top of her cleavage. A hint of colour peeked out from the edge of the material near Blake's collar, and it led Freya to wonder what tattoo was hidden beneath the fabric.

"I did wonder if you brought laptops on all of your dates."

Blake had a small smile on her face as Freya moved her gaze back up to meet Blake's eyes.

"How else am I supposed to capture my research?"

Blake laughed and Freya had a sudden warmth at being the cause of the melodic sound. Her heart picked up its pace a little at Blake's reference to their date. How long had it been since Freya had been on a date? Most of her encounters were at Blaze, their local queer bar. Those rarely entailed more than flirty conversation over a drink that was definitely not coffee.

"Hey, Blake. What can I get you?"

Freya turned to the young employee who had appeared beside their table with a big smile. Freya hadn't known they did table service here, and suspected it wasn't a standard occurrence. Did Blake come here often, too? Had she been another one of the random faces in the periphery of Freya's life, and it took a head-on collision to bring her into focus? A niggling feeling lodged in Freya's gut that she couldn't quite place, but something about that idea didn't land well with her.

"Hey, Lana. Good to see you. I'll take a latté, please, but I can come up and grab it from you. Do you want a refill?"

Blake directed the question to Freya as she nodded toward the long-empty cup on the table between them.

"I'll take a tea, please," Freya said as Lana smiled at her with a nod.

"Stay where you are, I'll drop them down," Lana said to Blake as she cleared the empty cup.

"Have you been here much?" Freya asked as she worked to settle the churning in her gut.

"First time, actually. I teach over at the university, though. Lana is one of my students."

Freya smiled and the churning eased a little. Her reaction was unusual, but something about the idea of having been around someone like Blake week in, week out, and not having noticed had unnerved Freya.

"What do you teach?" Freya asked.

It was another surprising development for her. When she had suggested meeting for coffee, Freya had been unsure of where it would lead. Her past would indicate that the coffee would become to-go as they found themselves back in her apartment doing all of the things she had envisioned doing with Blake since she first laid eyes on her. But something about this woman had Freya wanting to know more than the feel of her skin or the sound of her voice.

"I teach creative writing and critical reading and writing along with a few other ad hoc classes that pop up. My degree is in creative writing and it's my main love, though. Getting to help people discover their style, voice, and power when they really dig into their pieces never gets old."

Blake's eyes lit up as she discussed her job in a way that captivated Freya. Her passion was evident, and it radiated from her in waves.

"Lucky students. Do you write, too?"

A hint of pink crept up Blake's neck as she shrugged softly.

"A bit here and there. Nothing much. I mostly write poetry, so not like novels and stuff."

Interesting.

"You don't think poetry is a valid writing form?"

Blake's mouth opened and closed, and she frowned at Freya's words.

"Of course I do. I've read some poetry pieces from students that have told more of a story than a hundred-thousand-word novel, and some that have moved me more in one page than some stories have in two hundred. Poetry is absolutely valid."

The passion was back in Blake's voice, and Freya nodded.

"Ah, so it's less about the poetry and more about your belief in your own creations?"

Blake's eyes widened and she stiffened in her seat. Lana picked that moment to appear with their drinks and Freya worried she might have stepped over a line. She was used to the fact that she often said things without considering how the other person would receive them, but it was a habit Freya wasn't willing to change. How someone interpreted her words, and their intent, was their responsibility to deal with.

"Why do you say that?"

Blake asked the question neutrally, but her tone held a hint of defensiveness. It indicated to Freya that she wasn't the first person to broach this topic.

"You spoke about your students' work with such passion and excitement. It radiates from you. But when I asked you about your own, it wasn't excitement that came through. It felt more like embarrassment, or shame. For someone who understands and believes in the importance of poetry, that only leaves one other reason in my mind. Your belief in yourself."

Freya took a sip of her tea as Blake stared at her with a look of disbelief.

"You just say things how they are, I take it?" Blake eventually said, but her tone was light.

"Not sure my therapist would agree with that, but I try. Granted, she wouldn't agree with me being here either so screw her."

Blake laughed as Freya shrugged softly.

"Wouldn't agree with you being here why?"

Freya held the warm mug in her hands as she considered how much to divulge. It had been so long since Freya even considered talking to someone outside of therapy about anything personal. She wasn't quite sure she knew where the lines were anymore. What was too much to share? What was enough? This was part of why Freya kept to herself. It was too complicated figuring out expectations. But if she was going to open up to someone, it was better to do that honestly, right?

"I have commitment issues and apparently struggle with forming relationships. So, I'm tasked with not jumping into bed with anyone for a couple of weeks and working on the whole friendship thing."

Freya rolled her eyes exaggeratedly as she squirmed in her seat. Why had she said all of that? There was something about Blake that made her want to lay it all out there, and that was more than a little unnerving.

"How's that going for you?" Blake said with a hint of a smile.

"I invited you to a coffee shop instead of my bedroom, so it's progress."

Blake's eyes dropped to Freya's lips and Freya could practically see the images her words had evoked of exactly what they would be doing had Freya gone with the latter invitation.

"So…you invited me here to form a friendship?" Blake asked.

"I invited you here for research, remember?" Freya said as Blake shook her head with a chuckle.

"Honestly though. Obviously, I was under the impression this was a date, but I wouldn't want to get in the way of your progress. Figuring your shit out isn't something everyone is willing to do, so I'm impressed."

Blake raised her cup to her lips and took a sip as Freya considered her words. There was nothing platonic about the way she thought about Blake and hadn't been since the moment their eyes met. But if Freya was serious about working through her issues and avoiding one-night stands, what did that leave?

"I don't really know. What I do know is that I crashed into you, and something made me need to see you again. That's not a line to get you into bed, it's the truth. I can't remember the last time I actually went on a date, coffee or otherwise, so I'm not lying when I say it's progress. I get that it's a lot of messy for our first maybe-date, but I'm just trying to be up front."

Blake studied her, and Freya wondered if this would all be too much for her. Freya wouldn't blame her if so, but she couldn't ignore the fact that she wanted to spend more time with Blake. That wasn't a familiar feeling for Freya, and not one she wanted to ignore.

"I'll be up front too since you're laying it all out there. I haven't dated in a couple of years. My last girlfriend was a player and didn't give up the game, so to speak, when we became official. I have a history of choosing people who don't choose me, and I'm not sure what I'm ready for. But I wanted to see you again, too. So how about we stay here, enjoy each other's company, and see where that leads? Two weeks isn't a long time, so we can use it to get to know each other more."

Freya nodded and dropped her gaze to Blake's mouth again. This woman had appeared in her life out of nowhere, accepted her mess, and wanted to know more. That made Freya's heart warm, while also having a distinct effect between her legs.

Two weeks suddenly seemed like a hell of a long wait.

Chapter Four

Blake's phone buzzed from where she had tossed it on the bed as she got ready to take a well-needed bath. Her heart skipped a beat and she tried to tamper her excitement. There was a chance it wasn't Freya, but there would be no denying the pang of disappointment if it wasn't.

Luckily for her, the disappointment never came as Freya's name lit up the screen. Blake compelled herself to continue to the bath or it was likely she would end up sprawled out on her bed in a text exchange while her water went cold. She brought the phone with her and slipped beneath the excessive amount of bubbles before finally opening the message.

Busy tonight?

Blake bit her lip and considered her reply carefully. Despite their obvious chemistry, they had done nothing but talk their entire coffee date. The afternoon had passed so quickly that it was dinner time before either of them knew, and the coffee shop was closing up. Blake hadn't ever spent that many hours simply talking to someone about anything and everything, but there hadn't been even a moment of awkwardness between them.

Freya's admission about her commitment issues should have had Blake running in the opposite direction given her own relationship history. But Freya's openness and the direct way she laid things out had touched Blake in a way she couldn't walk away from. The date had ended without even a kiss, and yet Blake had been on a high as if they had made out for hours. The rest of the week had been filled with both text and phone conversations, and Blake could hardly believe Freya had ever been a stranger.

Just taking a bubble bath. I go wild on Sunday evenings.

Mentioning the bath was probably a little cruel, but after a long week, Blake could use a little light flirting. She had been serious about not wanting to impact Freya's progress. Even if that meant their physical chemistry had to wait to be explored. At least, in each other's presence anyway.

Blake set the phone down on her bath tray and slipped a hand beneath the water. The slight sting of the heat took a moment to subside as Blake moved her hand along her skin and caressed her breasts. Her nipples were already aching for attention, and she stroked one between her thumb and forefinger as her phone buzzed again.

Pics or it didn't happen.

Blake laughed at the readout as the three dots quickly appeared again.

For research, obviously.

Blake bit her lip and typed with the hand that was still dry as she teased her nipples slowly with the other.

You can't use research for everything. Plus, I'm not sure that's allowed as part of your therapy...

The dots were back almost immediately, and Blake smiled at the idea of Freya eagerly waiting to reply.

Technically, the rule was no casual sex or one-night stands. Sharing photos with a new friend wasn't in the no can do list.

Blake moved her hand down over her stomach and between her legs. She stroked the soft skin as she imagined what would happen if she complied with Freya's request.

You share photos of baths with all your friends?

Blake wanted to take back the message as soon as she had sent it. Freya had made it clear within their hours-long conversation that friends weren't something she had. Blake winced at her insensitivity.

Only the ones who purposefully tell me that they are taking a bubble bath because they know I'll be picturing myself beside them.

Blake's skin tingled as she continued her exploration beneath the water and typed out a reply before she could think too much about it.

Is that all you're doing?

Her heart began to beat quicker as she reread her message and pressed her fingers to her swollen clit. Blake had basically asked Freya if she was touching herself, too, and she wasn't sure if her racing heart was out of nerves or excitement. Most likely both.

Well, I was going to ask if you wanted to grab dinner, but then you started talking about bubble baths and somehow my hand wound up beneath my pants. Is that what you wanted to know?

Blake's breath caught as she read the words. *Fuck.* Yes, that was what she wanted to know, but she hadn't expected Freya to state it so bluntly. Although in the short time Blake had known her, it fit with Freya's style.

Yes. Yes, it was.

Blake sent the quick message, not wanting to keep Freya waiting, but unable to think of anything more flirtatious as she picked up pace with her fingers.

Is the bath relaxing? Or a little too...hot?

Blake grinned and struggled to type while keeping up the pace of her fingers.

Definitely hot. Luckily, I had no pants obstructing my hand.

Blake had known mentioning the bath would likely lead to some light flirting, but she hadn't expected it to become this. Any thought of them maintaining nothing more than a friendship was surely out the window now, right? Not that Blake imagined a friendship being realistic with the electricity that buzzed between them constantly.

Neither do I anymore. And technically since I'm only touching myself while imagining it's you, I'm not breaking any rules.

Blake wanted to reply and say fuck the rules, but she wouldn't. That wasn't her decision to make. Plus, Blake would be lying if she didn't say the forbidden aspect of their encounter wasn't part of the thrill right now.

You're breaking them in my head right now, but fantasy probably doesn't count. Forbidding something has a way of making it much more enticing, though.

Blake was so close to the edge and had to stop her movements several times already. She wasn't quite sure why she was edging herself rather than letting go, but it was like she was waiting for something.

I'm not sure anything could make you more enticing, Blake.

Forbidden or not, I'm pretty sure I would want you this badly either way. Shit, I've never been this close this quickly alone.

That was it. That's what Blake had been waiting for. The pressure built in her thighs as she barely managed to type out a response.

Not alone. Together. Now.

Blake's scream was silent as she finally let the orgasm peak and ripple through her body. Denying herself had added to the force of her eventual release, and she sank back into the lukewarm water as her body twitched.

That was...hot as fuck. And I didn't even get my photo.

Blake blinked lazily at the message and smiled. She turned the camera into selfie mode and sent a quick shot before she lost her nerve. Her hair was piled on her head and her smile was quite clearly the kind that comes after a blissful orgasm. It wasn't as revealing an image as Freya had likely been expecting since Blake had only included herself chin up. But something told Blake that Freya wouldn't mind.

Happy?

Blake sent as a quick follow-up to the photo before setting the phone on the countertop above the bath. She reluctantly pulled the plug as she switched on the overhead shower to wash herself off. Her phone buzzed while she grabbed her towel. Any pretence that she hadn't been listening for the response went out the window as she grabbed it quickly.

Sorry for the delay...your photo made it pretty impossible not to need an encore.

Blake's mouth dropped open and her heart flipped. Freya had touched herself until she came again. This time while looking at Blake. The idea had the throbbing between Blake's legs starting up again.

So, dinner?

The second message came through before Blake had responded to the first and she blinked as she read it again. Dinner? Freya still wanted to go for dinner? Blake wanted to see Freya, but how would they sit across a table from each other and act normal after what had just happened? More importantly, how would they end the night going home to their separate beds? Their chemistry had already been palpable, but Blake suspected it would be even more heightened after what had just transpired.

You sure that's a good idea?

Blake couldn't just say no. She didn't want to. What she did want, though, was to know that Freya was thinking it all through first.

Well, I was already hungry and now I'm ravenous, and I have no edible food in the house. I could go eat alone if you're scared to share a meal with me, but I'd definitely prefer your company.

Blake scoffed as she finished towelling off.

It's not the meal part that scares me. It's what happens after. You've got rules, remember?

Blake went to her wardrobe and picked out a nice pair of jeans and a sweater while she waited for Freya's reply. They would be going for dinner because there was no way Blake was passing up the opportunity to spend the evening with Freya. If the opportunity arose, she wouldn't pass up the chance to spend the night with her either.

Just dinner. I promise. I have an early morning client, so I'll behave. I like talking to you, and I don't break promises.

Blake was surprised to find the idea of it just being dinner didn't disappoint her. Sure, she wanted more with Freya. More importantly, though, she liked the idea of being someone Freya wanted to spend time with outside of the bedroom. From the bits and pieces Blake had gleaned last week, that was far more unusual for Freya than simply bedding someone.

I can be ready in half an hour. Where will I meet you? I like talking to you too, Freya.

Chapter Five

Freya walked up toward the second-floor office for her therapy session. She finished typing out a message to Blake arranging their weekend plans before popping her phone on silent. Her therapist's office was located in a large building that housed a number of independent therapists of all kinds.

Need physiotherapy, occupational therapy, speech and language therapy? Look no further. Freya chuckled at the idea of a one-stop shop with clients moving from one to the other like a car maintenance check. If only they didn't have to pay through the nose for the pleasure, it could be a solid healthcare plan.

Freya had buzzed in below already, so she sat in the chair outside Moira's office and waited to be called in. Her ass had barely landed in the seat before the door swung open and Moira gestured her inside.

"Good to see you, Freya. How have the past couple of weeks been?"

Lust-filled. Euphoric. Exhilarating.

Two weeks had gone surprisingly quickly, despite the constant temptation in between. Freya had been surprised when her reminder went off yesterday about her appointment today. Time flies when you're having non-sex fun, apparently. Although non-sex-related wasn't totally true, considering their text activities from the weekend before.

"They've been…interesting."

Moira's eyebrow twitched slightly as she studied Freya's face.

"Interesting how?"

Freya grabbed the trusty cushion and crossed one leg beneath her.

Might as well get comfy while spilling your deepest, darkest secrets and all.

"I stuck to the rules. I think. Mostly."

Moira smiled as Freya tugged at the threads on the cushion.

"By rules, you mean my suggestion of forgoing casual sex?"

Freya nodded in response, although it had come across more like homework than a suggestion.

"Let's elaborate on the mostly part."

Let's not.

Moira already knew far too many details of Freya's sex life. Not nitty-gritty details, of course. It wasn't that kind of therapy. But the high-level ones she needed to understand Freya's casual sex situation. Freya wasn't getting into the details of mutual long-distance masturbation though, not with a woman who was old enough to be her mother.

"I met someone. We haven't slept together, but there's been a lot of flirting and…insinuations of that nature. But something is different."

Moira had yet to remove her pen from its place, and Freya wasn't sure if the lack of note taking was a good sign or a bad one.

"Different how?" Moira asked when a moment passed and Freya hadn't elaborated.

"She's just…I don't know how to describe it. We met two weeks ago, and I've spent more time talking to her in those weeks than I have with anyone in longer than I can remember. Something about her makes me want to know her, but even weirder, it makes me want *her* to know *me*."

Moira nodded and crossed her legs as she set her notebook to the side. No notes at all? That was unprecedented from Freya's experience here.

"How do you feel about that? Letting her know you?"

Freya took a moment to consider it. She wanted to answer as truthfully as possible because she was more determined than ever to make therapy work for her.

"Honestly, I feel like it should scare me. But it doesn't. We've met for coffee and dinner and talked on the phone countless times already and I've told her things I've never said to anyone. That should be absolutely terrifying, so why isn't it?"

Freya wasn't expecting a straight answer from Moira, but she desperately wanted one. Therapy didn't work that way, though. Freya had learned by now that therapy was more about uncovering the answers you already knew rather than getting new ones from someone else.

"Do you think the fact that you had decided not to sleep with anyone gave you the opportunity to explore a different sort of connection?"

"I think you saying it means that that's probably what you think," Freya replied with a smile.

"It's not about what I think," Moira said right on cue.

"If the sex ban hadn't been in my mind, would I have slept with her the first time we met and then not talked any further? Maybe. Something tells me that I would've wanted to know more about her no matter what, though. I can't explain it to myself, so I'm not sure how to explain it to you."

Freya was frustrated at being unable to encapsulate the thing that was tugging her toward Blake. Lust? Yes, absolutely. But it was deeper than that.

"Let's try not to focus on explaining it perfectly right now. You've met someone who it sounds like you've formed a connection with. The important part right now is working on how you retain that, if that's what you want, which it sounds like you do."

Freya nodded without hesitation. It had been such a short amount of time and yet she was already so sure she wanted to keep Blake in her life.

"That's the part I'm worried about, though. Not scared, exactly, but concerned."

Moira nodded as if she already knew where Freya was going with this, but she waited for her to get there anyway.

"If the chemistry between us continues, then we're going to sleep together. And then, what are the options? I don't know if I'm ready for a relationship. But a friendship alone seems unlikely. I want to keep her in my life, but I have no idea how to do that without fucking it up."

Freya took a deep breath and gnawed at her bottom lip as her chest tightened. Thoughts swam around her head of all the times she had fucked it up before. All the people who had come and gone, most of whom she had pushed away. Freya had gone this many years without managing to keep one connection that hadn't been tainted or destroyed. How could she believe that would be different with Blake?

"You're already so many steps ahead. You're planning the fallout of intimacy before the intimacy itself occurs."

"Yes, I am. How can I not? Is that not what therapy is supposed to be about? Stopping myself from repeating the same damn mistakes that wind me up alone every time?"

Freya's voice cracked and she held the cushion tighter as she waited for the emotion to subside.

"I feel like the work we've been doing is less about stopping you from repeating patterns, and more about helping you understand why the patterns occur. Freya, the things you call mistakes are defence mechanisms that once helped you survive. They are tools that got you to where you are now, the good and the bad. The point of this isn't to show you why they were wrong, it's to help you see you don't need them anymore. That if you put those tools down for a while and let people in, you can still be safe."

Freya blinked but she couldn't stop the stray tear that trailed down her cheek. Crying wasn't something she was comfortable doing around anyone, and it was the first time it had happened here.

"It must say something that I could talk at length about my absent parents, and my shitty childhood, but hearing you say I can be safe is what finally causes tears."

Moira smiled softly as she nudged the box of tissues on the table in front of them.

"Sometimes, people can't let down their guard enough to show emotion until they feel safe. Crying is an act of vulnerability, and it doesn't strike me that you've had many chances to be vulnerable."

Freya wanted to tell Moira to stop before the slow tears became wracking sobs. She held the tissue between her fingers but made no move to wipe the tears from her face.

"So, if I'm not supposed to jump too far ahead, does that mean I just need to see how things go with her? Is the sex ban lifted?"

Freya wagged her eyebrows and grinned. If this weren't a professional appointment, she was certain Moira would be rolling her eyes.

"That's still up to you, Freya. Do you want it to be?"

Do I?

On one hand, Freya wanted nothing more than to finally explore the palpable passion radiating between them with Blake. On the other, the thought of sex being off limits and out of her control had been somewhat freeing. It had given her the chance to explore their connection in a way she might never have done otherwise.

"I know it's not the point of your job, but can you tell me what to do? If I'm the one to decide, then I'll know it's not a real rule and then I'll ignore it. I don't think I'm ready to make this a relationship yet. But I don't want to stop seeing her. Can you break the rules and tell me your opinion without making me tell you mine?"

Moira let out a small laugh and Freya pumped her fist internally. She was winning this one.

"I think you want the rule in place to allow you to continue this connection. Since all of your sexual encounters have ended in the same way, with no follow-on relationship, you're worried this one will follow suit. With that in mind, I think it would be advisable to continue as you have been, building this connection without sex, and we can check in again at the next session."

Freya groaned despite the fact that she had been the one to ask Moira to say it.

"In saying that, you also need to trust yourself, Freya. You don't feel afraid with this woman because you already know you don't need to. That's an important thing to keep in mind."

It was telling that Freya already felt lighter with the rule back in place. It was silly. She was an adult capable of deciding who and who not to sleep with, and when or when not to sleep with them. Yet the idea of abstaining for a legitimate reason, while working toward a better connection, comforted her.

Freya spent the remainder of her session mainly updating Moira on work and the other minor ways she had made an effort with what they had discussed. Apart from her connection with Blake, Freya had also had a non-work-related conversation with a colleague during the week. Granted, it was initiated by said colleague at the end of a work call. The woman had begun talking about her recent weekend trip away and Freya had listened. She had even participated in the conversation with follow-up questions and had refrained from pulling them back on topic. Baby steps.

By the end of the session, the tissue was in shreds on the equally tattered cushion. Freya gathered up the pieces to dispose of on her way out. The small white shreds floated their way into the bin, and Freya had a moment of emotion resurfacing. That one tissue, now torn apart, was a reminder that not only had Freya let tears fall today, she also hadn't rushed to make them disappear.

Maybe, just maybe, baby steps weren't so little after all.

Chapter Six

Blake pulled up outside her parents' house and switched off the ignition. She turned her phone off handsfree and pulled it to her ear to savour another moment of conversation before dinner.

"You should get going. You're going to be late."

Freya's voice was already so familiar to her and yet still had the same effect as the first time she had heard it.

"If I wasn't late they would think something was wrong. It's my brand."

Freya chuckled, and the silky laugh sent shivers down Blake's spine. They would be seeing each other again tomorrow, and still Blake didn't want to end the call.

"Should I expect you to be late tomorrow, then? Because the movie will start with or without you, Blake."

"We've given buffer time, so it'll be fine. Plus, cinemas have popcorn and slushies, so that's extra motivation to show up on time," Blake replied.

"Oh, so *that's* your motivation for saying yes to seeing a movie with me?"

Blake grinned at the bait Freya had taken. Their back-and-forth teasing was far more exciting than it should have been, and Blake was always looking for ways to bring it out.

"It's definitely one of them. Dark movie theatre, cosy seats, copious amounts of salt and sugar…What more could I want?"

Blake glanced up as the curtain twitched from her parents' living room window. Her mom peered out at her with a questioning look.

Caught red-handed. Blake was more than aware that her face was giddy and no doubt her mom would want to know exactly why.

"What more, indeed. You better go to dinner before we end up talking about other motivations and keep you from going altogether. See you tomorrow, Blake."

"See you then, Freya."

Blake ended the call and smiled at her phone for a moment before exiting her car. Despite their goodbye, Blake was almost certain they would end up texting again tonight and probably tomorrow before they made it to their…date? Was it a date? If so, it would make it their third counting coffee and dinner.

"Is dinner with your parents so dreadful that you have to sit in your car and brace yourself?"

Blake laughed at her mom's dramatics as she ushered her through the door.

"Yep. Absolutely horrifying. That's why I willingly do it every week despite being an adult who can choose not to."

Blake hung her jacket on the hook in the hallway and slung her backpack on the floor beneath it. She had come straight from her last class of the week and would likely end up spending the night in her childhood bedroom as she did most Friday nights. Blake occasionally wondered if it was weird that she had an apartment all to herself and still chose to sleep here occasionally, but she wasn't one to try turning a positive into a negative.

She was more than grateful that her childhood home, and her parents, were a safe and comforting environment that she was welcome in. It was a gift, and one she wasn't willing to squander because someone decided adult children should live alone to be considered successful.

"You make a good point. Your father is still busy cooking, so let's go chat and you can tell me who had you too busy giggling to get out of your car."

Her mom gave her a knowing smirk and Blake's cheeks began to heat immediately. She stopped by the kitchen to give her dad a hug and grabbed a cold bottle of water from the fridge on her way. It was a stalling tactic, but no amount of stalling would stop her mom from getting the answer she wanted. Blake followed her mom into the living room and curled up in her usual spot on the two-seater couch. The couch itself had been updated numerous times throughout the years, but regardless of which fabric or colour it had, Blake still occupied the same spot.

"So, who's the lucky individual getting all my only child's attention these days?"

Blake rolled her eyes and kicked off her shoes so she could pull her legs up under her.

"Not my fault you and Dad gave up after having me. Was I really that bad as a baby?"

It was a running joke between them that teetered between them stopping at one because Blake was perfect, or because they never wanted to go through it again.

"No comment," her mom said with a grin and Blake gasped in mock horror.

"It's the same person I told you about when I came to get my bag at your office. The one you pushed me to text, remember? And if I remember correctly, you said you'd get off my back about dating if I did. So there."

"I said I'd get off your back for a week. It's been at least three since that day, so you're out of luck. Seriously though, how is it going?"

Blake should've known her mom would recall the specifics of the conversation. Blake rarely got away with anything as a teenager because her mom remembered the most inane detail that caught Blake out on a lie. Luckily for her, her parents understood lies as developmental learnings rather than moral failings, and Blake had learned that the truth was often easier anyway.

"It's going well. We've been talking a lot the past few weeks. We're actually going to see a movie tomorrow night," Blake said.

"That's great, Blake. I'm glad you're putting yourself out there again. Will this be the first date?"

Blake considered her words carefully. She had no desire to talk to her mom about Freya's no casual sex rule, or the reason behind it. As much as her mom wanted her to get back out there, Blake was fairly sure knowing it was with someone who had a history of commitment issues would not make her happy. Blake's mom was rarely judgemental of anybody, but she was also a protective mother who wanted to keep her daughter's heart safe. Blake had no idea how to explain that despite Freya's track record with relationships, or lack thereof, Blake was surprisingly not at all concerned about her heart. Maybe she should be, considering her own history of ignoring warning signs, but this time wasn't the same. Blake wasn't ignoring anything, and neither was Freya. That was the key difference.

"Not exactly. We met for coffee already, but I guess we were exploring whether we were better as friends or whether there's something else there. I'm not even certain if tomorrow *is* a date."

Blake's mom raised her eyebrows sceptically.

"I'm not sure what there was to explore. I've seen the way you talk to and about your friends, Blake, and this isn't it."

Her mom waved a finger toward Blake's face, and Blake chuckled softly.

"It's complicated. Especially after everything with Linda, I just… think I need to take things slow. One day at a time and all, which if you remember correctly is usually your motto."

Blake's dad called out from the kitchen to let them know dinner was almost ready. Blake stood to walk to the dining table and her mom reached out to squeeze her hand as she passed.

"I'm not saying you're wrong to take it one day at a time, Blake. But there's a difference between taking it slow, and letting fear hold you back. If you feel the way it looks like you do about this woman, then don't hold back. You make sure tomorrow is a date if you want it to be, because any woman would be lucky to have the chance to take you on one."

Blake pulled her mom in for a tight hug. She was grateful for this woman, who often frustrated her no end with her all-knowing abilities but who loved her in a way that Blake had never had to doubt.

"I'll go wash up and meet you there," Blake said as she pulled out of her mom's arms and was met with the knowing twinkle in her eye.

Blake pulled out her phone on the way to the washroom and typed a message to Freya before she could think about it too much. She set the phone on the counter without hitting send and washed her hands as she studied herself in the mirror. Blake had never considered herself insecure growing up. She had never spent hours critiquing herself like she had heard some of her friends do, or worried that she wasn't smart enough or pretty enough or funny enough.

Blake's parents had instilled such a strong sense of self-worth in Blake that it had knocked her for six the first time she was left questioning it. When relationship after relationship ended with Blake heartbroken and her counterpart seemingly unaffected, it was inevitable that Blake would begin to wonder if it was her. What about her made someone seek something else or treat her like she expected too much by wanting to be respected?

Blake saw the good in people, because her parents had seen it in her, and not everyone had gotten the same. Truth was that the world was full of people hurting, and Blake had to learn that sometimes it was easier for them to hurt someone else than to heal themselves. More importantly, Blake learned that understanding behaviour didn't need to equal accepting it, and that was the biggest lesson of all.

Blake grabbed her phone and reread the message as she walked back toward the dining room. Freya was hurting, that was for sure. Between all of their teasing and flirting and laughing, Blake had seen the pain in Freya's eyes as she spoke about her lack of relationships of any kind. Blake didn't know all of Freya's story, but from the parts she did know, it was a vastly different one to her own. Freya's hurting was obvious, but her determination to heal was just as clear. That was why Freya's past didn't scare her. Blake wanted to know every deep, dark part of Freya, and she had a feeling that once Freya let her, there would be no turning back.

Chapter Seven

Freya smiled at the figure hurriedly moving toward her as she waited outside the cinema.

"I'm not late, right?" Blake said as she reached Freya and paused to catch her breath.

"Just five minutes. So, I guess you can still get popcorn and slushies," Freya replied with a smile.

"Glad you added on that last part, or my rushing would've been for nothing. Should we go get tickets?"

Freya held her phone out showing the already purchased tickets she had secured online.

"Got it covered, so we can head straight to the good stuff."

Freya nodded toward the concession stand. Blake grinned and beelined toward the forming queue.

"You got the tickets, so the treats can be on me. What do you want?" Blake asked as she rummaged through her shoulder bag.

"Nope. I organized this date, so I'm paying. What'll it be?"

Blake stopped her rummaging and looked as if she were about to protest. Freya gave her best *don't mess with me* face, and Blake chuckled.

"If you insist. Popcorn and mixed slushy, please."

"Mixed slushy?" Freya asked in confusion.

"Yup. They fill the cup with fifty percent red and fifty percent blue, and it becomes one hundred percent delicious."

They moved up and were next in line as Freya checked the concession menu on display behind the counter.

"That doesn't seem to be one of the flavour options," Freya said.

Blake looked at her as if checking she was serious before laughing lightly.

"This isn't my first rodeo, Freya. You know you can order things that aren't specifically stated on the menu, right?"

"Honestly, that hadn't occurred to me," Freya said with a shrug. The customer ahead of them left with their goodies and they moved to the counter. Freya ordered Blake's requested items for both of them and was grateful that the cashier didn't seem bothered about the off-menu item.

"Figured you seemed to know what you were doing, so I'd get the same," Freya said as they gathered the food. They walked toward the screen showing the latest romcom that Blake had mentioned wanting to see, which was what had prompted Freya to suggest they go together. It had been said casually, and Freya had been unsure about whether it constituted a date or just two friends watching a movie together. Luckily for her, Blake cut out any confusion with one simple message to Freya the night before.

Is tomorrow a date? I want it to be, by the way, just putting that out there.

Freya's face had almost hurt from smiling after the message had come through, and she had readily replied that she wanted the same. So here they were, in search of their pre-booked seats in the already darkened theatre on their confirmed date.

"These seats are amazing. I knew they had refurbished but I didn't realize it was this much of an upgrade," Blake said.

"What was it like before?"

The seats were standard. They were comfortable, but she couldn't imagine paying to watch a movie in seats less comfortable than this.

"What do you mean?" Blake asked as she set the slushy into the convenient cup holders beside them.

"The seats. How much worse were they?"

Blake set her popcorn down and turned more fully toward Freya.

"Have you never been to this cinema before? There's only two in the city, so I just assumed you would have been to both at some point."

Freya shrugged and took a piece of popcorn to pop in her mouth.

"Nope. Also, this popcorn is very good."

Freya reached down to grab more from the tub. The salt clung to her fingers as she made quick work of the handful.

"Wait. Hold up. You've never been *here* before, or you've never been to the cinema before?"

Blake's eyes widened and Freya laughed at the incredulous look on her face.

"I've never been to the cinema before. I have access to a million movies from the comfort of my home. I even have a pretty large TV across from my bed, so what's the point?"

Blake's eyes got wider, and she shook her head slowly.

"I don't think I've ever met someone who has never been to the cinema. There were no movies you wanted to see badly enough that you couldn't wait till they were out of the cinema to watch at home?"

Freya was enthralled by the popcorn and had pulled the tub back into her arms.

"Not really. I don't watch movies often. I can binge ten forty-minute episodes easily, but sitting through a couple-hours movie never appealed to me much."

And I've never had anyone to go with.

Freya added that part in her head, not wanting to kill the mood with information Blake already knew. Freya had no issue doing enjoyable things alone, but the cinema hadn't ever appealed to her enough to do solo.

"What about when you were a kid? You never went with family or friends or…"

Blake trailed off as if answering her own question in her head. Freya smiled reassuringly to ease some of the discomfort building.

"No, my parents weren't the *activities with their kid* type. So, you get to be the one to introduce me to this experience, and this popcorn. I see now why it's worth showing up for."

Freya wagged her eyebrows hoping to lighten the mood back up as Blake gave her a soft smile. The already dim lighting darkened further as the screen lit up.

Blake leaned in until her lips were pressed against Freya's ear and Freya's stomach swooped at the contact.

"I'm honoured. And just to clarify, you're worth showing up for, too."

Freya's breath caught as Blake placed a soft kiss against her cheek before turning back to face the screen. Blake's hand moved to the armrest where Freya's arm lay, and she entwined their fingers together. Freya's heart thrummed in her chest as the adverts filled the screen and Blake's thumb caressed her hand in slow circular motions. At that moment, Freya was sure that the cinema was about to be her new favourite place.

❖

"So, what's your verdict?"

They walked out of the cinema with their hands still interlocked, and Freya blinked against the onslaught of light.

"It's like another world in there. I forgot it was still daytime."

Blake chuckled as they walked past the queues of people getting ready for the next showings.

"I can see why it appeals to you," Freya said.

"Rom coms, or the cinema?" Blake asked.

"Both. I mean, I've seen rom coms before, so I was already a fan. But there was definitely something different about experiencing them in a room full of people there to do the same. Hearing everyone laugh collectively and even dreamily sigh collectively was something I hadn't realized I was missing out on. All these strangers sitting in one room just to escape real life and enjoy the unfolding of a story together is kind of beautiful."

They stood outside the cinema facing each other as those same people exited around them. Freya's cheeks heated as Blake stared at her a beat longer than was comfortable before reaching up to place a kiss on her lips. The kiss was over before Freya had even registered it was happening, and she wanted to rewind and savour it more.

"What was that for? Not that you need a reason," Freya said.

"I've been going to the cinema for so long that honestly I never thought about it that much. I guess I took it for granted, but you're exactly right. It is beautiful, and I love that you enjoyed the experience."

Freya didn't want the date to be over, and she hoped it didn't have to be. It was early evening, and the last thing she wanted after this was to spend the rest of her night alone in her empty apartment.

"Want to get dinner?" Freya asked as Blake opened her mouth to speak.

"I was just about to ask where to next. You sure you're not too full of all of your popcorn and half of mine?"

Freya gave her a sheepish look.

"It was so good, and you were wasting it. I'm not hugely hungry but I just didn't want the date to end, and I lack ingenuity when it comes to ideas of what to do."

Blake chuckled and squeezed Freya's hand that had yet to uncouple from Blake's. Freya was hoping it didn't have to anytime soon.

"We could go back to my place and hang out for a while and then get food delivered later?" Blake asked. Her voice was hesitant, and a blush crept up her neck. "When I say hang out I mean hang out. I know you mentioned about taking things slow and I respect that, but I thought we could talk or—"

Freya leaned in and placed a soft kiss against Blake's lips.

"I'll go wherever means I get to do more of that," Freya murmured against Blake's mouth as she pulled back from the kiss. Blake smiled dreamily and Freya wanted to pull her back in for more despite their public setting.

"My place is only about a twenty-minute walk if you're up for it. The bus is across the road, but I have no idea when it's due, and that's ten minutes anyway."

Freya readily agreed to the walk. She hated buses that were always crowded and noisy and would rather walk the whole city than take one, so it suited her. It would also give her body time to calm down before they reached their destination and she forgot all about her taking it slow rule. Although, with Blake's hand still firmly in hers and her thumb stroking lazily back and forth, Freya was sure her body was fighting a losing battle.

"Does the no-sex rule leave room for making out on my couch?"

Freya startled out of her thoughts and repeated the sentence in her head as she looked into Blake's twinkling eyes.

"You think making out on your couch won't lead to breaking said rule?" Freya asked.

"Have you no self-control, Freya? I'm perfectly capable of controlling myself if we have set boundaries," Blake said with mock offence.

"I very much want to test that theory and see how long it takes for that self-control to waiver," Freya replied.

Her mind filled with images of all the ways she wanted to

make Blake lose control and beg her to break those aforementioned boundaries. Even if the boundaries were Freya's to begin with.

"I can see the gears turning in that head of yours, Freya. Just remember, I won't feel good if I'm the reason you break rules that you've set for a reason, and I'm pretty certain you want me to feel good about what we do. Right?"

Blake was exactly right with that. There was one common thing that Freya had held on to through all of her past encounters that she did not want to lose wherever this new path took her. No matter what, Freya made damn sure her companion felt good about their experience and themselves, even if it was only for a night. Enthusiastic participation was a must, and Freya wanted that and more with Blake. So much more.

"I definitely want to make you feel good," Freya said, and she thrilled at the darkening of Blake's pupils. Blake's eyes dropped to Freya's lips and back up before she took a deep breath.

"My apartment is just up on the right. But before we go in there, I need you to understand something."

Freya nodded to indicate that she was listening.

"I want you, Freya. And I have no doubt in my mind that you can make me feel good. But I don't want one night with you. If sleeping together means I won't hear from you again tomorrow, then I don't want it. I'm not ready for you to disappear from my life, but I'm not sure I have the willpower to hold back if things go in that direction tonight."

Freya opened and closed her mouth. She had no idea what to reply, and the mix of emotions swarming her was confusing. She was excited that Blake wanted her and touched that more than that, Blake didn't want to lose her. Freya couldn't imagine walking away from Blake after one night together, but was she ready for more?

"I'm not asking you for commitment right now, Freya, but I am asking you for honesty. If you can't keep us in check with just making out, and you're not ready for more than casual sex, then we can kiss here and say good night. I want you to know that I'm okay with waiting as long as you need, Freya. You're worth it."

Chapter Eight

Blake squirmed under the intensity of Freya's stare. Freya had yet to utter a word after Blake's statement, and they were standing exactly in the same spot for what felt like hours but was likely only minutes. Blake wasn't sure if she had said too much, but she was confident in her words. She would rather wait for Freya to be sure than spend one night together and lose her. As electric as that night would be, Freya already meant too much to her in a short amount of time to lose.

"We need to go to your apartment."

Blake was relieved as Freya finally spoke.

"We can go, but what I'm saying is we don't need to. I'm good with whatever you're comfortable with."

Freya reached a hand out and pushed Blake's hair behind her ear. Blake's breath caught as Freya leaned in close, pressing their bodies together as she moved her lips to Blake's ear.

"We need to go to your apartment because I don't want to be arrested for public indecency. And the ways I want to respond to your extremely thoughtful words are definitely indecent."

Heat flooded through Blake's body and pooled between her legs as Freya brushed her lips over Blake's earlobe before she pulled back. Freya's pupils were dark with lust, and Blake lost all ability to be the voice of reason.

"Let's go."

Blake uttered the two words and turned to walk up the steps of her apartment block as Freya followed closely behind. So close in fact that the heat of Freya's breath tingled against her neck as she unlocked the door with a shaking hand.

Blake was suddenly overcome with self-consciousness. She hadn't exactly planned to have anyone over, and she hoped the place was at least somewhat presentable. The door opened directly into a combi kitchen/living space. Her bedroom that held the en suite, and only, bathroom was through a door to the right. It was small, but plenty big enough for her.

Blake shrugged off her jacket and threw it over the chair as Freya closed the door behind her.

"Welcome to my humble abode. Do you want a drink? I'm not sure what's there but I can guarantee at least water, coffee, and tea."

Freya reached out and placed a finger beneath Blake's chin before lifting her head softly.

"You're nervous."

It was a statement rather than a question and Blake nodded her confirmation.

"Why?" Freya asked softly.

"I don't know. I just started thinking that my place might be a mess and it's small and…"

Blake shrugged. Saying it out loud made it sound silly, and the truth was they both knew her nerves stemmed from a lot more than the condition of her apartment.

"Blake, your apartment could be in shambles, and I probably wouldn't notice. My focus is solely on you."

Blake let out a breath and smiled.

"You are very charming, Freya."

"I'm honest," Freya said before leaning in to place a soft kiss against Blake's lips.

The simple action awoke the hunger in Blake that silenced the nerves that had stifled it. Blake wrapped her arms around Freya's neck and deepened the kiss until every nerve ending in her body was screaming for more. Freya's hand slipped beneath the hem of Blake's shirt to caress her back, and Blake's skin tingled at the contact. The kiss moved from soft to sensual to desperate.

Freya walked them forward until the bare backs of Blake's thighs hit the small wooden dining table. Blake gasped as her linen skirt rode up to make way for the thigh Freya slipped between her legs. The rough denim of Freya's jeans pressed against the thin material of Blake's underwear. Blake dug her fingers into Freya's shoulders as her sensitive clit begged for more.

"Fuck," Blake whimpered as Freya's thigh pressed more firmly against her centre.

Freya pulled back enough to look into Blake's eyes. She gripped Blake's hips on both sides to steady her as she slowly moved her thigh in teasing motions. The intensity of Freya's gaze made Blake's breath catch, and she bit her bottom lip to hold back another whimper. Freya moved a hand from one of Blake's hips and ran it slowly up her body. She stroked her thumb over Blake's bottom lip and released it from its hold.

"Don't hold back," Freya whispered as she continued to stroke her thumb along Blake's lip. Blake closed her lips and placed a kiss against the pad of Freya's thumb before Freya replaced the digit with her lips. They kissed slowly and deeply as Blake moved her body to the rhythm of Freya's thigh and allowed herself to gasp and moan unabashedly at every stroke. The sounds she made had a tantalizing effect on Freya. Each one sped Freya's movements up and had her grasping to pull Blake closer in any way possible.

"Freya, fuck, I need you."

Blake choked the words out as Freya kissed her way along Blake's neck while her fingers teased their way along Blake's exposed thigh.

"Now," Blake said with more force. Freya hummed her approval against Blake's neck as she quickly replaced her thigh with her fingers. Freya slipped Blake's soaked panties to the side and stroked the slick skin between her legs as Blake threw her head back with a gasp. Freya's thigh had already worked Blake's clit into a swollen, pulsing state. She twitched as Freya stroked her thumb across it before her palm pressed more firmly against it.

"You okay?" Freya breathed softly against her ear as she nipped at Blake's earlobe.

"Almost. Please, Freya," Blake said. It was as much as she could muster, but there was no doubt about what she was begging for. Freya placed light kisses across the curve of her face until she was back eye to eye with Blake.

"Don't look away."

Blake nodded in acknowledgement of the demand because there was no doubt in her mind that that's what it was. Not a request, not a flippant remark, but a demand. One that Blake was all too happy to oblige once Freya provided the release she so desperately needed. Freya slipped one finger inside Blake, closely followed by a second as the evidence of Blake's need became all too obvious. Freya's palm stroked against Blake's clit as her fingers moved in a steady rhythm. Blake clung to Freya's shoulders as pleasure began weaving its way up her legs.

"Fuck, I'm close," Blake said with her eyes still on Freya's. The demand that had been an easy one to agree to was proving more difficult to maintain. Blake fought the urge to close her eyes to revel in the orgasm that was close to eruption. There was something intimate about letting go and tumbling over that edge while you watched someone watch you. Blake was exposed and vulnerable, but somehow safe. Freya looked at her with a clear longing and hunger, but beneath all of that there was something else in her eyes. Something soft, comforting, and ultimately that was the thing that made Blake keep her eyes right where Freya wanted them.

"You are so beautiful."

The words were little more than a whisper, and if Blake hadn't seen Freya's mouth move she might have wondered if she imagined them. The pleasure peaked and Blake cried out as it pulsed through her body in wondrous waves. Freya didn't move her eyes away even as Blake slumped in her arms as her body twitched from the aftershocks. Blake pressed her forehead to Freya's as she caught her breath. Freya stroked soft circles on the small of Blake's back, and Blake wanted nothing more than to stay in that moment.

"I think you broke your rules."

Freya chuckled as Blake pulled back and gave a face she hoped said *whoops, but I don't care.* Freya stepped back to give Blake room to straighten up as she regarded her with an amused smile.

"I've never been one to say rules are meant to be broken, because I'm a pretty good rule follower. However, I've perfected the art of finding loopholes to rules throughout the years."

Blake nodded toward the two-seater couch against the back wall and went to sit in it. Her legs were still feeling the effects of their rule-breaking, and she wanted to pay full attention to what Freya had to say. Freya sat next to Blake and they both turned to face each other.

"So, what loophole have you found? If you say anything about you giving me an orgasm not being real sex I think we'll have bigger problems."

Freya rolled her eyes with a smile. Blake's insides warmed as Freya's hand landed on her bare leg. The action seemed absentminded, as if Freya subconsciously needed to be touching her somehow.

"No, that was definitely sex. The thing is, technically my rule was to abstain from casual sex. Which at the time of making the rule meant all sex, since it was the only kind I had."

Blake held her breath against the hope that was blooming without her permission. The direction Freya's loophole was going in wasn't what Blake had expected, and she tried to stay in the moment rather than jumping ten steps ahead.

"So, you're saying…"

Blake trailed off and hoped that was enough to prompt for the clarification she needed.

"I'm saying that I didn't break the rules because I didn't have casual sex. Nothing I feel for you is casual, Blake. Terrifying, exhilarating, unexpected…all of those things, yes. But casual? No."

Blake let the smile she had been holding back appear and shook her head slowly.

"For someone who isn't used to the whole romance thing, you're pretty damn good at it. And as much as I want to bask in those words and accept them all at face value, I have to ask. Are you ready for something more than casual?"

Blake's gut twisted at her own question as fear gnawed at her insides about what the answer might be. She wanted to be the same carefree person who years ago would've swooned at Freya's statement and pushed aside her own concerns. But that person had been burned too many times by sweet-talking women who dodged real conversations, and Blake had promised herself that wouldn't happen again. Her rose-tinted glasses needed to stay well and truly off, and she needed to see Freya for who she was, good and bad and everything in between. That meant asking questions even if the answers could lead them in the opposite direction of where Blake wanted to go. Which right now was a dozen steps to her bedroom.

"I won't lie to you, Blake. I've never been very good at it anyway. I can't tell you I am one hundred percent certain I'm ready for a relationship. I've gone my whole life without ever having a meaningful one. I have no idea if I'll be any good at it, and I have a lot of baggage I'm still working through. But what I do know is that from the moment I knocked that cup out of your hands, I've wanted you in my life. And that has to mean something. You're the first person who doesn't make me want to run from the idea of becoming attached to you, and the truth is, I already am. It would already hurt to turn and walk away from you, but being just friends isn't an option either when I can't seem to keep my hands off you."

Freya's eyes wandered down to where her hand had begun playing with the hem of Blake's skirt, and she smiled softly.

"I don't know if I'll be any good at this, Blake. But I want to try."

Chapter Nine

Freya blinked open her eyes and waited as they adjusted to the dimly lit room. Her heart began to pick up pace as her surroundings came into view and she realized the room wasn't her own. It was smaller and had a large colourful print on the wall where the television sat in her room. Soft, even breaths puffed against her shoulder and reminded her of exactly where she was, and who she was with.

Freya turned her head gently so as not to wake Blake. Her heart maintained its accelerated rhythm as she took in Blake's curves beneath, and on top of, the quilt. Blake was sleeping on her side with a bare thigh flung over the covers that hid the rest of her naked body. A body Freya had gotten to explore every beautiful inch of last night here, in Blake's bed. Where she had stayed.

What the hell am I doing?

Freya closed her eyes again and took slow, deep breaths to quell the panic trying to claw its way up her throat. It was inevitable that it would rear its head at some point. Freya wasn't naive enough to think that the calm and certainty that had been with her last night would remain. Her attachment issues didn't magically disappear because she found true love and would ride off happily into the sunset, trauma free.

True love.

Freya's eyes flung open again as she replayed the words in her head. Did she love Blake? Was that what this was? It was entirely too soon to be considering words of that magnitude. Then again, how long did it take to love someone? Freya's parents had done things the *right* way. Dated for an acceptable amount of time before deciding it was love, moving in together, getting married, and having a child. They had followed the carefully laid-out steps, and in the end, love hadn't really been in the picture at all. Not for each other, and certainly not for Freya. One thing Freya was certain of was that she had no desire to follow in either of their footsteps. So, if there was no well-trodden path to lead the way, there were no rules to be adhered to either, right?

Love.

The pounding of her heart was so loud that she was sure it would wake Blake with its attempt to escape her body. Freya had considered why none of her feelings for Blake had terrified her before now. Part of her worried that it was the calm before a storm, lulling her into a false sense of security. She took a moment to utilize some of the tools she had learned in therapy. Expensive tools that Freya might as well get use of. She focused on her breathing and tried to pinpoint her feelings, something that didn't come naturally to her.

Freya had always used words like sad, happy, angry, the big feelings that were easily identifiable based on external indicators. Turned out there were a multitude of feelings beneath all of those, and that was the key to understanding them. It wasn't that Freya struggled to know that she was feeling *something.* The struggle lay in identifying exactly what that something was. The racing heart indicated fear, perhaps anxiety, and Freya tried to dig deeper and see what else made sense.

"You're thinking so loud I can almost hear it."

Freya turned her head and smiled softly at the still-sleepy-looking Blake. Her chestnut hair was tousled around her head, and her eyes were struggling to focus on Freya.

"You look adorable," Freya said.

"You look terrified. Have you been awake long? Trying to figure out how to sneak out without waking me?"

Blake smiled but Freya suspected the question wasn't wholly a joke.

"Nope. Trying to figure out what I'm feeling. Sneaking out would probably be an easier feat," Freya said with a smile. She heard the words after saying them and hurried to clarify. "Not that I wanted to sneak out. I just meant—"

Blake leaned in and cut Freya off with a soft kiss.

"I know what you meant. Is it a good or bad feeling we are trying to decipher?"

Blake drew back and Freya followed her in search of more of the far too chaste kiss. Blake reached out and placed a finger over Freya's lips, halting her in her tracks.

"Nope. You're not going to find the answer that way," Blake said.

"How can you be sure? It's worth a shot," Freya replied with a grin.

Blake gave her a mock stern look which only had Freya grinning even more.

"We both have morning breath, which is never sexy, and you have important feelings to figure out. I'm going to go brush my teeth, and when I come back we're going to make breakfast and talk. With clothes on."

Freya managed a faux pout which lasted for about two seconds. Blake rose from the bed and sashayed her way toward the bathroom with not a hint of self-consciousness to be seen. Freya watched every deliberate sway of Blake's generous hips. She practically whined as Blake disappeared through the bathroom door and shut it behind her.

Freya wanted nothing more than to drag Blake back into this bed and discover every dip and curve of her body over and over all day long. Partly because she wanted to avoid confronting the feelings surfacing, but Freya was sure mostly it was pure, unadulterated desire. Freya listened to the water running as Blake presumably brushed her teeth.

Freya had nothing with her to deal with her own morning breath. It was something Freya had never had to consider with a lover, considering the fact that she had never spent the night with someone that actually included sleeping and waking up together. It was a small thing, but it was another reminder that this was new territory for her, and she had no idea what to expect.

"Let's go get those loud thoughts out of your head over food."

Freya startled as Blake spoke. She had been wrapped up in her contemplations and had missed the sound of the door opening. Her body reacted immediately to the still naked Blake standing at the end of the bed watching her carefully. Freya's eyes wandered down to the equally ample curves of Blake's breasts. She couldn't help her satisfied smile at the still-reddened skin from Freya's explorations the night before.

"You gonna stare at my boobs all day or join me for breakfast?"

Freya looked up at Blake's face that clearly indicated her enjoyment at being ogled.

"Depends. Can we skip the clothes part?"

Blake laughed and grabbed an oversized T-shirt from the end of the bed.

"Nope, because then we'll get no talking done. But I'll skip pants."

"Deal," Freya agreed.

She hopped up and looked at her clothes strewn on the floor. The last thing she wanted to do was get back into jeans. Her face must've spoken for her, and she smiled in relief as Blake handed her a pair of comfy lounge pants and T-shirt from a drawer.

"Thank you. My body isn't ready for jeans yet."

Blake grinned in clear self-satisfaction knowing that she was the cause of Freya's still aching body.

"I don't have a toothbrush for my morning breath," Freya blurted out as she stood holding the clothes.

"There's a spare in the cupboard beneath the sink. I'll start breakfast, and come out when you're ready."

Freya opened the still-packaged purple toothbrush and had a fleeting thought of whether Blake had gotten it for if someone stayed over. Freya knew from their previous conversations that she hadn't been in a relationship in a couple of years, but that didn't mean there hadn't been other people here within that time. A stab of jealousy surprised Freya at the thought of anyone here in this space with Blake.

She eye-rolled at herself in the mirror as she finished brushing her teeth. Freya couldn't be jealous of Blake's past when she had bedded more women than she could count the past few years. But the little sliver of jealousy remained nonetheless, and in a weird way Freya was glad for it. Once she didn't let it affect things negatively, it wasn't necessarily a bad thing. Jealousy wasn't something that Freya was familiar with, and it certainly wasn't a casual emotion.

Blake had set out an impressive array of bagels, fruit, and coffee, and Freya's stomach rumbled at the display.

"I didn't realize how hungry I was," Freya said as she joined Blake at the small dining table.

"Well, we did forgo the takeout last night, and I don't think the random snacks we foraged at midnight were a great substitute," Blake replied.

"Good point. But I can't say I regret sacrificing real dinner with hours of sex instead."

Blake chuckled and they sat in comfortable silence as they satiated the hunger that had gotten ignored until now.

"When did you get the tattoo?"

Freya broke the silence with the question that had popped into her mind.

"Which one?" Blake replied after swallowing the bite that was in her mouth.

"All of them, but I meant the one peeking out from the edge of your T-shirt," Freya said with a nod toward Blake's collarbone.

She had spent time tracing the black lines last night but had been too distracted to ask more about them. The design was a small but detailed flower with what looked like a tiny bee perched on its stem.

"I got that one at nineteen after my nan passed away unexpectedly."

Blake was smiling as if in memory, but unmistakable sadness passed across her features.

"I'm sorry. You were close?" Freya asked. She had never had any sort of relationship with her own grandparents, but the grief was still evident in Blake's words over a decade later.

"Very. She practically lived with us when I was young. My parents bought a house only a few doors down from hers. They worked quite a bit, so she took care of me after school. I adore my parents, but my nan was my favourite person."

Freya reached out and squeezed Blake's hand softly as she spoke.

"Her name was Rose, and she called me her little bee. Hence the tattoo."

Blake pulled her T-shirt to the side to reveal the design again, and Freya registered it clearly with the context.

"It's beautiful. Really smart design idea too."

"I can't take credit for it. It was actually my nan's drawing. She's a big part of why I got into creative writing. She would tell me stories and we created this sort of running one about adventures little bee would take. As soon as I learned to write, I began writing them down and she would draw pictures to go with them. I still have most of them in a box in my parents' house. The tattoo was a copy of one of the drawings."

Freya's eyes welled, and she was embarrassed at the unexpected reaction.

"You okay?" Blake asked with concern.

Freya had no idea how to explain her sudden response to a simple story of Blake's childhood.

"Yeah, sorry, I'm not sure what's come over me," Freya said with a small laugh. Her cheeks were hot, and she had too many swirling emotions to pick apart.

"Maybe it's those pesky feelings you keep trying to distract yourself from, hmm?" Blake said as she reached out a hand to cover Freya's.

"It's okay to get emotional, Freya."

Was it though? It was a story about Blake's life, not Freya's.

"I don't know why, honestly. I don't think I'm sad. The meaning behind the tattoo and the drawing and picturing little you writing stories and your nan drawing them and supporting you, it just…got to me. It's beautiful."

Freya choked up at the end and almost fled the table from embarrassment. What in the world had gotten into her?

"It is beautiful. I was fortunate to get the time I did with her and to have the memories I do. It's okay for that to make you feel things, good or bad. It's like when you watch videos with people reuniting at airports or dogs reacting to their owners and tear up even if they are strangers."

"You watch videos of strangers?" Freya asked in confusion.

The reply made Blake laugh, and Freya joined her as the room filled with their combined mirth.

Chapter Ten

Blake whistled to herself as she dressed for her picnic date with Freya in an hour. It had been a couple of weeks since their first night together, and although they had agreed to take things day by day, Blake was hopeful. They had spent hours after breakfast talking about their feelings and fears and everything in between. Pausing only to explore each other again multiple times.

They had spent a few passion-filled nights together since, and Freya seemed to get more relaxed with each one. Blake had awoken the morning before last to Freya already up preparing breakfast for them both. Blake smiled as she grabbed her toothbrush and glanced at the second one beside it. The one that had become Freya's. There were reminders of Freya everywhere. The smoking hot red dress Freya had worn for their last date was in Blake's laundry hamper. Blake had almost drooled upon seeing the dress and had enjoyed peeling it off Freya even more. Freya had left the next day in Blake's more comfortable clothes, leaving the dress behind. It warmed Blake to know there were remnants of her in Freya's place too, even if she had yet to see it.

Despite how comfortable Freya was getting while they were together in Blake's space, she had yet to invite Blake into hers. Truth be told, Blake had yet to be introduced to Freya's life at all. She was content to take it at whatever pace Freya needed, but she couldn't help her curiosity.

The ding of Blake's phone drew her attention, and she snapped out of her daydreams.

I'm heading your way now. Ready in fifteen?

Blake checked the time and baulked at how much of it had passed since she started to get ready. She shot back her agreement and pulled her stuff together. No more than five minutes later, there was a knock on her door, and Blake rushed to grab her light jacket.

"You're early," Blake said as she pulled open the door.

"Early for what?"

Blake looked up from where she was shoving her keys into her bag at the sound of her mother's voice.

"Oh, sorry, I thought you were Freya."

"Freya?"

Her mom repeated the name with what sounded like confusion.

"My date. Remember? The one you practically forced me to go out with weeks ago? You'll be glad to know your meddling worked. We're sort of…dating now."

Blake smiled and expected her mom to do the same but was met with a look that bordered on concern.

"You never mentioned her name. And we've barely spoken since the night you weren't even sure if it was a date or not. So, what's Freya like?"

Blake was confused by her mom's reaction. She expected excitement, not hesitance. True, Blake had spent most of her free time with Freya the past few weeks, so hadn't spent much time with her parents, but she figured her mom would understand, if not encourage that.

"She's great, but she's actually about to arrive for our date, so…"

Blake trailed off sheepishly. She wasn't the type of person who could tell her mom to leave nonchalantly, but her mom was good at picking up on hints.

"Oh yes, sorry. I was just passing by after my last appointment of the morning and thought I'd drop off the memory boxes you asked me to root out for your project. I'll get going."

Blake took the bag her mom held out and set it inside the door. She pulled her mom in for a quick hug.

"Thank you. I'm sorry I've been so busy. I promise to make time for dinner next week. Things have been going so well, I can't wait to tell you about her."

Her mom squeezed a little tighter before pulling back with a smile. It wasn't a real one. Blake knew her mom well enough to know that. Something was up and Blake had no clue what it could be.

"Do you need to talk? I can message Freya and reschedule if you want to come in."

Her mom shook her head and waved Blake off.

"No, not at all, enjoy your day. I need to get going anyway."

She turned to leave, and Blake stepped out to close the door behind her.

"I'll walk out with you. Freya should be here any minute anyway."

Her mom looked briefly as if she was about to protest, but she stopped herself and they fell into step together. Something was not right, but her mom wasn't one to be pushed about things. She would tell Blake whatever it was when she was good and ready, and she always gave Blake the same grace.

Her mom walked out of the main building door first with Blake following closely behind. She spotted blond curls at the end of the building steps and grinned. Blake stepped out beside her mom, and Freya's eyes seemed to flick between them. Confusion marred Freya's features, and Blake winced.

"Hey. Sorry, I didn't intend to spring the whole meet the parent thing on you, but my mom just stopped by to drop something off. She's leaving now, so we can forgo formalities until another time, right?"

Blake directed the last part to her mom as the confusion on Freya's face gave way to something akin to panic. Freya hadn't divulged a huge amount, but enough that Blake understood that parents were a touchy subject for her. That coupled with the fact that they had barely begun dating made it understandable that she would find it far too early for introductions.

"Sorry, what?"

Freya responded, but her eyes were still on Blake's mom. Blake quirked an eyebrow and walked closer to Freya.

"This is my mom, Moira. She was dropping by the old stories I was telling you about that I wanted to show you later. You okay?"

Blake reached out a hand to Freya's. The contact snapped Freya out of whatever internal panic she had going on and she blinked before turning toward Blake.

"Sorry. Yeah, I'm okay."

Blake wanted to point out that the quiver in Freya's voice said otherwise, but she refrained.

"I'm going to get going. You two have a good day. Nice to meet you, Freya."

Blake's mom spoke for the first time since they bumped into Freya outside. Her voice was steady and clear, but her face was masked with forced politeness.

Shit.

Blake wasn't concerned about Freya making a bad impression. Her mom would never hold it against someone, especially someone who was blindsided by her barely-girlfriend's mother. However, her mom's reaction was far from warm and inviting, and Blake didn't want Freya to kick herself about this later.

"Bye, Mom. I'll be over on Friday, promise."

Blake smiled at her mom as she got into her car where it sat in front of the building. She turned back to Freya, who still looked as if she had seen a ghost.

"I'm really sorry. I would have warned you, but I put my phone into my bag when I heard the knock because I assumed it was you. My mom doesn't generally drop by unexpectedly. I think she was checking on me because I haven't been over much the past few weeks."

Blake squeezed Freya's hand and smiled reassuringly.

"I've been a little caught up with staring at you and all. I know she seemed a little off, but honestly, she will be happy about it. She's been pushing me to date again for ages."

Freya gulped and nodded slowly. She looked like she was still trying to gather herself, and Blake was fine to give her whatever time she needed. The sun was out, the breeze was light, and they had a whole day to push past the initial awkwardness.

"You want to walk there? It's a beautiful day."

"I…can't."

Blake turned toward the direction of the park before Freya's words registered. Blake turned back to Freya with a frown.

"What do you mean? We can get the bus if you'd prefer."

Freya shook her head and looked around her as if waiting for someone to pounce.

"No, I mean, I can't go. I'm sorry. I don't feel well, I need to go home."

Freya's breathing was quicker than usual, and Blake's confusion turned to concern.

"What's wrong? We can go inside. I have medicine or I can grab whatever you need."

Blake's eyes widened as she stepped toward Freya only for Freya to step back.

"I'm sorry."

It was all Freya said before she turned and walked in the opposite direction. Blake stood stock-still and watched her go while holding what was obviously a picnic basket in one hand.

What the hell just happened?

Blake urged her feet to move, follow Freya, make sure she was okay. But her brain urged her to stay where she was. Whatever was up with Freya, Blake was certain it wasn't illness. She reminded herself of the promise she made. No more chasing, no more begging people to want her.

Blake walked back into her apartment and slumped onto the couch. Less than an hour before, she had been so hopeful about their day together and, beyond that, the direction their relationship was going. Now all Blake felt was deflated.

It was understandable for Freya to be a little surprised by the unexpected introduction to Blake's mom. It wasn't understandable for her to hightail it out of there without even talking to Blake about it. If this was her reaction to the first uncomfortable situation they had, it wasn't a good sign. Blake was done being the one who ended up broken by trying to fix people who didn't want to be fixed. At least, not by her.

Chapter Eleven

What were the damn odds?

When Freya got back the brain power to think clearly, that was the first thing that came to mind. Considering the fact that she had bumped into Blake outside her therapist aka Blake's mother's office, the odds were probably high. Freya was more than aware that all her therapy tools had vanished, and she had dealt with it all horribly, but it was too much. Being faced with the person who knew so many of her deepest scars and insecurities out of context was hard. Then finding out she was the mother of the person who Freya had her first real connection to ever had thrown her body into complete panic.

Freya had gotten home, curled into bed, and sobbed in a way she hadn't done in longer than she could remember. Every wound that had yet to heal, every memory etched behind her eyes, every lonely moment that led her to that day poured out of her until her head pounded and her chest ached. It was all too much, and she had shut down.

Now, two days later, a feeling she could only assume was grief choked her until she couldn't sit alone with it anymore. That's how Freya had found herself back to her old haunting spot, Blaze. It was barely late enough for the drink she was sipping all too quickly. The warm liquid gave her something to focus on as the place got busier with the evening rush. She sat in her usual spot, between the bar and the dance floor with her back against the wall and a perfect view of the door. Freya had always assumed it was because it made it easy to look out for potential companions, but in reality it was another unpacked trauma. Nobody could sneak up behind or in front of her, it was the prime place for control of her surroundings. Another lesson Freya had learned from Moira.

Blake's mother.

What a shit show this had turned out to be. The only two people in the world Freya had ever truly opened up to, and they happened to be mother and daughter.

"Hey, Freya. Long time, no see."

Freya startled and a surprised laugh left her mouth as she looked up into Robyn's familiar brown eyes twinkling in amusement.

"Sorry, I didn't mean to scare you. I can go."

Freya shook her head quickly.

"No, you're okay. It was just funny timing. I was only thinking about how I usually pick this spot to sit because nobody can sneak up on me, and then you do that."

Robyn sat in the unoccupied chair across from Freya and smiled softly. She had a comforting smile, the kind that made you want to return it. Once upon a time, Freya had wondered if they could have something more than the one-night stand they had shared. In fact, she had even suggested a second night, something she rarely did. Robyn had shot her down and was now married to the reason why, and it was obvious to everyone who met the couple that it had been the right choice.

"I thought I'd say hi. I haven't seen you here in a while."

Robyn and her wife Lexi had a group of friends that hung out in Blaze quite often. The group were probably the closest acquaintances that Freya had, and she had always envied their tight-knit relationships as she watched from a distance.

"Yeah I've been…seeing someone, I guess," Freya said. She didn't miss the quick flash of surprise on Robyn's face even though her features shifted quickly into a smile.

"That's great. Who's the lucky lady?"

Freya's mouth opened and closed as she considered exactly what to say. Talking about her personal life wasn't her forte, and doing so was what had led to her feeling how she felt today. Opening up to someone else didn't seem wise, but Freya had so much inside that she was sure if she didn't get it out she would burst. Her therapist wasn't an option, so who else?

"Listen, it's okay if you don't want company. I've got an hour to kill before my second shift starts, but I can go sit over there and play on my phone and I won't be offended. You just looked like you could use an ear, and I've been told I'm a pretty good listener. Or something like that," Robyn said with a chuckle.

Freya smiled and took another sip of her drink as she tried to gather her thoughts.

"Won't Lexi mind you talking to me?" Freya asked to buy some time.

Lexi, Robyn's wife, had been Robyn's roommate when they hooked up and had seen Freya walk out of the apartment after their one and only night together. Yet Lexi had been nothing but polite, if not kind, to Freya anytime they had interacted since. Still, she didn't want to cause any unnecessary drama for anyone.

"Why would she? Lexi knows we had sex, and that's all it was. Hell, if she got mad at me talking to women I slept with, I'd have to shut my mouth every time I came in here," Robyn said.

Freya laughed lightly and nodded.

"Touché. You and I both. I forgot you and I shared a lot of… proclivities before you figured out you already lived with your one true love," Freya replied.

"Yep. Pretty sure we've decimated the five degrees of separation thing between us."

They sat in comfortable silence for a minute as Freya gathered the courage to say something, anything to make sense of the mess in her head.

"How did you do it?" Freya asked quietly.

"Do what?"

"Deal with your commitment issues and put it all on the line for Lexi. I mean, I get it, you two are perfect for each other. But how did you go from one-night stands to forever with one person?"

The question barely scratched the surface of what Freya wanted to know, but it was a start. Truthfully, though, she didn't need an answer to that last part. Giving up casual sex to spend every night with Blake didn't concern her. If anything, it thrilled her. That wasn't the part that made her heart pound and had her hightailing it to safety.

"Honestly? It wasn't difficult. The first night I spent with Lexi, I knew that was it for me. She was it. The hard part was trusting that I was good enough for her. Even when I wasn't being strong or the one to fix everything. Letting her take care of me and still feeling worthy of her, that was hard. It took time and patience on her end for me to work through those things. And a lot of talking. Luckily for me, Lexi has a way of making anyone talk to her," Robyn said.

Freya was quiet for a moment as she took it all in. So much of what Robyn said resonated.

"Blake's like that. She has this way of making me say things I never expected to say. Our first date we spent hours in a coffee shop, just talking, and I felt closer to her than I ever have to anyone."

Freya's chest filled with emotion at the memory. Why did there always have to be a catch?

"Sounds like you got yourself a good one. I'm happy for you, Freya."

Tears pricked at the corners of Freya's eyes, and she shut her lids as if that could prevent them from falling.

"Shit, sorry. I gather that was the wrong thing to say."

Light pressure landed on Freya's arm, and she let the warmth settle against her skin before opening her eyes again. Robyn's face was full of concern and compassion, and Freya wanted to run away from it all. But where exactly had that gotten her so far? She was pushing mid-thirties, alone in a bar that she had frequented for years now, without even one real friend in the place, or the world for that matter, to turn to about all of this.

"She is a good one. Too good for me, you know? I've got so much baggage that I'm still wading through. Then it turns out the person helping me wade through it, who knows all about my past and my numerous one-night stands, is none other than her mother."

Robyn's eyes widened and Freya almost laughed at the comical nature of the unfiltered reaction. Saying the words out loud sounded about as preposterous as it had felt standing on that street hearing it from Blake.

"You told her mother about your one-night stands? I'm not judging, just want to make sure I'm following," Robyn said in a tone that sounded as confused as Freya felt.

"Her mother is my therapist. Which I only found out when I went to pick Blake up for a date on Saturday and bumped into her outside."

Robyn blew out a breath and shook her head slowly.

"That's…"

"Ridiculous? Horrifying? The plot of a cheesy rom com starring a mediocre dude and a ridiculously out of his league boss bitch?"

Robyn sputtered a laugh and Freya smiled at her own dramatics.

"Oddly specific but yes, all of that. Are you the boss bitch or the mediocre dude, though?"

Freya shrugged as she took a sip of her drink.

"Who knows. What I do know is that Blake and her parents are really close. How am I supposed to go to Friday dinners and sit across the table knowing that her mother knows more about my sex life, my attachment issues, and my many shortcomings than my girlfriend does?"

Robyn didn't reply right away, and Freya half expected her not to bother. What exactly did you say to that? She didn't expect anyone to have answers, especially given the fact that nobody knew Freya well enough to know what she needed. Nobody apart from Blake at least, and she wasn't an option.

"I don't know how you go about handling a situation like that. What I do know, though, is that things are rarely as impossible to deal with as they seem. And if Blake makes you feel the way I can see she does when you even mention her name, the details are worth figuring out. What did she have to say about it all anyway? It must be weird for her too."

Freya fidgeted with the paper coaster on the table as heat crept its way up her neck.

"I…didn't stick around long enough to find out."

Freya kept her eyes on the table as shame consumed her.

"Tell me what happened. You might as well, in for a penny and all."

Robyn's voice was still soft with compassion, and it gave Freya the courage to glance up at her. There was no judgement apparent on Robyn's face, or any reflection of her own shame.

"Blake introduced us and Moira, Blake's mom, played it off as if we had just met. I mean I guess she sort of had to, client therapist confidentiality or whatever. I could see she was as taken aback as I was, so I am sure she didn't know either. I started to panic internally and stayed silent and then I told Blake I didn't feel well. I could tell she didn't buy it, but I turned and left before she pushed any further. I know it was a shitty way to deal with it, but my brain was running in overdrive, and I felt like I couldn't breathe."

The replay of the moment had Freya's breath quickening and she focused on taking a few deep breaths to slow it down.

"You panicked. That's understandable. It must have been a shock. Have you reached out to her since?"

Freya shook her head and glanced at her phone face up on the table between them. As silent as it had been since that day.

"No. I sort of expected her to message or ring. To be mad at me, or confused, or demand answers. Anything. Once I got home and calmed down, I was ready for that, and I planned so many answers in my head. But I didn't expect nothing. It's been two days and radio silence. Maybe her mom told her to stay away from me. I wouldn't blame her if she had."

Robyn prodded the top of Freya's phone toward her.

"There's only one way to find out. You walked away, so you're the one who needs to reach out. She deserves answers, and you deserve to give yourself a shot. Talk to her."

It was so simple when Robyn put it like that. But the worries still flooding Freya's brain had her hesitating as she reached for the phone.

"What if she wants nothing to do with me? Or what if she does? This whole commitment thing was hard enough without all this extra complexity. I'm terrified."

Robyn picked up Freya's phone and placed it into her hand where it had frozen in midair.

"I'm not going to pretend it's going to be sunshine and roses. But I can say that you're already pretty miserable not talking to her, so you need to decide if the risk is worth the reward."

If that reward was Blake, then Freya had the answer. She tightened her grip on the phone and smiled softly at Robyn.

"Thank you. For wasting your hour off listening to my drama," Freya said. She laughed lightly to lighten the words, but the gratitude was sincere.

"It's been far more interesting than mind-numbingly scrolling on my phone. I'm definitely going to need an update, too. In fact, Lexi and I are meeting Brooke and Sam here Saturday evening at eight for drinks. If you're not busy, then join us. If all goes well you should bring Blake. If not, you can drown your sorrows among friends."

Freya opened her mouth and closed it again. No words would truly encapsulate everything the sentiment meant to her. From its casual delivery to the specificity of the invitation. Freya had often gotten a vague *we should catch up sometime* semi-invitation from acquaintances and colleagues throughout the years. Sentiments that never led to anything concrete, which was as much her fault as theirs. The mental effort to figure out if they actually meant it and prod herself to follow up with plans held too much uncertainty for her to follow through on. Robyn had so easily given a day, time, and place while leaving the ball in Freya's court to accept or not. A tiny seed of hope blossomed when Freya realized that she wanted to.

"I might just do that. Thank you. Again."

Robyn hopped up from her chair and nodded in response.

"I need to run. I'm glad we got the chance to chat. See you Saturday."

Freya smiled at the reiteration of the invitation as Robyn turned to walk toward the door.

"Freya?"

Robyn had stopped and turned back toward her.

"Yeah?"

Freya's gut twisted as she waited for the catch. Robyn's smile was still soft and kind and her eyes twinkled as she spoke.

"Even mediocre guys and boss bitches in cheesy rom coms get happy endings."

Chapter Twelve

Can we talk?

Blake stared at the three simple words as if they would morph into all the answers she had been waiting on for days now. She had ignored the message when it appeared on her screen the night before, but her willpower only lasted so long. Her eyes had barely opened this morning when she caved and opened it. The problem was Blake had absolutely no idea what to reply. Could they talk? Sure. Did she want to? That was a different question.

Blake placed the phone face down on the bed and pushed it away. She buried her face in the pillow to drown out the noise from passing cars. If only drowning out the noise in her own head were as easy. The pillow wasn't doing a great job anyway as the gentle knock on her door reached her ears.

"Honey, you up?"

The concern evident in her mom's tone unreasonably irritated Blake. She had been the one to show up on her parents' doorstep last night with a presumably tear-streaked face. Her mom had fed her dinner followed by ice cream and given her space to hole up in her room with her thoughts. Blake was grateful that she hadn't prodded for details last night, yet the niggling annoyance still resided in her chest.

"You can come in," Blake said.

Although there had been no further knocks, she was sure her mom was still hovering outside. A suspicion confirmed by the immediate turn of the doorknob as her mom entered the room.

"Your dad's gone fishing for the day. I have breakfast prepared if you feel like joining me. Do you have classes today?"

Blake threw her legs over the side of her bed and pushed them into the slippers she kept beside it.

"No classes this week, it's midterm. I'll just wash up and come down for breakfast."

Blake smiled, but the concern etched into her mother's features didn't waver. She hovered for a moment before nodding.

"Okay, I'll take the food up."

Blake waited for the door to click shut after her mom left before she sat back down on the bed. She slid her hand beneath the pillow and retrieved the phone from where she had pushed it away. Her heart thumped as one new message waited for her.

Good morning. If you want me to back off, just say and I will. But I wanted to say I'm sorry for bailing on our date. I'd like to try to explain if you'll hear me out.

More words this time at least. Blake left her phone on the bed and walked into the adjoining bathroom. The message replayed in her head as she washed up and brushed her teeth. Her gut twisted as she recalled brushing her teeth in her own apartment the morning after the first night Freya stayed over. Blake had woken up that morning and had seen the thoughts running a million miles an hour across Freya's face.

She had suggested talking over breakfast and gone to wash up to give Freya time to get her thoughts together. Part of her had expected to walk out of the bathroom to find Freya dressed and ready to bolt from her apartment. From what Blake knew about Freya's past, that wouldn't have shocked her at the time. She had been prepared for it. The more they had talked after that, the less prepared Blake was for Freya to flee. She had become comfortable, safe, vulnerable. Again.

Blake grabbed her phone before leaving her room and typed out a quick reply.

I want you to back off.

She stared at the words as her anger ebbed and sighed before deleting them. It wasn't true. Blake locked her phone and popped it into her pocket as she followed the smell of home-cooked food toward the kitchen. A small, spiteful part of her hoped that Freya saw the dots appear and disappear in their message thread. She eye rolled at her own pettiness before flopping into her usual seat at the table.

"Rolling your eyes at my display?"

Blake frowned before she glanced down and spat out a laugh.

There on her plate was a large pancake with bacon for hair, pudding for eyes, and a sausage smile.

"Ms. Fry," Blake said as her mom took the chair across from her.

"You looked like you needed her today."

Blake couldn't quite remember when it had begun, but anytime Blake had a hard day growing up, she would wake to what she had dubbed as *Ms. Fry* on her plate for breakfast. The silly pancake face had never failed to raise a smile from her, even in the worst of her teenage moods.

"I did. Thank you."

They ate in silence for a while before her mom gave up on subtlety and went back to her preferred method of direct communication.

"So, what happened?"

Blake set down her fork and sat back as she wondered what to say. When her apartment had gotten too quiet, and with Sadie away for midterm, Blake had weighed up the pros and cons of coming here. The fact that her mom would make her talk it out had been on both sides of the list.

"Freya happened," Blake said with a light shrug.

Her mom nodded and looked as if she was struggling to find words. Not a usual occurrence for her. "What did she say?"

Blake frowned and studied her mom. That was a strange follow-up. The niggling that had been with her since that afternoon outside her apartment got louder and Blake couldn't shake it.

"She didn't say anything, that's the problem. We were supposed to go on our date when you met her outside the apartment. You both acted weird, you left, and she suddenly had to go home. I haven't seen her since. What's going on?"

Blake's mom shifted uncomfortably in her chair, and alarm bells rang in Blake's head. She thought back to that day and remembered that her mom had been off since before even meeting Freya. In fact, she had been off since Blake first mentioned her name.

"You know her. Is she a client?"

Bingo.

It was all clicking into place now. Blake had known from the start that Freya was in therapy.

"Oh my God, how did I not realize? I bumped into her outside your damn office and still didn't put two and two together. You are her therapist."

Blake's mom didn't confirm or deny, which meant Blake was on the money. She couldn't confirm because of confidentiality, but she could deny if it weren't true.

"You're the therapist who put her on the sex ban. Ironic since you were basically pushing me to jump her bones," Blake said with a laugh devoid of humour.

Her mom opened her mouth as if to protest, and then closed it. Her mom was strict about client confidentiality and wouldn't even hint at anything throughout the years. Ireland was a small place, she would always say, and Cork even smaller. Someone always knew someone who knew someone, and a story without identifying information could still end up in the wrong hands. Blake respected that, even if right now she wanted her mom to throw it all aside and talk to her.

"I know you can't confirm or deny anything. Which makes it kind of difficult to actually talk it through with you."

"I'm sorry. I want to help, I hate seeing you hurting."

She reached a hand out to cover Blake's and squeezed gently.

"That's why she left, then. She must've been shocked when I introduced you. I knew she was panicking about something, but I figured it had more to do with her parental issues. Which I'm sure you know all about."

Her mom didn't flinch, and Blake admired her strength. Blake could never have followed in her footsteps. She would have caved by now and at least nodded.

"I get that it must be weird for her knowing that you know everything about her. But she didn't have to run away. She could have talked to me and explained, or at least tried to make a better excuse. She could've made more of an effort not to leave me in the dark."

Blake's mom sighed as she stroked her thumb over Blake's hand softly.

"Sometimes when people are put on the spot and panic, they… react in the ways they're most accustomed to. It's like that saying old habits die hard. It can take a long time to do something differently to how you've always done it, but it doesn't always mean someone isn't trying their best, you know?"

Blake tilted her head and watched her mom's face carefully.

"So, you're saying that Freya is used to running away and dealing with things alone, but I should be patient because she's trying to change that?"

Blake's mom sighed and Blake sympathised with how hard it must be to know most of the answers and not be able to give them.

"I'm saying that maybe you should talk to her to see if you feel that's true or not. Have you tried to since she left?"

"No. I promised myself I wasn't going to be the one to do the chasing anymore. You saw what happened before, I won't go through that again. I'm sympathetic with Freya's issues, but she's the one who needs to decide if she wants to deal with them."

A flitter of a smile crossed her mom's face and Blake suspected it was one of pride.

"That's fair. So, you haven't heard from her?"

Blake glanced down at her phone and then opened the message thread, holding it out for her mom to read the two messages that had come through.

"She reached out last night and then this morning. I haven't replied yet."

"Are you going to?"

Blake shrugged as she put the phone back down.

"I'm scared."

The words slipped out before she could stop them, and her mom walked around the table. She sat in the chair next to Blake and pulled her in for a tight hug. The familiar comfort had Blake welling with emotion again.

"Tell me what to do."

The soft, rhythmic movement of her mom's palm up and down her back calmed Blake's breathing.

"I can't. But I can tell you what you said, which I think answered your own question."

"What?" Blake said with a sniff. Despite not being her therapist, her mom could never stop herself from using Blake's words to teach her stuff.

"You said that Freya is the one who needs to decide if she wants to deal with her issues. From the messages you've shown me, it looks like she's trying to make that decision. Now it's your turn to decide if you want to be a part of that or not."

Blake pulled back and wiped her eyes as she looked at her mom.

"Before a few days ago the answer would've been yes, absolutely. And I know that one mistake shouldn't make me write her off. But she left and I had no idea if I'd ever see her again and it hurt. So bad. How can I trust that she won't do it again?"

"Focus on what you can control, which is you. The only thing you need to trust is yourself."

Blake sighed at the words she had heard a thousand times before and should have seen coming.

"Stop being a therapist for one second and just tell me the truth. You know me, and you clearly know her. If I let her explain, is she going to break my heart?"

Blake stared at her mom, hoping that she would find the answer written in her face even if she wouldn't say it with her words.

"I am telling you the truth. I don't say these things just because they are the way a therapist talks, I say it because it's the truth, Blake. I can't tell you she won't break your heart. If I could make sure your heart was always safe from harm, my love, I'd give anything to do that. I can't control that, and neither can you. What I do trust, though, is that I have raised an amazing, compassionate, strong human who I have no doubt can deal with what life throws at her. Even if that's a broken heart. Trust that, Blake, and you have your answer."

As much as Blake wished her mom would tell her what to do, she understood that was the best she was going to get. She also knew from experience that her mom was careful not to influence Blake even if she had the power to do so. It was a gift Blake often took for granted, being given the space and support to make her own decisions, for good or for bad. There was never an *I told you so* or a *You should've listened to me* waiting for her at the end of a mistake, and it meant she could always come here when things went wrong.

Something Freya had never had, Blake understood. Blake turned to pull her mom into another quick hug.

"Thanks, Mom. For everything."

Chapter Thirteen

Freya took her usual seat on the couch and pulled the familiar frayed cushion into her lap. She marvelled at the way it was all the exact same while being infinitely different. Freya could hardly believe it was barely over a month since she left this office and bumped into the woman who turned her whole world on its head. The woman who happened to be the daughter of the person sitting across from her right now.

"I wasn't sure if you'd keep today's session," Moira said.

The words were spoken in the same way Moira had always spoken to her, and Freya was a little surprised by that. As if Freya were any other client and this was a routine session. Moira was good at her job, that much was clear, but Freya hoped for a hint of how she truly felt about the situation.

"I wasn't either, honestly. But my calendar reminder went off and, well…I figured it was better than running from this problem, too."

The flicker of a smile that Moira gave sparked a thrill of pride. She wanted this woman's approval. As her therapist, that wasn't something to strive for, but as the mother of her…

Her what? Girlfriend? Lover? Oh God, don't say lover.

Freya glanced up and hoped the panicked thoughts weren't written all over her face.

"So, that must've been as much of a shock to you as it was to me. I don't really have a manual that tells me what to do in this situation, but I will try my best. Firstly, are you okay?"

Freya blew out a breath and shrugged her shoulders.

"I have no idea how to answer that. Are you asking as my therapist, or as Blake's mom?"

Moira set down her notepad and pen on the table beside her and crossed her legs slowly.

"You've already paid for this session, so right now I'm your therapist. But I won't pretend I'm not also, and always, Blake's mom. I'm good at separating my professional from my personal life, Freya, but I understand these are quite intricately linked for you too."

Freya nodded. She appreciated the honesty of the statement.

"This is the last session of the group I prepaid for, right?"

Moira nodded her reply.

"Okay, so, I think I need a recommendation for a new therapist."

Moira picked the notebook back up and tore a page from the front of it. She passed over the single sheet with a list of names and numbers scrawled in neat handwriting.

"I assumed you would ask for that, so I got it ready."

Freya read the names and tried to ignore the quiet voice in her head that taunted her by saying that Moira was all too happy to unburden herself from Freya. It was a voice that used to be far louder before Freya had begun therapy, and one she wouldn't give more weight to than the woman who had helped her quieten it.

"I've already spoken to my first recommendation on the list. She works from this office too, so no change of location, and she has availability coming up. I'm also happy to have a transfer session with her in advance to get her up to speed so you're not starting from scratch."

The voice was drowned out by the gratitude that swelled inside Freya at the thoughtfulness of Moira's gesture. Freya had been wrestling with her doubts about how she would manage to drag herself to a new therapist with the idea of restarting from the beginning.

"Thank you. That's…I don't really know what to say."

"You've made great progress, Freya, and it's important you continue that," Moira said.

Freya placed the sheet of paper in her bag and turned back.

"So, should we leave it at that? I know there's time left in the session, but you can use that for the transfer stuff or whatever. I mean, I'm not sure it's appropriate for me to discuss any of my current shit with you."

Freya laughed weakly and bit her lip to stop its shaking.

"That's up to you, Freya. I don't want to sway you either way, but in here I am your therapist first and foremost."

"Does Blake know?"

Freya asked the question that had been on her mind in a multitude of ways over the past few days.

Does she know I'm your client? Does she know why I walked away? Does she know how much baggage I have? Does she know you're probably never going to want your daughter getting caught up with someone like me?

"My daughter is astute. So yes, she figured out why we were both acting strangely that day. I haven't told her anything, though, and I won't. Anything you say stays here unless you choose to take it elsewhere."

Freya nodded again as she tried to gather the words she needed to say and hoped they would come out in the right order.

"I really miss her."

None of those words were any that Freya had been planning to say, but the truth spilled from her lips regardless.

"How does that feel? Missing someone?"

Freya considered the question. In the context of their previous sessions, it was a relevant one.

"It hurts. It's scary. All of my fears of people leaving if I let them close are right there at the surface and it's hard. But…"

Freya tightened her hold on the cushion and steadied her breathing before she continued.

"But mostly it's this constant desire to see her. To talk to her. I'm not sure how much you know, but the truth is I didn't leave because I let her close. I left because I panicked. And I can continue to beat myself up about that, or I can do something differently. I can show her that my initial reaction was one of fear, but that every day since then all I've wanted was to fix it in any way possible so I can be with her again. In the way she deserves."

Freya took a deep breath as the silence stretched between them.

"Like I said before, you've come a long way, Freya. If I told you six months ago that you'd be saying this now you probably would've gotten up and walked back out."

Freya laughed at the accurate observation.

"This might not be fair to say, and I understand as a therapist you have to do the whole not give me direct answers thing, but it's in my head so I'm saying it anyway. I guess I worry most about the fact that you know so much about it. Mostly all the ugly things that I have spent so long moving away from. Not to mention far too much about my… casual encounters. Which is all fine as my therapist, but as Blake's mom? I know how important you are to Blake, and vice versa. How do I sit across from you at dinner and wonder if you're judging me because I'm not good enough for your daughter?"

Freya's heart pounded in her chest as she sat and waited for Moira's reply. She had absolutely no idea what it would entail, but suspected it would be kind, if not curt and professional.

"I know I mentioned this, but I don't have a guidebook for how to deal with this situation. Since this is our final session anyway, I'll do my best to *directly* address some of what you said. Even if that's not the therapist way," Moira said with a wry smile.

"Anything ugly from your past that you've told me, Freya, has not been because of you. None of what you went through was your fault or painted you in any kind of negative light. Aside from that, my daughter is a smart, capable woman. Her decisions are, and always have been, her own. I would never attempt to sway her away from someone that she cared about deeply, even if I wanted to. And let me be direct, I don't want to. Blake deserves someone who cares for her in the way she cares so deeply for everyone else. And it's clear to me that you care deeply for her, Freya."

Freya blinked back tears and willed herself not to cry here, again.

"I hope she can see that too," Freya said softly.

Moira sat forward in her seat and smiled.

"She will if you show her. My daughter can be stubborn, but in this case her reluctance is more fear than obstinacy. Blake has always been the one to give all of herself to a relationship, and I think she just needs to know someone is willing to meet her halfway."

"I can do that. I want to," Freya said.

"I believe you. Now, I happen to know she has no classes this week and she went back to her apartment this morning. And I wouldn't suggest bombarding her unannounced if I didn't think it would be well received…"

Freya hopped up from the couch and dropped the cushion back in its place.

"I owe you," Freya said.

"You can repay me by joining us for dinner when you figure this all out and facing that new fear of yours."

Freya grinned and nodded in response. Suddenly the fear wasn't quite so scary anymore. Apparently, facing them sometimes worked. Who knew?

Chapter Fourteen

Blake grabbed the popcorn from the microwave and dumped it into the waiting bowl. She was in her comfiest lounge pants and had prepared her favourite binge-worthy, queer, demon-slaying TV show. Popcorn bowl in hand, she curled onto the couch and picked up the remote to press play. Her hand betrayed her and grabbed her phone again. The lack of message from Freya this morning had her heart panging unreasonably. Blake had yet to reply to the latest messages, so why would she expect another? Yet some small, hopeful part of her wanted proof that Freya wasn't giving up on her.

Blake chastised herself and pulled up the message thread. They were both adults, and she shouldn't be playing games to make Freya prove herself. Freya didn't deserve it, and Blake deserved answers. She typed out a quick message agreeing to talk and sent it before she could overthink. The soft rapping on her door was almost immediate, and Blake frowned at her phone as if it was the culprit.

"Blake?"

Freya's voice carried through the paper-thin walls of the apartment, and Blake jumped. She hopped up from the couch and walked to the door. Her hand stalled on the doorknob before she pulled it open.

"Hey," Freya said with a shy smile.

"Hi. Um, did I summon you?" Blake asked as she nodded to the phone in Freya's hand.

Freya chuckled and nodded. "Somewhat. I was standing out here trying to work up the courage to knock. I was worried you'd send me packing or that I'd seem like a stalker, but your message gave me the nudge I needed. I know it's short notice, but how about now for that talk?"

Blake stood back and gestured for Freya to come inside. She was not prepared for the conversation to happen so soon, but she was glad Freya was here. Seeing her again brought everything rushing back. More than anything, it had Blake's heart leaping to attention.

"Do you want anything? Tea, water?"

Freya shook her head and glanced down to the nest Blake had made herself on the couch.

"Sorry if I interrupted your plans. I'm not sure I can offer better company than *Wynonna Earp*," Freya said with widened eyes.

Blake smiled and walked back to her spot on the couch.

"Well, if you bore me I'm just going to press play. Be warned."

Blake picked up the popcorn and popped a bit into her mouth as Freya sat across from her on the one-seater chair.

"That's definitely one way to end a conversation," Freya said wryly.

Freya fidgeted with her hands as Blake sat expectantly. She fought the urge to fill the silence. Freya wanted to talk, and Blake was willing to listen. She needed to let Freya take that step herself.

"Firstly, I want to say that I'm sorry. I know that you know why I panicked by now, but I dealt with it badly. I've never had anyone who I could be vulnerable and panic around, and I didn't know how to manage that with you. It wasn't okay and I want you to know that I do know that."

Blake wanted to pull Freya close to her and wrap her up tightly. She wanted to say it was all okay and that she understood, all was forgiven. But the niggling hurt at the memory of Freya turning and walking away from her still lingered, and she would be doing no one any favours by ignoring it. Blake wanted to release Freya from the guilt that quite obviously gnawed at her, but she had to ensure she was doing so with eyes wide open and not clouded by her deep feelings for Freya.

"It wasn't okay. I do understand why you panicked and left. It must've been a shock for you seeing my mom, your therapist, completely out of context. But you left and didn't contact me for days, Freya. I had no idea what was going on until I put two and two together when I went to visit my mom. It took days for you to reach out to me, so it feels like a little more than in the moment panic, you know?"

Freya nodded her agreement and Blake was glad that there was no immediate defensiveness.

"You're right. I panicked in the moment, but after that I was so filled with shame and fear. I couldn't really piece it all together properly to even understand, much less explain coherently. I knew you deserved answers, but I was trying to figure them out for myself first."

Freya picked up the cushion that Blake had gotten as a housewarming gift when she first moved into the apartment. It had *New Adventure* embroidered across the face of the cushion, and Freya played with the tassels that adorned each edge.

"That's the thing, Freya. You don't need to figure it all out alone before letting someone know something is going on. I don't expect you to be able to explain every reaction, every feeling you have perfectly in the moment. It's enough to tell me something is going on for you and that you either need space to work it out or that you want to work it out together. Either option is okay, but silence and confusion is not."

Freya frowned as she absorbed the words.

"You'd be okay with me saying there's something going on and I need time alone to figure it out?"

Freya's scepticism was evident, and Blake understood it wasn't about her.

"Of course. Just because we're seeing each other doesn't mean I expect you to change how you deal with things to suit me. Obviously, I am more than happy to help you work through things if that's what you want, but it's also okay to need time alone to do that. I need to know that that's what's happening, though. Otherwise, I have no idea if this is a blip or if you're just...gone."

Freya hesitated for a moment before moving to join Blake on the couch. She reached out a tentative hand, and Blake turned her palm up to reassure Freya that the contact was welcome. As the soft skin of Freya's hand landed in hers, Blake's stomach flipped. Her body responded so innately to Freya even with something as simple as holding hands.

"I'm sorry. I know how it feels to be left wondering, and I never wanted to do that to you. I have a lot of shit I still need to work through, Blake, but I want to. With a new therapist, though," Freya said with a light laugh.

"I was so concerned with messing up your therapy journey with sex that I didn't consider I might do that with my parentage instead," Blake said.

She was only half kidding. Her mom was good at her job, and Blake hated the idea of Freya losing someone who had been helping her heal.

"I saw Moira, your mom, this morning. She gave me a recommendation for a new therapist, and she's even going to get the new person up to speed so I don't have to trudge through my parental issues from the start. She also nudged me to come here, so there's that."

Blake wasn't at all surprised by the fact, but Freya was, judging by her widened eyes.

"She likes to meddle in my love life sometimes, but it's usually for the best."

"What about this time?" Freya asked as her eyes dipped to Blake's lips.

Blake pulled her bottom lip between her teeth and enjoyed the way it made Freya's pupils dilate almost immediately.

"I guess we will find out. But before you kiss me the way I can see you want to…are you sure you're ready for a relationship, Freya? Because that's what this is if we continue."

Blake's heart thudded and she was sure her anxiety was clear by her sweat-slickened palm that Freya still held.

"I am sure that I want to be your girlfriend, Blake. I am as sure of that as I am of the fact that your lips are begging to be kissed right now. And that I am aching to put them out of their misery. So, can I?"

Freya whispered the last words as she brought her face mere centimetres from Blake's. Blake's lips tingled from the heat of Freya's breath and her tongue darted out of its own accord.

"Yes, you can."

The words were barely out before Freya's lips were upon hers and Blake melted into the kiss. It was soft, then desperate and filled with the kind of longing that Blake had been filled with since the moment Freya turned her world on its head. It was over too quickly, and Blake pouted as Freya pulled back.

"You're cute," Freya said with a smile as she ran a finger across Blake's protruding bottom lip.

"This is the making up part, Freya. It's not supposed to stop with a quick kiss."

Blake raised her eyebrows, and Freya grinned before kissing her again quickly.

"First I have a question."

Blake's lust-filled brain took in the words and she nodded to indicate she was listening.

"Will you come to Blaze with me this evening and meet some friends?"

Blake tried to hide her surprise. It was not the question she was expecting, at all. Freya didn't have many people she called friends. She had kept Blake at arm's length from any part of her life until now, so this was a welcome, if unexpected, request.

"I think they are friends, anyway, or they could be. I'll explain properly beforehand, but I like these people and I'm trying to put myself out there and not run away from potentially meaningful connections. I think that'll be a lot easier to do if I know you're there with me."

Blake smiled and pulled Freya's hand to her lips. She kissed her knuckles softly.

"Of course, I'd love to come with you. What time?"

"They are meeting at eight," Freya said.

Blake glanced at the clock on her wall and smiled salaciously.

"That leaves at least five hours before we need to start getting ready. How shall we fill the time?"

Blake yelped in surprise as Freya pushed her back and was on top of her before Blake even realized they had moved. The full weight of Freya's body pressed against her had Blake smiling at the familiar feeling. Her eyes met Freya's, and the depth of emotion reflecting back at her was breathtaking.

"I can think of a few ideas," Freya said before capturing Blake's mouth with hers as they got lost in each other once again.

Chapter Fifteen

Freya sighed contently as she followed Blake through the door of Blake's apartment. The door closed behind them, and Blake whirled to pull Freya in for a long, deep kiss. Freya wrapped her arms around Blake and gripped her ass to pull them closer together. She wondered if this overwhelming urge to be ever closer to Blake would fade, but so far it hadn't. Even in their quiet, everyday moments together, the need to be close was constant.

"My parents love you," Blake said as she pulled back with a smile.

It had been a few weeks since Freya's final session with Moira. A few blissful, Blake-filled weeks. Tonight, Freya had bit the bullet and joined Blake for Friday family dinner. Her fears had been put at ease not long after they arrived. It had been a little awkward at first, mostly on Freya's part, but once they began chatting that worry disappeared.

"The feeling is mutual. They are awesome people, which should be no surprise considering they created you," Freya said with a wink.

Blake smiled as she pressed closer until Freya's back pressed against the door. She stroked a soft thumb along Freya's bare thigh where her pencil dress ended.

"True. But I'm also keenly aware that not so awesome people can create remarkable humans, too. I am who I am largely because of my parents, and you are who you are despite yours. I know which one I'm most impressed by."

Freya's breath hitched at the depth of the words contrasted with the teasing touch against her skin.

"You're saying beautiful things while trying to get up my skirt, which is causing very mixed emotions, darling."

Blake smirked and nudged Freya's thighs with her knee as she teased her fingers beneath the tight material of Freya's dress.

"I'm multifaceted. And you are ruining my plans with this sexy as hell dress that gives little leeway for my advances."

Freya chuckled at Blake's failed attempts to move her fingers higher and reversed their positions.

"Lucky for me, your dress is a lot less confined."

Freya quickly lifted the chiffon fabric of Blake's dress and dropped to her knees.

"Shit," Blake murmured.

Freya eagerly peeled her already damp panties down her thighs as Blake stepped out of them. The glistening evidence of her effect on Blake increased the ache between Freya's legs. She parted Blake's thighs farther and leaned in to trace her tongue across Blake's clit. Blake whimpered at the contact and placed a hand on Freya's head to steady herself.

Freya smiled before pressing her lips more firmly to Blake's centre and placing hungry kisses over every aching inch. She had planned to take her time teasing and caressing Blake, but an urgency overcame her, and Freya couldn't hold back. The sweetness of Blake engulfed her senses, and she wanted to hear the cries of pleasure that were almost enough to send her over the edge, too.

"Fuck, Freya, right there."

Her name from Blake's lips was as much an aphrodisiac as the way Blake asked for exactly what she needed. Freya kept her lips wrapped around Blake's clit as she stroked her tongue in an even, steady pace. She reached one hand up to grip Blake's hip and used the other to tease her opening.

"Yes, Freya, I need you inside me."

Freya moaned against Blake's clit at the instruction and eagerly complied. She pressed her fingers inside Blake and moved them in a steady rhythm that matched her tongue as Blake's legs began to shake. Freya continued her actions as the melodious cries of Blake's orgasm reached her ears. She continued until the shaking of Blake's legs ebbed and the cries turned to whimpers. Only then did Freya pull back in time to gather Blake into her waiting arms as her knees sagged from the pressure.

"You are still not happy about your ruined plans?" Freya murmured as she kissed the top of Blake's head.

"Mmm, plans change. But I plan to recommence mine when I get the feeling back in my legs and get you out of that dress."

Freya chuckled as Blake looked up at her with a satisfied smile.

"I have no objections to that," Freya said as she placed a soft kiss on Blake's lips.

When Freya pulled back, Blake's eyes fluttered open, and a feeling hit Freya square in her chest at the depth of emotion in them. If she wasn't already sitting on the floor with Blake in her lap, Freya was sure it would have knocked her with its intensity.

"You okay?" Blake asked as she reached a hand up to cup Freya's cheek gently.

Freya turned her head to place a soft kiss on Blake's palm.

"Definitely. I was so worried about how tonight would go, and it was perfect. And then to come back here and end the night like that, it's…much more than okay."

Freya was sure there were better words for how she was feeling, but those ones would have to do, for now. Blake hopped up and held a hand out to Freya.

"You got one thing wrong with that," Blake said as Freya joined her.

They were both still fully dressed, sans Blake's underwear, which amused Freya.

"What did I get wrong?" Freya asked as Blake took her hand and began leading them to her bedroom. They entered the room and Blake pulled Freya in front of her. She tugged at the zip on the back of Freya's dress and pulled it down slowly. Freya's skin tingled with anticipation as Blake placed soft kisses on every inch as it was revealed.

"*That* was not the end of the night," Blake said.

She pushed the dress to the floor and wrapped her arms around Freya's body. She caressed Freya's braless breasts and teased her already pebbled nipples. Blake continued to kiss her way along Freya's back as she moved them forward. She pressed her hands against Freya's back until Freya was bent over and gripping the edge of the bed.

"I plan to end the night wrapped up in each other after our bodies are sore and exhausted from pleasure. That okay with you?"

Freya gasped as Blake traced her nails lightly down Freya's back and pressed them between her legs. Her underwear was on the floor swifter than the time it took for Freya to respond.

"Yes. More than okay."

Freya curled the bedsheets in her hands as Blake stroked her pulsing clit from behind.

"You've said that a lot tonight. More than okay."

Freya pressed her forehead against the bed as Blake's fingers inched deep inside her in slow, teasing motions.

"My vocabulary is limited when I'm focused on how fucking good this feels," Freya panted.

Blake pulled her fingers out before pressing them in again, faster and deeper this time.

"I'm sure we can find ways to work on that. You might find other ways to describe how you feel…with incentive."

Blake withdrew her fingers again and teased a circle around Freya's most sensitive spots.

"Shit. Don't stop," Freya pleaded.

Blake had a way of making her want things she never expected to want before. Like now, for instance, despite her pleas, Freya wanted Blake to continue teasing her until she couldn't take it anymore. Something Blake had picked up on and played with quite early on.

"Tell me how you feel. And the word *okay* is banned," Blake said as she dipped a finger in and out of Blake again. Just one, not enough to get Freya to where she needed, but it kept her right where she was.

"Horny as fuck?" Freya said with a groan.

Blake murmured and curled her finger in a way that had Freya arching back for more.

"I can see that. How about you try something that isn't as obvious from the way you're soaking my hand."

Freya turned her head to see Blake's eyes trained between her legs, quite obviously enjoying the view.

"I'll tell you whatever you want to hear when you finish what you started," Freya said as Blake's eyes flicked to hers. The small smile that played on Blake's lips had Freya dying to kiss her.

"Only if it's the truth," Blake said.

The smile was still in place, but there was a hint of vulnerability in her tone.

"I promise. And I don't break promises," Freya said.

She would've said damn near anything to get Blake back inside her at that moment, but it also happened to be the truth. Freya kept her eyes on Blake's as Blake pressed her fingers back inside. Her body moved in response to the steady thrusts of Blake's hand as the pace increased. She fought against the urge to bury her face in the bed so that Blake could see exactly what she was feeling. Freya had no doubt that it was written all over her face as she cried Blake's name. The waves of pleasure continued for what felt like an eternity before she turned and pulled Blake on top of her.

They kissed languidly as Freya traced her hand up and down Blake's back.

"I love you."

Blake pulled back and stared at Freya as if not quite believing that the words had come from her. Freya smiled at the surprise on Blake's face. She held Blake's face in her hands to keep it in place and ensure there was no room for doubt.

"That's how I feel. I love you, Blake. I have from the first night I woke up in this bed and saw you sleeping beside me. I probably have since the first time you ran into me."

"*You* ran into *me*," Blake said automatically before she followed up with, "That's probably not the most important part of that sentence, though."

"Let's say we ran into each other, and since that moment, my life has shifted in so many ways. I had already begun to understand myself better and work on the things I needed to do to begin to really live, but I expected that journey to take a lot longer. But the thing is, you've made me truly live since the moment I laid eyes on you. I didn't understand it, or have words for it then, but I do now. I love you."

Blake's eyes welled as she kissed Freya until they were both breathless. She pulled back and stroked a stray tear from Freya's cheek as they both took in the other in awe.

"I love you, too, Freya. And I am in love with how you love me. Don't ever stop," Blake said with a grin.

Freya pulled Blake closer whispered and softly against her lips, "I don't plan to, darling. I promise."

"And you don't break promises."

Blake echoed Freya's earlier words as their lips met again and they sealed the promises with much more than simply a kiss.

Her Brother's Girlfriend

Aurora Rey

Chapter One

Hadley folded her arms and blew out a breath. The restaurant sat empty, the dining room dark and the kitchen quiet and pristine. What might have been a moment of welcome calm on a Monday afternoon hit differently on a Friday night. The quiet had an eeriness to it, a sadness.

"Welcome home," Brad said.

She glanced at her twin, her best friend for as long as she could remember and the manager of Devine's, the restaurant that had been in their family for three generations. "Thanks."

She'd actually been home for the better part of a week. After getting the phone call that their father had been in a serious car accident, she'd barely managed to finish her shift before booking it the hour and a half north to the hospital in Poughkeepsie where he'd been taken. The days since had been a blur of hospital rooms, medical jargon, and big talks about the future of the restaurant.

Jimmy Devine would be in no shape to run the kitchen he'd helmed for close to twenty years—not for several months at least and maybe not ever, at least not at the level and pace he'd maintained before. Her mother and brother insisted she take a few days to think on it, but she'd made the decision to come home the instant her dad's prognosis was known. She loved her career in the city, but she loved her family—and Devine's—more.

"It won't be the end of the world if we stay closed another week. It won't bankrupt us."

It wouldn't. But it would put an unnecessary pinch on cash flow when they could use the opposite. Not to mention the staff. They'd maintained payroll for the week, when everything felt uncertain and they didn't want to lose people on top of that. That wasn't sustainable, though, and the loss of tips meant the waitstaff were still running at a substantial deficit. "Are you offering that for my benefit or yours?"

He lifted both hands. "Yours. I'm ready when you are."

Of course he was. Brad was nothing if not reliable. He had one of those steady, nice guy personalities, authentic enough to save him from being irritating, at least most of the time. "If I don't do something with my hands soon, I might actually short-circuit."

Brad chuckled. "You sound like Dad."

She didn't regret getting that trait, or a host of others, from him. Or the calm steadiness she'd inherited—or perhaps learned—from their mother. Her family wasn't perfect by any stretch of the imagination, but they tried to do right by each other and the world around them. And there was no shortage of love. "Thanks."

"Are you sure you don't want to stay with Brianna and me? You know she'd love to have you as much as I would."

The sentiment was sweet, and not wholly unexpected, but the innuendo she couldn't help but read into the delivery struck her. Struck her as in made her choke on her own saliva and cough until her head ached and her eyes watered.

"You okay?" he asked.

She nodded feebly.

"I was just trying to spare you your childhood bedroom. Unless maybe you've been missing that Alanis Morissette poster."

Hadley shot him a simpering smile because that was easier than getting into why the dated decor and collection of basketball trophies were preferable to a guest room in the condo he and his girlfriend shared. "Don't hate on Alanis."

He smacked a hand to his chest, all faux offense. "I would never."

"Besides, being at the house will make Mom's life easier when Dad gets released." He'd have a physical therapist stopping in to support his recovery, but all the basic care would fall to the family. Cheaper than a rehab facility—not to mention better for their dad's spirits—but it would be a ton of work. In addition to keeping the restaurant afloat, she wanted to help with that as much as possible.

"Yeah." Brad frowned. "Maybe Brianna and I should stay over, too."

"No," she said, too quickly and too loudly to stand any chance of being taken at face value.

"What's going on?"

Just, you know, being in love with your girlfriend. The prospect of all living under one roof tipped the scales from weird into complete torture territory. "Nothing."

"Not convincing."

"I just mean, you don't want to disrupt your life like that. You've got enough on your plate. And the dogs. That would make for a very full house." She cleared her throat, still a bit froggy from before. "And it's not like you won't be over all the time anyway. At least give yourself the benefit of sleeping in your own bed."

"What about your own bed?"

A loaded question if ever there was one. She'd quit her job in Manhattan, given her roommate license to move his boyfriend in to cover her share of the rent indefinitely. Based on their father's injuries—and age—it was entirely possible he'd never return to the kitchen. But renting a place of her own in Pine Creek implied a permanence she wasn't quite ready to commit to. Not to mention an expense. "Ask me again in three months."

He pulled out his phone. "Don't think I won't."

"Are you seriously setting a reminder to harass me?" she asked.

"No, I'm setting a reminder to check on the health and well-being of my sister who uprooted her whole life to come home and save the family business."

She didn't wait for him to finish typing the note to grab his arm. "I want to be here. I need you not to doubt that."

Brad blew out a breath. "I don't."

"Not convincing."

"It's just, well, Brianna said something about how much she admired you for chasing your dreams and hoping you wouldn't wind up resenting putting them on pause to come back."

She could spend hours dissecting the fact that Brianna gave more than a passing thought to her dreams, her feelings. But that was an exercise better saved for the comfort and privacy of her own thoughts. Preferably at three in the morning when she should be asleep. "What makes you think coming back wasn't part of the dream all along?"

"Was it?" He seemed both surprised and pleased at the possibility.

She might not be ready to own it as her grand plan, but she definitely hadn't ruled it out. "Let's just say I'm not sad to be here, sucky circumstances notwithstanding."

He seemed to take her words to heart. "I'll take that."

"Okay, then. I'm going to go sort through the cooler so I can chuck anything that's no good anymore and make an order list." Because it needed to be done and because she was reaching her limit of heart-to-heart conversations for the week.

"And I'll make sure you have everything you need for service."

For all that she hated what brought her home, she was looking forward to it—getting to run the kitchen, getting to make the recipes she'd learned before she was legally old enough to be on payroll, getting to flex her creative muscles with a special here and there. "I'm sure you will."

"Brianna has offered to help however she can. Don't hesitate to pull her in if you need her."

In addition to being Brad's girlfriend since the tenth grade, Brianna was the pastry chef at the restaurant. Though she refused to call herself that, since she hadn't gone to culinary school. Hadley was equal parts ecstatic and aghast at the prospect of spending so much time together. "I know she's got plenty on her plate, but tell her I said thank you."

"I will. But seriously, she could cover the standard offerings with one arm tied behind her back. She's happy to divert her mad scientist energy for a little while."

She'd heard Brianna had started to branch out, putting twists on some of the classic recipes and introducing new ones here and there. Her chef heart loved it as much as her hopelessly in love one did. Not that she'd had much opportunity to sample Brianna's concoctions. That was about to change, though. Despite her inconvenient romantic feelings, Hadley had strong other feelings about the head chef and pastry chef working together on menu items that complemented each other, not to mention making efficient use of perishable ingredients they might both want.

No, she'd resigned—reconciled?—herself to getting over her feelings for Brianna once and for all. It might prove painful at times, but this level of exposure therapy would likely be her best chance, as absence had in fact made her heart grow fonder. She needed to get over it and get on with her life already.

"You're imagining bossing Brianna around, aren't you? Or are you trying to figure out how to turn the tables so you can boss me around, too?"

Of all the things she'd imagined when it came to Brianna, bossing her around had never made the list. But like so many things, Brad didn't need to know that. "Totally. Now let me get to work so I can conjure up a list of things for you to do."

"Yes, Chef." Brad offered a playful salute and headed in the direction of his office.

Hadley rolled her eyes but without irritation, since Brad meant neither true sarcasm nor true deference. She pushed through the swinging door and stopped short. The woman who'd been occupying far too many of her thoughts hunched over the worktable at the dessert station, a parchment paper piping cone in one hand and a look of fierce concentration on her face. Mad scientist, indeed.

She didn't say anything, but Brianna looked up with a start. "Hadley."

Did she have to go and say her name like that? "Hey, Brianna. I didn't realize you were here."

Brianna smiled and Hadley's chest constricted at the sight. "I wanted to be here in case you needed anything. And, you know, see you."

And say things like that on top of it? "You're really sweet."

Brianna blushed, which did little to aid Hadley's efforts to play it cool. "We're family, right?"

Indeed they were, at least in practical terms. She wasn't sure why Brad hadn't popped the question, but she'd never brought herself to ask why. Either way, Brad and Brianna had been together for more than a decade, and Brianna was part of the family in every way that mattered. Facts she'd do well to remember. "For sure." She lifted her chin. "What are you up to?"

"Don't laugh, but I'm trying to teach myself chocolate work."

"Yeah?" Because of course she was.

"Nothing over-the-top, but I love the way little chocolate doodads finish a dessert. I can never get them as shiny as I want, and half of them break along the way."

"Are you tempering the chocolate?" A fussy step, but one that made all the difference.

"Trying to. Maybe you could give me a few pointers." Brianna laughed. "Hopefully ones that don't involve buying a giant marble slab."

"There are some hacks that work for most applications. You haven't started building showpieces when I wasn't looking, have you?"

Brianna smiled at that, but a flush rose in her cheeks. Different, though, than when Hadley complimented her. "I'm a long way from that sort of thing."

"More trouble than they're worth most of the time." She waved a hand and hoped it didn't make her look like she was trying too hard. "And certainly for the likes of Devine's."

"So, um, do you need anything?" Brianna asked.

If she didn't know better, she'd swear she had the same effect on Brianna that Brianna had on her. But she did know better. Brianna didn't give her a second thought, at least not in the ways Hadley spent way too many of her thoughts on Brianna. "I'm just cleaning out the walk-in and getting an order together so we can be ready for service next week."

Brianna nodded with the sort of eager enthusiasm that had the potential to get Hadley into trouble. She needed to get a grip, and she needed to do it fast. "I can help," Brianna said.

"Don't stop what you're doing. I'll be here a few hours at least. There will be plenty to do whenever."

"Okay, I'll come find you in like twenty. Is that okay?"

It was her turn to nod, and while she didn't want to come off as eager, she couldn't help but wonder if the sparks zinging through her were visible to the naked eye. "Cool."

She turned to go, but Brianna called her name. She resisted a groan at the way it made her skin tingle. God, if she didn't chill the fuck out, it was going to be a long however long. She turned back with a raised brow, not entirely trusting her voice.

"Welcome home," Brianna said with enough feeling that Hadley knew she wasn't imagining it.

"Thanks." She made a beeline for the walk-in, hoping the refrigerated air would chill the blood now pumping through her as though she'd just run a mile. She closed the door behind her and slumped against the cold metal. Damn. So much for playing it cool.

Chapter Two

After her run-through with the kitchen crew, Hadley headed to the dining room to brief the service staff. Half of them had worked at the restaurant for as long as she could remember, which proved comforting. She ran through the night's specials, which she'd kept simple until she got a feel for things. Brianna did the same but with show-and-tell, passing around a slice of ricotta tart with lavender and honey that had everyone scrambling for a bite. Brad ran down the reservations list, pointing out the anticipated pinch points.

"Anything else?" she asked. When no one piped up, she wished everyone a good service.

Jack, who'd taught Hadley how to carry a tray of eight entrees without dropping it, lifted a hand before the group scattered to their respective stations and tasks. "Just want you to know we're glad you're here."

Murmurs of agreement and a chorus of nods followed.

Hadley sucked in a breath and willed herself not to get emotional. "I am, too. And I'm deeply grateful to all of you for sticking around and trusting we'd make it work."

"You're not going to turn the menu all chichi, are you?" Paulette, another old-timer, folded her arms.

"I can't promise I won't get a little wild by Jimmy's standards, but I won't go rogue. And if any of you feel like I have, consider this a standing invitation to call me out."

That got her a few chuckles. She decided to quit while she was ahead. Back in the kitchen, it struck her that no one on the line asked her about changes to the menu. Did they assume she wouldn't? Or secretly hoped she did? Questions for another day, preferably one after she had a week of service under her belt.

The early birds trickled in, and the main dinner crowd followed hot on their heels. Muscle memory kicked in, formal training and experience buttressing the years she'd spent taking direction in this exact kitchen. She barked out orders, mostly because the kitchen got loud and that was how communication over the clang of saucepans and the sizzle of food happened. And because that's what everyone was used to—the staff and her alike. Still, she went out of her way to keep the vibe upbeat, joking about her dad setting up his recliner next to the cold station so he could keep watch over things.

It mostly worked, though she got some side-eye when she insisted a steak be redone and sent back a plate of chicken marsala that had been plated a bit too free and loose for her liking. It made her wonder if her dad had loosened his standards in the last few years or if people who remembered her as an acne-riddled teen had trouble with her telling them what to do.

"How are you holding up?"

Hadley turned at the sound of Brianna's voice—gentle without crossing the line into patronizing. "I'm good."

Brianna came closer. "You don't have to put on the brave face with me, you know."

She knew absolutely nothing of the kind. "Maybe I am brave."

That got her a smirk. But even then, Brianna managed to be easy about it. "I have no doubts about that. I'm saying you don't have to be, at least not all the time."

Such a simple observation. Innocent, too, really. And yet it left Hadley feeling seen in ways she rarely experienced outside her family. Hell, even inside her family a lot of the time. Here, in this moment, it made her feel shaky and more than a little vulnerable. None of which she was inclined to confide. "I'm fine. Really. I appreciate you checking on me, though."

Brianna's eyes narrowed. "I see the Devine stoic macho bullshit is not gender specific."

A snort of laughter escaped before she could stop it. "Okay, I love my brother to death, but there isn't a drop of macho in him."

Brianna offered a sniff of disapproval, though Hadley couldn't tell if it was directed at Brad or at her.

"And I'm not macho, either. I'll have you know I have a therapist and a meditation practice, and I cry at pretty much every *StoryCorps* segment."

Rather than laugh—which was what Hadley intended—Brianna's whole face softened. "Of course you do."

"But I've got a full dining room and a kitchen staff not quite convinced little Hadley can pull it off, even if she did land one of those fancy city jobs." Not that anyone had given her a hard time. It was simply that Jimmy ran a tight ship and she'd yet to prove herself as the right blend of confident and competent to get the job done.

"Okay, fine. But I reserve the right to ask you about your feelings at a time to be specified later." Brianna winked and returned to the dessert station without waiting for a reply.

Hadley might have been tempted to follow, but a slew of tickets came in and had her searing, sautéing, and saucing for the next hour without a break. She slipped into the zone, calling orders and pushing plates out the door. The pace was on par with Champignon, but the vibe never hit that frenetic hum she'd grown accustomed to. Perhaps because she was in charge here and could tend the line and the people on it without worrying about whether her head chef would get his boxers in a bunch about something and launch into a mid-service tirade. Or, perhaps, Devine's was simply different, for better or for worse.

❖

It was just after midnight when Hadley padded from the bathroom in an old T-shirt and a pair of boxers—the closest thing she owned to pajamas these days. Since her mom had already gone to bed, she headed straight to her room. It felt more like her college days than her childhood, back when she'd come home for a long weekend or a school break and put in a shift at the restaurant so her father could have a night off. She'd scrub off the smells of service and then crawl into bed, texting with her other restaurant crew night owl friends until the adrenaline wore off and she could fall asleep.

No messages waited for her tonight, though. Oh, a few of her friends had checked in. But things at Champignon had another hour to go still and would be followed by late dinner and too many drinks. She already didn't miss that part, or the hookups and drama that came with the territory.

"I'm barely thirty and I'm too old for that," she said to Carmine, who'd made himself at home in the center of her bed.

The orange tabby stirred at the sound of her voice but managed little more than a yawn and stretch before closing his eyes again.

"A lot of help you are."

Hadley nudged him over a few inches and slid between the sheets. He let out a meow of protest.

"You have to share. It might be your bed now, but it was mine first."

She thought he might leave with an indignant flick of his tail—it wouldn't be the first time—but he circled a few times, curled into a donut against her leg, and started to purr.

"See? Sharing's not so bad."

He continued to purr.

She picked up her phone, though it had only been thirty or so seconds since she'd checked it. A notification popped onto the screen, and the sight of Brianna's name made her pulse trip. She unlocked the screen but lifted her head to look at Carmine for a second. "You want some advice? Don't fall for a girl you'll never be able to have."

Purr, purr, purr.

"Again, no help." She shook her head and returned her attention to her phone.

Hope it's not too late to text. Just wanted to say you were amazing tonight. I love seeing you back in the kitchen.

Brianna had added the smiling emoji with heart eyes at the end. Hadley groaned. Carmine let out an irritated sigh.

She stared at the ceiling for a moment, considering a plethora of things she'd like to say in return. Sexual innuendo, confessions of undying love. So many options. And yet, so few. *It feels good to be back, even if the circumstances suck.*

That got her a heart in return. The red one. She groaned again and let the phone drop to her chest.

Since there was nothing to say to that, she didn't try, and Brianna didn't text again. She and Brad were probably in bed themselves. When

Hadley's imagination threatened to go down a path that had the two of them still awake but otherwise occupied, she shut off the light and flung an arm over her eyes.

It didn't help.

She grabbed her phone again and doom-scrolled for a bit. But true to its name, the activity left her antsy and even more angsty than before. She toggled to her meditation app instead and pulled up ten minutes of guided relaxation. It made her feel hokey, but it worked. Well, sort of at least. Enough that her therapist would be proud and she might stand a chance of falling asleep sometime before dawn. She'd take it.

Hadley gazed into the near darkness. Despite Brad's teasing, the Alanis Morissette posters were long gone. Still, the walls and the bed were the same. And the way the light slanted in from the streetlight on the corner felt so deeply familiar, it was hard not to reminisce. She'd spent so many nights in this room, fantasizing about her future. Fantasizing about Brianna.

She'd come a long way since those angsty teenage nights. And yet, in some ways, she was exactly the same. A little more mature, a little more successful. A lot more jaded. At least when it came to matters of the heart. She hadn't given up on finding love, but she'd stopped believing it would fall into her lap. Stopped believing that the right woman would come along and make her forget the fact that she'd spent more than a decade coveting the one woman she couldn't have.

Maybe coming home would force her to wrestle those demons once and for all. Not that they were demons per se. She'd spent enough hours in the chair with her therapist to know that emotions themselves weren't inherently bad. They simply ran counter to one's goals and priorities sometimes. Finding a way to hold them without letting them run roughshod was the key. Hadley believed it intellectually if nothing else, which gave her something to hold on to when that imagination of hers had a mind of its own. Just like those guided meditations her therapist had turned her on to.

She let out a sigh, picked up her phone, and cued up a second meditation.

The soothing voice—female, British accent—encouraged her to fill her lungs slowly and release the breath completely. She noticed and let go of little pockets of tension in her body as the woman walked her through a scan of her limbs, torso, and jaw. The result left her calmer and several steps closer to sleep. She switched over to the gentle waves soundtrack that lulled her to sleep through the ambient city sounds most nights. After all, sometimes silence was the loudest.

She relaxed and drifted, letting the day and all the thoughts and what-ifs of the day fade into oblivion. And if it was Brianna's encouraging smile she took with her, well, no one but her needed to know.

Chapter Three

Hadley emerged from her room to the aroma of coffee and let out a hum of pleasure. Since she was invariably too lazy to prep it the night before, waking up to a hot, fresh pot was a true treat. She padded down the stairs and into the kitchen, making a beeline for the drip pot she was pretty sure was as old as she was. She poured herself a cup, adding the flavored creamer that tasted like home, and didn't even bother sitting down for the first sip.

"You're just like your father," her mom said from the breakfast nook where she sat with her own cup.

"Why, thank you." Hadley grinned and settled into one of the chairs, specifically avoiding the one where he always sat.

"How was service?"

"It was good. No disasters, the staff seemed glad to get back to work, and Mr. Fabretti said my piccata was different but good."

"Was it?"

"Of course not." Some recipes were sacred. Her dad's chicken piccata was one of them.

Mom laughed. "That sounds about right."

"Everyone misses Dad, and they're worried about him, but I think being back feels like something they're doing for him as much as themselves." A different vibe from most restaurant jobs, though she'd considered her own experiences less toxic than most.

"Your father's already talking about when he can go in. 'Not to work, mind you, just to see everyone.' "

Hadley laughed at the spot-on imitation of her father. "It would probably lift his spirits."

Her mom wagged a finger. "Don't you start, too. He's not even home from the hospital. Can we hold off on his plans for gallivanting for a little while yet?"

"I won't breathe a word. He is still coming home today, though, right?" He might have a long recovery in front of him, but being able to do it at home rather than the hospital or some facility would make a world of difference.

"That's the plan. As long as the doctors give him the all clear and the medical equipment place delivers as promised."

As if on cue, the doorbell rang. Hadley glanced at the clock on the microwave, wondering if she'd slept later than she intended. But no, it was 8:09. "Pretty early for a delivery."

Mom headed to the door and Hadley got up to hide in her room, for at least as long as it took her to put on pants. But she'd no sooner put her foot on the first stair than a familiar voice sounded behind her—one belonging to the woman she'd spent half the night thinking about—cheerfully wishing her mother a good morning.

"Why on earth did you ring the bell?" Mom asked.

"Well, Brad's not with me, and it's early." Brianna paused. "And I wasn't sure if Hadley would be, um, dressed."

Since there was no way to escape without being seen, Hadley turned. Should she be more worried about her hair or how obvious her nipples were in the threadbare shirt she'd slept in? "Hey."

Brianna's gaze flicked almost imperceptibly to Hadley's chest before locking on her eyes. "Hi."

Mom, bless her, seemed oblivious. "That's just silly. You're always welcome here. And Hadley doesn't stand on ceremony any more than the rest of us."

She both loved that sentiment and wanted to punch it in the throat. "For sure," she said like an ass.

"Okay. I won't next time." Brianna lifted a basket covered with a dish towel. "I just wanted to drop off some muffins."

"Oh, honey, that's so thoughtful." Mom looked at Hadley to concur.

"So thoughtful," she parroted.

"I figured you both could use a little boost. And, really, Brad and I don't need to polish off two dozen just the two of us."

Hadley laughed at that because how could she not? "I'm not sure he'd agree, but I respect your commitment to moderation."

Brianna quirked a brow. "With some things at least."

"Will you come in for a cup of coffee?" Mom asked.

Hadley resisted a groan.

"Only if I'm not interrupting," Brianna said warily, as though she'd sensed Hadley's hesitation.

"Not at all." Mom waved a hand like it was the silliest caveat in the world, then headed for the kitchen. "We were just discussing when the medical equipment company would get here."

"Oh, Brad mentioned that was today. A bed, right? And a chair with a lift?" Brianna followed, leaving Hadley to pull up the rear, covering her chest without making it obvious she was covering her chest.

"Yes, we're sequestering him to the first floor for at least the next month." Mom clicked her tongue. "He's going to hate it until he realizes he gets to hold court while his friends and family come and go."

"That sounds like Jimmy to a T." Brianna's smile held fondness.

In the kitchen, Hadley got out plates while Mom poured Brianna a cup of coffee. They'd no sooner sat down than the doorbell rang again. Since Hadley had never made it upstairs for pants—or a bra—Mom went to see to it. That left Hadley sitting at the table all cute and cozy with Brianna. Well, Brianna was cute at least, with her boatneck sweater and messy bun that managed to look anything but. She didn't even want to think about how frightful her hair must look.

"The rolled out of bed look suits you," Brianna said, as though reading her thoughts, and gave her a long, slow once-over.

Hadley stuffed an absurdly large bite of lemon blueberry muffin into her mouth, a strategy that saved her from having to reply but did little to help her in the play it cool department. A reasonable tradeoff as far as she could tell because how the hell did she respond to a comment like that? Well, respond in a way that didn't make her sound like her goal was to get Brianna into bed with her.

When Brianna frowned, Hadley's plan went to pot. Because of course Brianna would read her silence as unamused or, worse, offended. She took a swig of coffee that burned her tongue and smiled. "That's a generous assessment."

The frown melted, a smirk taking over. "Eye of the beholder and all that."

Was Brianna flirting with her? Because she legit struggled to imagine this conversation with anyone else and not having that be the case. Well, that wasn't entirely true. Brad would make that exact comment. A little more sarcastically, perhaps, but he'd make it. And since Brianna was practically her sister, she should file this whole interaction squarely in that category. Right? Right. "Like I said. Generous beholder."

Brianna laughed and Hadley did, too, hating herself for being unable to pull off playing it cool with anything even slightly resembling authenticity. Even after all this time. Ugh.

Mom swept into the kitchen, a look of panic in her eyes. "The bed won't fit."

"Won't fit where?" Hadley asked.

"Through the office door."

The small bedroom on the first floor had been a playroom for Brad and her when they were kids, mostly to keep their chaos contained. But by the time they'd started high school, the toys had given way to a home office setup and had been that way ever since. "Okay, let's think," she said.

Rather than shifting into brainstorm mode, her mom seemed to be on the verge of a meltdown. "They won't let him come home without it."

In that instant, it hit Hadley the toll this ordeal had taken on her mother. Yes, it had turned all their lives upside-down. But for Mom, it was her soulmate who'd had a brush with death. The person she'd never spent more than a few nights apart from who'd been in the hospital for more than a week and whose coming home depended on having everything set up just so. "What if we put it in the living room?"

Mom looked horrified by the prospect.

"I know it feels weird, but it might work out great. He'll be able to move from the bed to his chair more easily, and he'll have the television." She went for a winning smile. "We'll just have to be quiet when he wants to take a nap."

Her mother—calm and rational almost to a fault in other circumstances—nodded slowly.

"Talk about holding court," Brianna added, and Hadley wanted to hug her.

"Yes, okay. That could work."

It would because it had to. But there was no reason her mom couldn't feel good about in the meantime. "And he'll be less secluded for the first week or two when he has to spend more time in bed than his chair."

Mom's nodding took on the decisive quality it had when she'd set her mind to something. "I'll move the coffee table and the love seat. It can go there."

"Do you want a hand?" she asked, already standing.

"No, no. There are already too many cooks in the kitchen." Mom waved her off and disappeared the way she'd come.

"Thank you," Hadley said, looking squarely at Brianna. "She's so unflappable, but this has thrown her."

"I can't even imagine." Brianna shook her head.

Hadley's mind conjured where Brianna's imagination might be. Fears of Brad getting hurt? Fears of finding herself injured and dependent on others for every single thing? It struck her—not for the first or even the hundredth time—that Brad had yet to propose. She'd have put a ring on that ages ago if given the chance. And not that she wanted to reduce Brianna to a stereotype, but it felt equally strange that Brianna didn't seem to be putting any pressure on, didn't seem to be in a hurry.

Maybe being together for more than a decade had given them both enough security and comfort that they didn't feel the need to make things any more official. Maybe they'd yet to start talking about kids and that served as the impetus for a lot of straight couples. Well, opposite sex couples. Brad was as straight as they came, but Brianna identified as bi. A fact that didn't help Hadley's unrequited feelings one bit.

Whatever it was, it wasn't any of her damn business. She'd continue to love them and support them and be happy for them, at least as long as they continued to do the same for each other. And she'd do her pining in the privacy of her own thoughts.

Chapter Four

For as long as Hadley could remember, Mondays meant family dinner. As a kid, it was the only day of the week the restaurant was closed and the only night all four of them were able to sit at the table together and enjoy a meal. The tradition continued even after Hadley moved to the city, and since her schedule was often the same, she timed many of her quick trips home to coincide with it.

Today was no exception. And with Dad home and well enough to start physical therapy, the energy in the house held an air of celebration. Yes, he had a long and painful path ahead of him, but milestones were milestones, and everyone could do with a reason to make merry.

Despite having every intention of helping, Mom essentially shooed her out of the kitchen, claiming even a chef needed a day off from cooking now and then. So she found herself in the living room, entertaining her father with Brianna and Brad. He was being a good sport, despite his obvious nerves about starting PT.

"What if he's one of those barking coach types? I don't do well with that," Dad asked out of the blue when conversation lulled.

"You prefer to do the barking yourself, huh, old man?" Brad lifted his chin in playful challenge.

"Damn right I do," Dad said without missing a beat.

"For what it's worth, I think most physical therapists are women." Brianna shrugged like she wanted to help but wouldn't stake a whole lot on her assertion.

"Maybe she'll be pretty and flirt with you," Hadley offered. "Take your mind off the fact that she's making you do exercise."

Dad seemed pleased by the possibility and changed the subject back to his method for the perfect prime rib. Hadley knew perfectly well how to make a prime rib—both his way and the way she'd learned in culinary school—but she nodded with all the serious intensity of someone learning a big secret.

The lesson kept them occupied until a knock came at the door, followed by the doorbell. Aggressive or flighty? Could go either way. Dad's expression turned, reminding Hadley of a kid coming to terms with the pile of brussels sprouts on his plate.

Brad hopped up from the sofa. "I'll get it."

Hadley couldn't hear exactly what was said, but Brad's greeting sounded halting. A stark contrast to the bubbly response of the person she presumed to be the physical therapist. A moment later, a knockout of a woman in dark teal scrubs appeared, Brad right behind her. "This is Shelby," Brad said.

"And you must be my new patient, Mr. Devine." She extended a hand to Dad.

"How'd you guess?" Nerves or not, Dad turned on the charm. "But please, call me Jimmy."

Shelby introduced herself to Brianna, then Hadley. She talked about her background and her role in the recovery process—a script to be sure, though she didn't make it feel that way. She'd be coming three times a week to start, then go down to twice and eventually once per week as Dad gained the strength and stamina to do the exercises on his own. "I'd love to walk the family through what I'm doing," she said. "Some of the basic range of motion stuff should be done every day, but Mr. Devine—sorry, Jimmy—will need someone with him in the beginning."

Hadley and Brad volunteered. Brianna offered to tend things in the kitchen so their mom could watch, too, but she returned saying they should take the first round. Her eyes said more than her words, though Hadley wasn't sure Brad picked up on it. He was too busy staring at Shelby.

"Why don't you keep her company, then?" Hadley asked. "We can handle this."

Brianna shot her a knowing nod and returned to the kitchen.

Shelby started with a series of questions about Dad's pain level, his physical activity before the accident. She took copious notes, adding to the extensive file she already had on the exact procedures done to repair his spine. Hadley didn't consider herself squeamish, but the talk of rods and fused bones had her just this side of dizzy.

Brad seemed unfazed, asking questions and looking every part the eager student. She took that as permission to fade into the background, paying enough attention that she could assist on days Shelby wasn't there but not enough to count for making conversation. Between her father's penchant for winning over everyone who crossed his path and Shelby's effusive praise for his efforts, the hour-long session went swimmingly.

"We won't always go this long," Shelby said as she packed up her things. "But I will work you harder."

That got a chuckle out of Dad and an almost too loud laugh from Brad. Hadley resisted an eye roll and opted against jockeying for the job of walking Shelby to the door. "You did good, Pops," she said.

"I figure I might as well be stubborn about getting back on my feet instead of stubborn feeling sorry for myself."

It was the sort of dad-ism that made her smile—simplistic but it packed a punch of wisdom that made her reflect on her own ways of handling adversity. "Ever the sage."

"I do what I can. Now, go check on things in the kitchen. I'm hungry enough to eat a bear."

She did, but not without noticing that Brad still hovered at the front door with Shelby. God, she really hoped he didn't make an idiot of himself. For his sake, obviously, but for Brianna's as well. Men could be such boneheads when a beautiful woman paid attention to them.

Not that the failing was unique to men, obviously. She'd had plenty of her own moments through the years. Most of them with Brianna. She chuckled. Maybe she should cut Brad a little slack.

❖

There wasn't room for the lift chair in the dining room, and with the extra furniture in the living room, there was no hope of squeezing the dining table in. Mom's logic to resolve the matter had been to go out at the crack of dawn and buy a set of folding TV trays so everyone could sit in the living room together without having to eat off their laps.

The setup reminded Hadley of trying to eat on a plane, since meals in front of the television had been reserved for Saturday morning cartoons and the occasional pizza night. At least in this scenario they all had elbow room. And real utensils. Oh, and real food.

"I can't believe you finally caved," Brad said to their mother, drumming his fingers on the surface of his. "How hard did we beg for these as a kid?"

Mom chuckled. "Hard enough that I started refusing on principle."

Brianna laughed and Hadley shook her head. "I love that you're willing to admit that as a parenting style," Hadley said.

That earned her a shrug. "I'd say you two turned out all right."

Dad pointed with his fork. "Too late to lodge complaints now. The statute of limitations is expired."

Hadley lifted both hands. "Who's complaining? Not me."

"That's more like it." Dad shoveled a bite of pot roast into his mouth.

Brianna, who sat on the sofa next to Brad, gave his knee a squeeze. Then she leaned over and did the same to Hadley. "I think you both turned out perfect."

Hadley was too busy ignoring the jolt of electricity zipping up her spine to come up with a witty retort. Fortunately, Brad seemed to suffer no such affliction. He bumped his shoulder to Brianna's. "Aren't you glad you fell in with this crew?"

Brianna's shoulders drooped and she gave a soft smile. "Yeah."

It was no secret that Brianna had neither a happy childhood nor loving parents. Her father had left when Brianna was in middle school, and the man her mom had married a few years later was a real tool. They'd moved to New Jersey a few years prior, and the general sentiment was one of good riddance. Or that was the gist she'd gotten—mostly from Brad. Brianna didn't seem to let it bog her down too much, but it didn't spare Hadley the twisting sensation in her chest or the urge to pull Brianna close and tell her a million times she deserved to be loved and cherished always.

A round of laughter yanked her back to the conversation at hand. She joined in, hoping no one would notice she'd zoned out.

"Come on," Brad said. "You've got to have my back on this one."

Since he was looking directly at her, Hadley cringed. "Yes?"

Brianna lifted a hand. "Don't worry, you don't need to spare my feelings."

Shit. Shit shit shit. "Uh."

"She's hot. It's okay to say. And if you don't want to, I will." Brianna poked her fingers into her own chest. "I think she's gorgeous."

Who were they talking about? Context clues would imply Shelby, but she'd gotten herself in trouble assuming rather than knowing what was being discussed. "I'm going to plead the Fifth."

Brianna's eyes danced with humor. "Chicken."

"Yep." Which was true, even if not in the way Brianna meant. But no way in hell was she going to admit she found Brianna's more subdued beauty a thousand times more compelling than Shelby's more model looks.

"What?" Brianna lifted her chin. "She's not your type?"

Hadley tipped her head. "She's very pretty, but nah. Not really."

Brianna regarded her with curiosity. "What is your type? It's weird that I've known you as long as I have and I have no idea."

Hadley lifted both hands in what she could only describe as self-defense. "This is not appropriate family dinner conversation."

"Doesn't bother me," Dad said. His tone made it clear he knew full well that wasn't the real issue.

"Me either," Mom said cheerfully.

She shot her mom an "Et tu?" look before taking a deep breath and blowing it out. "I don't know. I mean, in queer terms, I'd say more femme than masc like me."

"Sure, sure." Brianna nodded.

"Um. Curvy, I guess, rather than really thin. I don't really care about hair color or anything."

"That's Hadley's way of saying she's a boob woman," Brad said, proving he could be actively unhelpful when he wanted to.

Hadley squeezed her eyes shut. "Dude."

He shrugged. "Tell me I'm wrong."

She blew out another breath, this one full of exasperation. "I like a woman who's real. Both how she looks and how she is in the world. Authentic. Sensitive. Passionate."

Brianna chewed her lip, and Hadley had literally no clue how to interpret it. She looked to Brad, then her mom, desperate for a lifeline.

"Girl next door," Mom offered.

"Yes, exactly." She glommed onto the descriptor, loving that it conveyed plenty while staying completely vague.

Brianna looked right at her then and seemed to debate what to say.

Eventually, she smiled. "Well, those of us who fall into that plain Jane category appreciate your appreciation."

"There's nothing plain about you," Hadley said before she could stop herself.

"I'll drink to that." Brad lifted his glass of iced tea.

Both her parents did the same. Brianna, too. Whether Brad meant to save her ass or was simply jumping on the bandwagon since he should have been the one to say it first didn't really matter. Hadley picked up her own glass, happy to toast girls next door, not putting her foot in her mouth completely, and anything that would change the subject sooner rather than later.

Chapter Five

Hadley got to the restaurant early, hoping for some relative peace and quiet. She loved that her dad was feeling good enough to have visitors, but damn. He might as well be the mayor for the number of people who'd stopped by in the last couple of days.

The back door was propped open to let in the cool spring air. Jose and Mila, the morning prep cooks, bustled around in companionable silence. Salsa music drifted from a portable speaker she couldn't see, reminding her of her first kitchen job in the city and the crash course in Spanish that gave her at least as much credibility as her culinary degree. "Morning," she called.

Mila looked up from the pile of mushrooms she was cleaning and waved. Jose offered a nod on his way to the walk-in with a pot of stock. "Morning," he said.

"Anything exciting?"

They both shook their heads, and Hadley smiled. Excitement was the last thing anyone wanted during morning prep.

"Oh." Mila raised a hand. "The produce guy threw in some endive because the baby greens weren't up to his standards. Said his greenhouse supplier would be hearing from him."

Hadley nodded and followed Jose to the walk-in. She snagged the door for him and went over to inspect while he arranged and rotated product on the sauce and stock shelf. She peered into the cardboard flat of lettuce. Not the best she'd seen, but she wouldn't have given it a second look. The endive, on the other hand, was gorgeous.

She didn't normally do a special salad, but today might be the day to make an exception. They had avocado and a crap ton of citrus. Well, technically the oranges and grapefruit were Brianna's, but perhaps Hadley could convince her to share.

She headed over to the dessert station where Brianna was already whipping up something. Hadley stopped short and didn't say anything at first. She simply watched, enjoying the way Brianna's confident fingers handled the ingredients and utensils. She'd be right at home in any of the kitchens Hadley had worked in through the years. Sure, Brianna might not have the training for elaborate sugar or chocolate work, but her flavors and technique reflected an instinct that even Hadley didn't possess when it came to pastry.

Brianna's hand stilled, the rhythmic tap and scrape of the whisk against the metal bowl coming to an abrupt stop. "Are you trying to make me nervous?"

Hadley cleared her throat and tried to ignore the flush that crept up her neck. "Like I could even if I wanted to."

Brianna canted her head and offered an enigmatic smile. "You absolutely could, and I'm pretty sure you know it."

She swallowed hard and reminded herself that, while this might feel like flirting, it one hundred percent wasn't. "Well, that certainly isn't my intention." Because if it was, she'd be in trouble.

"Want me to teach you a few things about meringue?" Brianna held up the whisk, a billowy white cloud clinging to it and forming a perfect soft peak.

"You could, probably, including why you're whipping it by hand instead of in the mixer." She lifted a finger. "But that's not why I'm here."

"What can I do for you?"

So, so many things. "Would you hate me if I stole some of your oranges and grapefruit?"

Brianna's eyes narrowed. "How many?"

"Two dozen?"

"Hmm." Brianna chewed her lip. "How popular do you think a grapefruit curd tart will be?"

"Not a fair question, since I'd personally inhale whatever doesn't sell and would inflate your numbers on principle."

"Well, I wasn't going to do that until tomorrow anyway. Order me some more and I'll bump it to next week."

"Deal." Hadley folded her arms. "What will you make instead?"

"Pavlova, maybe. With lemon curd and blackberries." Brianna nodded slowly. "I got those in today and they were a total splurge. Too nice to cook down."

If Hadley hadn't been so busy being smitten, she'd have been impressed with Brianna's ability to adapt and be creative on the fly. "I approve this message."

"Though…"

"What?"

Brianna shrugged. "I sometimes wish we were more seasonal in our sourcing. More local."

She'd certainly thought the same thing on more than one occasion. Her father wasn't opposed in theory. He simply liked having whatever ingredients he wanted at his fingertips—whenever he wanted them. "Yeah?"

"I don't think it's a trend, you know? People care about where their food comes from, and they're willing to pay when thought and care has been put into it."

"You're preaching to the choir."

"And it's a challenge, right? Finding inspiration when the pickings are slim."

It sounded like a challenge, and damn if she didn't like it. "Give me a few weeks to get my bearings before I upset the apple cart." Hadley smirked. "But feel free to bring it up again."

"I'll take that." Brianna smiled.

"Are you happy?" Hadley asked without really thinking about it.

Brianna's eyes narrowed. "Happy how?"

The fact that she bounced the question back told Hadley the answer wasn't yes, at least not unilaterally. But getting into the specifics—or what the hell she might do with whatever revelations came from it—was another matter entirely. "Sorry. Weird question to ask in the middle of the kitchen."

Brianna nodded, but her expression remained serious.

"Not that I don't want to know the answer," Hadley said quickly. "Or care about it or want to help if the answer is no."

That got her a chuckle. "Thanks."

"But it's still a weird way to ask, not to mention shit timing." God, could she get out of her own way maybe?

More nodding, along with a sigh.

"You work at my family's restaurant. And you're with my brother. If you're not happy, I definitely want to know."

"I'm not unhappy," Brianna said eventually.

The space between the two could be vast, and it usually implied room for improvement. "We should talk." Hadley swallowed. "I'd like to talk. More, I mean. About this."

"I'd like that." Brianna's eyes met hers and conveyed a lot more than her words.

Her mind raced for a time and a place that didn't include Brad or her parents or half the restaurant staff, with little success.

"Do you want to go foraging with me? Brad tries to be a good sport, but he has zero interest."

Hadley liked the idea of foraging, even if she'd never taken the time to learn enough to be good at it, save her annual pilgrimage to score wild ramps during their notoriously short season. "That sounds great."

Brianna regarded her with suspicion. "Do you mean that, or are you just humoring me?"

"I'm not," she said more emphatically than the situation warranted. "I mean, I'd totally humor you, but that sounds fun."

"Monday? If the weather is decent?"

It was both the next day they had off and a mere four days away. And yet somehow it felt like an eternity. "Perfect."

Chapter Six

The week managed to drag and fly by at the same time. Service went smoothly, including Brianna's grapefruit tart. Hadley had to hide a piece to make sure she got one before it sold out. Her own creative juices were flowing, too. She'd done a miso salmon that even a couple of the stalwart regulars tried and a duck breast with a cherry and port reduction that Brad insisted should be added to the menu permanently.

At home, Dad improved slowly but steadily. Brad and Brianna came over practically every day before the restaurant opened. They had lunch together and played cards, reminding Hadley a little too much of her high school days.

And now here she was, for better or worse, spending her day off with Brianna. They'd driven a good twenty minutes out of town, parking in a tiny lot she wouldn't have even noticed on her own. Brianna assured her it was public land where responsible foraging was allowed, then handed her a basket and tromped into the woods with purpose. Hadley followed, not confident they'd find anything but happy to have some time alone with Brianna. Even if it felt a little bit like torture.

A few minutes along what passed for a path, Brianna stopped to study their surroundings. Hadley took advantage of the pause to look up rather than down. The trees remained bare, allowing most of the sunlight to reach the ground. She turned her face to it and closed her eyes, letting it warm her cheeks. How long had it been since she'd done that, or stopped long enough to appreciate the colors that danced across her eyelids?

That was one of the things she loved most about Brianna—her

ability to make Hadley slow down for more than five seconds. Stop and smell the proverbial roses. She wasn't exactly bad at it left to her own devices. She simply forgot to do it very often.

"Ooh, ooh."

Brianna's enthusiastic outburst pulled Hadley from her reverie. "Ooh?"

Brianna pointed.

Hadley squinted. A clump of wrinkly taupe-colored mushrooms peeked out from the blanket of dead leaves. "Are those morels?"

Brianna nodded and hurried over. She'd no sooner squatted near them than her arm stretched in a different direction, index finger signaling a spot near Hadley's feet. "And there."

She looked down and found an even larger clump just to her left. She'd been so busy soaking up sunshine, she almost missed them. Could have easily stepped on them. She shoved aside that annoying little voice in her brain that wondered about that being a metaphor for her life. "How do I pick them?"

Brianna abandoned her own patch and hurried over. She took a small knife from the pocket of her jeans and cut the mushroom cleanly at the base, close to the ground. "Just like that."

Brianna held the knife out to her, but Hadley grabbed the mushroom instead. "It's beautiful."

"It'll be really tasty, too, sautéed in butter and garlic." Brianna looked around. "And at the rate we're going, we might have enough for dinner."

Hadley's imagination instantly conjured a table set for two, complete with candles and a nice buttery chardonnay. But of course that's not what Brianna meant. She meant a nice family dinner, complete with Brad and their parents. Or maybe she did mean a romantic dinner, but with Brad. Ugh.

She shoved those thoughts aside and helped Brianna harvest a few dozen. Brianna was careful to take no more than half of any single clump, and the way she talked about making sure the underground mycelia remained healthy was the cutest thing ever. "When did you become a science nerd?"

Brianna spun the stem of a mushroom between her thumb and index finger. "When I realized it made me a better baker."

Hadley held out the basket. "Touché."

Brianna dropped the mushroom onto the pile. "I think that's probably enough for today."

She knew better than to admit she wasn't ready to leave. "A very productive outing."

"I thought you were going to make me talk about my feelings." Brianna smirked.

She hadn't forgotten. It was more that they were having a nice time and she hadn't wanted to ruin it stirring up trouble where none might exist. But that suddenly seemed cowardly. "Do you want to talk about your feelings?"

Brianna turned, her gaze on the trees instead of Hadley. "I don't know."

"I think that's code for yes."

"You can't say anything to Brad. I know that's not fair to ask, but I'm asking anyway."

A thousand doomsday scenarios swirled in her mind, but she didn't hesitate. "Whatever it is, it's between us."

Brianna nodded, then glanced at the ground before looking back at Hadley. "I can't help but feel sometimes like I'm not living the life I'm meant to."

"How so?"

"I don't know. I don't really have an urge to have kids. There's not someplace else I want to live. I'm just…" Brianna shrugged. "Restless."

Against her better judgment, Hadley reached out and grabbed Brianna's hand. "I think that's a perfectly normal feeling."

"Do you ever feel like your life is the way it is, not because of a decision you made, but because you never made any decisions at all?"

Hadley chuckled. "No."

Brianna nodded, a mixture of sadness and resignation in the gesture. "Yeah. You decided to leave, decided to come back. And I'm sure you made a million other decisions along the way."

"More good than bad, I like to think, but definitely not all good." And a few epically bad, especially in the realm of romantic entanglements.

"It's both, right? Always. And you don't always know it's a bad decision, but at least you're making it."

"Well, sometimes I knew it was bad but did it anyway." Though she chalked that up to a quintessential component of surviving one's twenties. "But you're worried about not making a decision in the first place?"

Brianna shrugged. "I didn't decide to stay in Pine Creek. I just never made a decision to leave. I didn't decide to become a pastry chef. I just kept doing what I started doing in high school and never bothered to try something new."

The anguish in Brianna's eyes had Hadley scrambling for something—anything—to say or do to make it better. "I think Devine's current dessert offerings would beg to differ. We weren't doing anything even half as inspired when you and I were in high school. And no one taught you that. You chose to learn, to experiment, to create."

Brianna nodded, but the haunted look remained.

"I can happily get my old boss to gush over your creations if you don't trust my objectivity. I should warn you he might try to woo you to his restaurant, though."

"Maybe I should let him."

Her usual unease anytime she and Brianna were alone together amplified by a factor of about ten thousand. "Do you not like working at Devine's?"

"No, no. It's nothing like that. I just feel like I need to shake my life up, change something."

In her book, changing one's job or changing one's scenery were the two most obvious ways to do exactly that. And maybe her first thought should be for Brad, for the heartbreak he'd surely suffer if Brianna up and left Pine Creek, but the only heart she could think about was her own. Her own sad sack of a heart that had yearned for Brianna for pretty much as long as she knew what that kind of yearning was. It was one thing to see Brianna, day after day, knowing her heart belonged to someone else. Now that she'd come home, though, and that was her lot in life, the prospect of not seeing her at all somehow hurt even worse.

Brianna's shoulders sagged. "You think I'm being foolish."

"I don't," Hadley said, too quickly to be convincing. "I'd just, I'd miss you is all. I mean, and Brad. Brad would obviously miss you, too."

Brianna looked even less convinced by that than Hadley's denial about her being foolish.

"But you should do what makes you happy. If going on some grand adventure is what you want, you shouldn't hesitate even one second."

It felt a bit like betraying her brother to say that, but she couldn't bring herself to lie.

"I don't need a big adventure. I just need…"

When Brianna didn't continue, Hadley tried to lighten the mood. "A little adventure?"

Brianna sighed. "I don't even need a little adventure. I just need whatever I do to be mine."

That was a language she spoke. Growing up in a family business, growing up with a twin. It would have been so easy to simply stay, to put on the apron and not think twice. Not think even once, really. It had been on the table—a nice and tidy future hers for the taking. She'd pushed back, not wanting to disappoint her parents, her brother, but knowing she'd be miserable if she didn't strike out on her own, at least for a while. The irony of it all was doing that made it so easy to make the choice to come home. To know it was a choice. "I get it."

"I'm not sure your brother does."

Hadley searched for traces of bitterness, something she could glom onto that demanded she swoop to Brad's defense. Or Brianna's. Only there wasn't any. That same resignation from before hung on Brianna's words like a dress several sizes too big, limp and lifeless. "Have you talked to him?"

Brianna shook her head. "I should. But between everything going on with your dad and the chaos of having the restaurant closed for a couple of weeks, it feels like such a selfish thing to do."

So many thoughts swirled in her mind. Her instinct was to play mediator because she loved Brad and she loved Brianna and wanted them to be happy. But even as the right and good thing to do paraded to the front of her mind, something much more selfish lurked in the shadows. Something that looked a lot like calling Brad out for being an idiot and dropping a not-so-subtle hint that, unlike Brad, she was the sort of person—the sort of partner—who paid attention to stuff like that.

"It's not selfish," she settled on saying instead. A wishy-washy middle ground to be sure, but not something she'd hate herself for later.

"Thanks." Brianna gave her a soft smile.

"Is there an area of your life where you can do that?" she asked.

"Do what?"

"Take control, feel like you're calling the shots."

Brianna considered for a long moment. "In the kitchen. And more so now that you've given me a nice boost of confidence."

Hadley released a shaky breath, oddly relieved and maybe even a little satisfied that Brianna's answer involved her, time they'd spent together. "You flex some major culinary creativity in that arena."

"Now if only I could apply that to my personal life?" Brianna laughed but rolled her eyes.

"Is there something you want that you've been afraid to go after?" She tensed even as she asked, knowing there was every possibility Brianna's answers might include words like house and wedding and babies.

"I'm not sure," Brianna said. She looked nervous, though, like maybe she did know and didn't want to say.

"Something to ponder, then. It's easier to be decisive when it's something you want." Hadley mustered a smile.

Brianna rolled her eyes. "And probably better than doing something rash on principle."

As much as Hadley agreed, she didn't want to concede. "It's hard to know you have the life you want if you don't have many points of comparison."

Brianna frowned.

For better or worse, Hadley plowed on. "Like, I knew coming home was the right decision because I knew what some of my other options were. You haven't really had that luxury."

"But what am I supposed to do? Run off to the city for a couple of years? Go get some other random job I don't want? Break up with Brad?"

Hadley's throat constricted at that last bit. Because as awful as it was to have the woman she loved in love with her brother, the prospect of not having Brianna in her life at all was even worse. "Do you want to do any of those things?" she asked.

"No!" Brianna all but screamed her response, then seemed to catch herself. "No."

"I'm sorry," Hadley said instinctively.

Brianna shook her head, a rueful smile on her face. "Why are you apologizing?"

She sucked in a breath and blew it out slowly, mostly to buy time. "Because those feelings are hard."

"Yeah, but they're not your fault."

"No, but you deserve to love your life. If you don't, I want to make it better. I'm sorry because I don't think I can."

Brianna took her hand. "You do."

Hadley wanted to read so many things into that simple statement, but she knew better. "You make my life better, too."

Brianna nodded slowly, as though doing her own reading into things that maybe she shouldn't. "We should get back."

Relief and disappointment pulsed through her. "Yeah."

Chapter Seven

Brianna didn't continue the conversation on the drive home, so Hadley didn't either. Nor did she bring it up at family dinner, as Brad and her parents oohed and ahhed over their foraged haul. In fact, she acted so much like it never happened that Hadley started to wonder if she'd made the whole thing up.

But then Friday morning rolled around, and Hadley woke to a cryptic text. *Can you meet me at the restaurant early? I've been... experimenting.*

She had no idea what it meant, but her gut told her it was going to be good. She threw on clothes, put way more effort into her hair than she would on a day she'd spend most of her waking hours in a chef cap, and slipped out of the house with little more than her wallet and a travel mug of coffee. Jose and Mila were at their usual tasks, leaving Brianna tucked alone in her little corner of the kitchen.

"What's the mad scientist up to this morning?"

"I'd rather show you than tell," Brianna said with a sly smile.

Hadley clapped her hands together and rubbed them back and forth. "Bring it on."

"Is it weird that I'm nervous?" Brianna asked.

Hadley had plenty nerves of her own, but something told her Brianna's jitters didn't come from the prospect of spending more time together. In close proximity. Alone. "Why would you be nervous?"

Brianna tipped her head this way and that. "You know. Calling the boss in to show off. Then worrying what you came up with isn't worth the fanfare."

"Brianna, it's me. You have absolutely nothing to be nervous about. Besides, if what you're showing me has anything to do with that, I'm all in." She pointed to the propane torch sitting on the table.

"You're right. I don't know why I'm being silly." Brianna pulled a ramekin from the cooler below her station and sprinkled it with sugar. Then she flicked on the torch and brûléed the top like it was what she'd been born to do.

After extinguishing the flame, Brianna held out a spoon to Hadley. Hadley made a sweeping motion, meaning to convey Brianna should go first. Brianna cracked the shell and scooped out a bite. But instead of taking it, Brianna lifted the spoon to Hadley's lips. Hadley swallowed thickly and wondered if her galloping pulse was visible to the naked eye. She accepted the bite, and her eyes drifted closed with pleasure. The caramelized crunch gave way to the silkiest custard, the undercurrent of dark maple playing perfectly with the burnt sugar topping. A savory note, one she couldn't quite put a finger on, rounded out the flavors and kept the curse of overly sweet at bay. "Oh, my God."

Brianna smiled. "I take that as a good oh, my God?"

"Good is not an adequate word. I'm not sure there is an adequate word. What is that flavor I can't pick out?"

"Maple?" Brianna asked in a way Hadley could only describe as coy.

"I got that," she said, feigning offense.

Brianna's expression went sly. "It's miso."

The second Brianna said it, recognition followed. Of course it was. "That's genius."

Brianna shrugged. "I didn't come up with it. Though I haven't seen it done with maple before."

"It's got more nuance than caramel, which I've seen paired with miso before." Any sweet, salty, and slightly savory fusion hit all her flavor wickets, and this took it to the next level.

"Yeah, I love that combination. I wanted to play with maple since it's one of the ingredients I can source locally without making it a thing."

Hadley smiled at the explanation, at Brianna's attempts to push the envelope without drawing any attention to herself. "So, why isn't this on the menu?"

Brianna sighed. "It's a little out there?"

"Are you telling me or asking me?"

"A little of both, I guess. I mean, Jimmy made a big deal of finally keeping soy sauce on hand. I'm not even sure he knows what miso is."

Her dad was a lot of things—good things—but adventurous didn't make the list. At least when it came to what he cooked and served. "Did you ask him? Please don't tell me he dismissed it as exotic." She shuddered. "Or Oriental."

Brianna laughed. "I actually just came up with this one, so no."

She didn't want to overhaul the menu in its entirety. One, because Devine's had a lot of loyal customers, and they kept coming back precisely because they liked what the menu had to offer. Two, it felt like a betrayal, changing everything the second her dad couldn't do anything about it. But little updates here and there? Specials that could get some traction and justify regular rotation? She'd fantasized about that since before taking over the kitchen was a blip of possibility. "I think we should offer it."

"Yeah?"

"Here's my reasoning. If we offer the old standards and some fresh new options side-by-side, we'll get a chance to see how much of an appetite folks have to be adventurous."

Brianna nodded slowly. "Okay."

"If you make a small batch and it sells out, it builds excitement and demand for the next time you make it."

"And if it flops?" Brianna quirked a brow.

"The waste will be minimal, and we'll get to eat the leftovers ourselves."

Brianna laughed. "I love you."

Hadley froze. Yes, she knew the context. Yes, she and Briana had expressed that sentiment to one another more than once through the years. And yes, she knew exactly how she was supposed to take it. But damn. Her poor heart stopped, skipped a beat, then tripped over its attempt to restart itself. "Uh…"

That got her an elbow to the ribs. "Come on. You know you love me back, even though I'm not as funny as you are."

"You're plenty funny." She swallowed. "And I love you plenty, too."

Brianna stared at her for a long moment. Hadley didn't even want to think about what unspoken truths were written all over her face. But instead of poking fun or asking what the hell was the matter with her, Brianna's smile softened. "Have I told you I'm glad you're back?"

Hadley nodded, not quite able to form words. At least none that wouldn't get her into serious trouble.

"Well, it bears repeating."

Another nod. Brianna's eyes remained locked on hers and Hadley would swear to God Brianna was thinking about kissing her. Was it a hallucination? Wishful thinking? Or was there the tiniest sliver of a chance that Brianna wanted her, too?

Impossible. And if not impossible, unthinkable. Right? Even as thinking about it occupied every neural pathway she had. Even if, the more time she spent with Brianna now—not to mention the more time she spent with Brad—the less and less she believed them to be meant for each other. Not that she had any business saying as much to either of them. Conflict of interest much?

"Please tell me I get to eat some of whatever smells so good in here." Brad's voice carried from the far end of the kitchen.

Brianna took an abrupt step back. Moment or not, they hadn't been standing all that close, so the move only reinforced whatever harebrained and half-baked notions Hadley's imagination had cooked up.

Brad appeared, his usual affable smile securely in place. "What is it and when can I have some?"

Brianna picked up the ramekin and handed it to him with a fresh spoon. "Hadley was just giving me feedback on some of my experiments."

Feedback. Was that what the kids were calling it these days?

Brad shoveled a huge bite into his mouth and let out a groan of pleasure. "Winner. Let's put it on the menu tonight."

He knew it didn't work that way, but it was his version of high praise, and Brianna clearly took it that way. "Hadley says I can soon, as a trial run."

"Absolutely. Yes." His eyes narrowed. "Have you felt like you couldn't be creative before?"

"No, nothing like that." Brianna blushed. "I come up with new things all the time. This, and some of the other stuff I'm showing Hadley, are a bit out there. I didn't know if they'd fly."

Brad frowned but didn't say anything.

As the silence crept into uncomfortable territory, Hadley's keep-everyone-happy sensibilities kicked it. "Dad's only willing to take innovation so far, you know?"

Whatever weird reverie Brad had fallen into broke, and he laughed. "When the cat's away, the mice will play?"

"Obviously." Brianna elbowed Brad lightly.

"Well, just remember I'm a mouse at heart, too," Brad said.

Brianna winced. Hadley coughed. "Says the guy who literally prowls around the restaurant like a cat making the rounds."

He laughed. "Yeah. Okay. Fair. Speaking of, I gotta go work on tonight's reservations."

"Better you than us," Brianna said.

"Actually, Shelby was telling me about this platform her friend's restaurant in Rochester uses. It has an interface that the hostess station can use to manage seating without having to chart it by hand every night. Maybe I'll have to do a little playing of my own."

Brianna nodded with enthusiasm. "That would be so cool."

Hadley agreed. A modern tabling system would save work but also give them the option to take reservations online. She also added a tick mark to the tally in her head of how many times Brad referenced Shelby. He was up to four in the last two days, and she'd barely spent an hour in the same room with him. She had no business being protective, of course. But that didn't stop her.

Brad offered a parting wave and returned to the office. Hadley watched him go, then turned to find Brianna staring at her intently. "What?" she asked.

"Thank you," Brianna said.

Hadley's mind raced. "What for?"

"For reminding me I can go for what I want without going anywhere."

She wouldn't have said she'd done anything of the sort. Nor was she sure the end result would bring her anything but more unrequited pining. But Brianna seemed genuinely pleased. For better or worse, that made it all feel worthwhile. "Anytime."

"You say that like it's no big deal."

"It isn't."

Brianna looked at the ground, then took a step closer. When she brought her gaze back to Hadley's, she kept her head tipped ever so slightly down. The result—Brianna's deep brown eyes looking up at her through those gloriously long eyelashes—just about brought Hadley to her knees. "It is to me."

Chapter Eight

By the time Hadley got to Brad and Brianna's, Brad's Jeep was already gone. She had a fleeting feeling of good riddance, but promptly gave her subconscious a smack to the head. She'd developed a strict no-tolerance policy for thoughts like that. Pining was one thing; undermining was another. She put too much stock in manifesting things, of having invisible vibes with the universe, to tempt fate.

Still, she knocked on the door clutching a bottle of chardonnay like it was a date. And she'd put on a nice-ish shirt after her shower. Oh, and the cologne that Brianna had complimented once several years ago and she'd worn faithfully ever since. She'd come to terms with picking her battles.

Brianna opened the door, wearing a dark green sweater with a deeply scooped neckline and jeans that hugged the generous swell of her hips. So much for picking battles. "Hi."

"Hi." Brianna's smile was as warm and welcoming as usual, but it seemed to have a playful edge, too. "You don't have to knock, you know."

She didn't wait for Hadley to respond, turning and heading for the kitchen. Hadley followed silently. Brianna's jeans did even more for her backside than they did for her front, leaving Hadley to wonder about the line between appreciation and objectification. "Where's Brad again?"

Brianna pulled out a pair of wine glasses, then handed Hadley a corkscrew. "Gaming."

"Right." He'd been an RPG guy since high school and had a monthly game night with a group of guys who still lived in town.

"Apparently, Shelby is a gamer, too. She's only had her online group since she moved here, so Brad invited her along."

Of course he did. Since she couldn't say that, at least not with the inflection she wanted, she settled for "Huh."

Brianna laughed. "Better her than me."

Hadley laughed, too. She'd tried once or twice but never managed to get into it. "There is that."

"Besides, I'm not complaining about dinner being just the two of us."

She'd balked at the prospect initially. Something in the category of dancing with the devil. But with her parents both down with a cold and Brianna's almost bashful invitation, saying no felt borderline rude. Especially after they'd had such a nice hike that morning. Still. What the hell was she supposed to do with a comment like that? That and the soft smile Hadley would swear was a mix of flirty and shy. Had she started to hallucinate? Was that it? Or was Brianna legit sending her signals?

Brianna frowned. "No?"

"Huh?" Hadley repeated, but this time in the form of a question. "No. I mean yes. I mean, I'm cool with just the two of us."

"Could have fooled me." Brianna smirked, and her tone remained playful.

"I'm totally cool. This is great. Who needs more time with Brad, anyway?" Hadley coughed. "Sorry. I'm a little out of it. Must be all that fresh air from earlier. My lungs haven't adjusted."

That earned her an incredulous look, but it also seemed to satisfy Brianna in some way. The smirk softened. "I'll have to get you outside more often."

Inside. Outside. In bed. Pressed up against a wall. Jesus Christ, what was wrong with her? Not a question she wanted to entertain tonight. "If anyone can, it's you."

"I'll remember that." Brianna lifted her chin toward the bottle. "You going to open that?"

Hadley managed not to say "huh" again, but barely. She went to work on the bottle, grateful for something to do with her hands. Just as she was grateful for that first sip of wine. There was no way it could affect her—such a small amount and so immediately—but the idea of it calmed her. Reminded her she was an adult as much as it softened the edges of her frayed sense of self. Fortunately, Brianna didn't seem to notice, putting Hadley to work on the vinaigrette for the salad while she steamed the mussels.

For all her nerves coming in, Hadley couldn't help but relax over dinner. That was the thing about Brianna. She was interesting and funny, all while making Hadley feel like the funniest and most interesting person in the world. It's what made Hadley fall in love with her all those years ago, what kept that love alive and kicking despite every logical reason to let it go.

Something about tonight felt different, though. Hadley couldn't quite put her finger on it, but it was like all of a sudden, all those feelings were mutual. The respect and admiration, the affection. The attraction.

It couldn't possibly be, but she could come up with no other explanation for the way Brianna leaned in to listen to her stories about New York, the way Brianna's hand lingered on her arm. And while she was certain she and Brianna had shared a dessert at some point in the years they'd known each other, there was something downright erotic about dipping their spoons into the bowl of silky creme anglaise and rhubarb compote Brianna threw together for them to share.

By the time they stood at the sink, washing and drying the few things that couldn't go in the dishwasher, Hadley started to wonder if the whole night had been a dream. She even pinched herself a few times. But each time she did, Brianna remained, looking at her with those Disney princess eyes and a come here and kiss me smile.

Hadley continued to pinch herself as Brianna flicked off the kitchen light and led them to the living room. If the sensation wasn't going to wake her up, maybe it would help her get a grip.

No such luck.

Brianna didn't sit, so Hadley didn't either. They just stood there, looking at everything but each other. Until Hadley couldn't take it anymore and let her eyes seek what the rest of her was already attuned to.

Brianna licked her lip, her gaze fixed on Hadley's mouth. By the time she looked into Hadley's eyes, Hadley was quite certain she'd spontaneously combust and prove every elementary school science teacher who swore such a thing couldn't happen wrong. "I should go," she managed to say.

Brianna nodded, but she didn't move. Her chest rose and fell, her breaths shallow and fast.

"I'm probably going to regret saying this, but the reason I should is because I don't want to. I want to stay. But staying means I'll probably do something we both regret. I can handle my own regret, but I'd hate myself over yours."

The nodding stopped. Brianna visibly swallowed. Hadley turned to go, unsure just how far she could push her resolve. But Brianna grabbed her arm. "Me, too. Everything you just said. And saying it might make things harder, might make them worse. But you deserve the truth."

If her life was a movie, that would be that. She and Brianna would fall into each other's arms. Fall into bed. Fall in love. Consequences be damned. But life wasn't a movie, and if it was, she'd more likely be the cartoon character whose head explodes after getting kissed by the pretty girl than the romantic hero who gets the girl and lives happily ever after.

Brianna leaned in, kissed her cheek. But instead of opening the door to more, it seemed to punctuate the moment. No exclamation point, no question mark. Just an understated and all too final period.

"Good night," Brianna said.

A thousand questions swirled in her mind, but none of them had answers. Or maybe they all had the same answer, one that filled her up and left her empty at the same time. One that gave her no indication of whether she'd wind up better or worse for knowing it. "Good night."

❖

There was little Hadley liked less than going to work on no sleep. Having to do that and see the person responsible for her restless night? Brutal.

And yet.

Last night might not have changed everything, but it sure as hell changed plenty. Whether or not they ever acted on it, Brianna shared her feelings. Well, at least the attraction part. It thrilled her even as it twisted her insides into knots. And it left her at a complete and utter loss.

By the time she parked at the restaurant and let herself in the back door, she'd settled on either pulling Brianna into her arms and kissing her—consequences be damned—or ignoring her completely. Brianna didn't seem to share her quandary. She made eye contact with Hadley the second she walked in and made a beeline for where Hadley stood, sketching out the night's specials.

"Can I talk to you for a second?" Brianna asked in lieu of a hello.

"Of course."

"Are we going to pretend that didn't happen?" Brianna asked.

She had half a mind to play dumb, but that would insult Brianna's intelligence. Not to mention her feelings, whatever they were. "I don't see much of an alternative."

Brianna frowned.

"Do you?" Not a fair question, by any stretch of the imagination.

Brianna's frown intensified, making Hadley feel guilty for posing it.

"Look, I'm pretty sure my efforts to hide the fact that I have feelings for you have failed spectacularly at this point. But I have zero desire to undermine your relationship with Brad, and if I've left you feeling like I have, I can only apologize and promise to back the fuck off." Which she should probably do even if Brianna denied feeling undermined.

"What if I don't want you to back off?" Brianna's gaze was so intense, Hadley would swear Brianna could see right into her soul.

"Um…" Even if she hadn't been rendered speechless, there wasn't much more she could have said. What kind of question was that? Did it imply Brianna's feelings were the same? Or, probably more likely, that she simply wanted to go back to the seemingly easy friendship they had before. Both felt almost impossible. Though sequestering herself from Brianna's company would be like depriving herself of, if not food or water or oxygen, at least some essential vitamin or mineral. The sort of deficiency that eroded her well-being and left her lethargic and lifeless.

"Not the right thing to say?" Brianna smiled, but a sadness clung to it.

"I guess I don't understand what you mean." Much less how to respond.

"You're right. It wasn't a fair question." Brianna chewed her lip. "But I'd feel like a coward if I pretended like nothing happened or that it didn't mean anything."

They were still dancing around even giving it a name. Was it an almost-kiss? An indulgence of the imagination? Or simply a wine-induced lapse of rational thought? She hated not knowing how Brianna would define it. Though, insisting it wasn't nothing counted for something. Even if that something proved impossible to pursue. "It meant something to me, too," she eventually said.

"I'd never cheat on Brad."

"I know." She wanted to say she'd never do something like that behind Brad's back, but she wasn't entirely sure it was true.

"But ending things with him feels, I don't know." Brianna sighed.

"Foolish?" Hadley offered.

"Impulsive." A smile played at the corner of Brianna's mouth. "You might be surprised to hear this, but impulsive isn't really my style."

She chuckled. "Same."

"So, I guess what I'm saying is I need time to think."

"Of course." Which made sense and was the right thing to say. Even if her pulse raced at the prospect of anything more than a complete shutdown.

"You seem to be taking this better than I am." Brianna chewed her lip again.

"Better?" *As in hoping against hope?*

"Like, not surprised."

Hadley laughed in earnest then. "Oh, I'm surprised all right."

"Oh."

"But not devastated. If that makes sense?" She hoped it did, without completely tipping her hand.

Brianna winced. "Not really."

"I mean it feels like it's more complicated for you. You've got more to sort out." She hoped Brianna took that because admitting she was hopelessly in love and ready to drop everything and go all in seemed like a less than ideal thing to put on the table.

"Yeah, okay. I'm not sure that's true, but I know what you mean."

"Or maybe I'm just saying I'm fine to give you some space. No expectations, no pressure." She scratched her temple. "But interest. Please don't mistake any of this for a lack of interest."

"I see."

God, she was literally the least suave human on the planet. Fortunately, other members of the kitchen crew started to arrive, saving her from digging herself any deeper. She tried for an encouraging smile, complete with head bob, and fled to the coffee station for a double shot of espresso. It was going to be a long night.

Chapter Nine

Hadley emerged from her room, groggy and desperate for coffee. Between the hectic dinner service and a series of too vivid dreams about Brianna, she felt like she'd been put through the wringer. A very aggressive and sexually frustrating wringer. She'd almost have taken another sleepless night instead. Almost.

She found her mom puttering in the kitchen, the smells of coffee and bacon making both her brain and her belly rumble. There remained a few perks to living at home. At least in the short term.

The warm and fuzzy feeling carried her as far as the coffee pot and to the fridge for a splash of cream. It came to an unpleasantly abrupt halt when she glanced into the living room and found Brad perched on the edge of the coffee table, enraptured with whatever exercises Shelby currently had their father doing. Though perhaps it would be more accurate to say she found Brad, once again, enraptured with Shelby.

It had all started innocently enough. Brad on Dad duty when Shelby happened to come by. Casual conversation in the kitchen about Dad's progress that meandered into more personal territory. Hell, she'd gotten herself caught up in it once or twice, too. Shelby had some magical elixir of bubbly personality with enough intellect and thoughtfulness at its core to save her from the sort of inane perkiness that grated after a while. More than that, she seemed to take a genuine interest in Brad. Nothing overly flirty or inappropriate, but Brad blossomed in the glow of her attention.

She said as much after Shelby left for the day. Brad blushed and blustered, more mortified than defensive. "Do you think I crossed a line?"

Hadley tipped her head, not wanting to make him feel like shit any more than she wanted to let him off the hook. Especially given her own recent developments with Brianna.

"Do you think she thinks I crossed a line?" he asked with more vehemence than before.

Hadley folded her arms and regretted saying anything. "Which 'she' are you talking about?"

"Shelby. Who else would I—" Brad cringed. "Oh. You mean Brianna?"

"Do you even love her?" Hadley asked, more harshly than she'd intended. More harshly than she should. Than someone without a deeply personal vested interest should.

"Of course I love her. She's…" Brad lifted a shoulder. "She's Brianna."

"Are you trying to convince me or yourself?" She managed to tone down the accusation, but it was hard for a question like that to land gently.

"I do love her," he said again.

"Are you in love with her?" She wanted to know, and she didn't.

Brad frowned. "I'm not sure I know the exact difference."

As much as she might like to throttle him for having a shred of doubt about being head over heels for a woman like Brianna, a pang of sympathy hit her chest, the sensation reminding her of taking too deep a breath on too cold a morning. "Seems like you owe it to her, and to yourself, to figure that out."

To his credit, Brad nodded, expression grave. "Yeah."

She couldn't help but think about her conversation with Brianna, that feeling of being not unhappy, but not entirely satisfied either. And the flash of chemistry between them that had her revving but probably left Brianna completely churned up.

She didn't envy either of them, really. Change was hard when there was nowhere to go but up. Giving up a nice, comfortable existence for the unknown? A tall order for even the bravest of souls. "I think talking would do you both some good."

His eyes narrowed. "What do you mean? Has she said something to you?"

Hadley shook her head. Brianna had asked her to keep what she'd said in confidence. Besides, it felt like they'd entered murky waters, and she didn't trust herself to be unbiased—either looking out for her own interests or trying so hard not to she went too far the other way.

But what if, for all their years together and all appearances of being a perfect couple, they weren't meant for each other after all? Even as the possibility thrilled her, she shoved it aside. Talk about a dangerous game.

"I'm not cheating, if that's what you're worried about," Brad said, as though the thought had only just occurred to him, and he needed to distance himself as far from the idea as possible.

"I know you're not." The fact of the matter was that perfectly decent people did. They got caught up and felt trapped and made stupid choices. But integrity was Brad's middle name, even if his birth certificate said Joel.

"I'm not going to pretend there isn't some spark with Shelby, but I haven't acted on it. And I won't."

Won't was such a funny word. It left so much room to be miserable. "Well, I'd suggest figuring your shit out instead of shoving it down and trying to be noble. Brianna deserves better than that."

"I know."

She punched him lightly on the arm. "You do, too."

❖

Hadley got to the restaurant, feeling more squirrelly than she cared to admit. It didn't help matters that Brianna seemed even cagier and Brad, God love him, had gone into full overcompensation mode. He kept checking in with her, and at least twice, she spied him sniffing around Brianna like an eager puppy. It was so bad that more than a couple members of the staff gave her questioning looks during prep.

After the pre-service rundown, she decided to do a little checking in of her own. On Brianna, of course. Not Brad. "You doing okay?" she asked, figuring vague would give Brianna options.

"I'm fine." Brianna's bright smile didn't hide the worry in her eyes.

Hadley resisted the urge to touch her. Not because a casual touch would draw attention, but because she didn't trust herself to keep it casual. "I can tell you aren't, but I won't press if that would make things worse."

Brianna laughed. "How do you know me so well?"

She lifted a shoulder, knowing better than to answer with the truth. "I just want to make it better if I can."

"I know." Brianna inhaled deeply. "I know."

It was a generous answer, given that she was the primary cause of Brianna's current agitation. Well, not cause exactly. Catalyst, maybe. "Nothing has to be sorted right now. Just give yourself some time. Nobody's going anywhere."

"Yeah. You're right." Brianna nodded slowly, but it was clear her attention had turned inward. "I'm, uh, going to finish prepping for service."

Better that than sticking around and asking more questions she wasn't sure she wanted the answer to. "Yes. Me, too."

Before they could go their separate ways, Brad strode over with his intense manager face firmly in place. "Don't hate me," he said.

She and Brianna exchanged a look. It was one they'd shared many times through the years—basically a who could possibly hate Brad, he's so nice expression laced with the tiniest trace of exasperation. "We'd never hate you," Brianna said, saving Hadley the trouble.

"I just accepted a last-minute reservation for fifteen at seven." He cringed. "We had the space and it felt wrong to turn away that kind of business on a Wednesday."

He had a point. And it wasn't like the staff couldn't handle it. "We might run out of specials, but I can wing something if we get desperate."

Brianna nodded. "Same. I got ahead on making tart shells and lemon curd, so I can dip into that."

Brad smiled his good guy smile. "You two are the best."

"We know," Hadley said.

He hurried off and Brianna shot her another look. More intimate than before. Hadley could happily read a thousand things into a look like that but knew better than to let herself. Especially if she was going to give Brianna all that time she promised there was to sort things out.

Fortunately, the pace of service kept both her body and mind hopping. The unusually large party threw her rhythm just enough that she had to focus to keep things running smoothly. It almost felt like she was back in the city—a welcome distraction, even if it made her glad she'd mostly given up working that way.

The kitchen finally quieted a little after eight, and Hadley wondered if she should seek Brianna out or give her space. Brianna saved her the trouble of deciding, catching her eye and tipping her head in the direction of the walk-in cooler. Oddly, it wasn't the first covert conversation she'd had in an oversized refrigerator.

"What's up?" she asked when Brianna pulled the door closed behind them.

"I lied earlier."

Hadley tensed, the words triggering even though she didn't know what part of earlier Brianna was referring to. "You did?"

Brianna looked at the ground briefly before lifting her eyes to Hadley's. "When I said I was fine."

She swallowed, guilt and longing swirling in an elaborate dance. "You're not fine?"

Brianna shook her head. "I can't stop thinking about you."

Fuck. Fuck fuck fuck. How could a sentence she'd waited practically her whole life to hear feel like a punch to the stomach? "I'm sorry."

"I'm not."

Blood roared in Hadley's ears, as loud as an approaching A train at the Washington Square station. "Brianna."

"I don't know what I'm going to do about it yet, so it feels kind of unfair to tell you, but…" Brianna looked down before looking into Hadley's eyes. "I needed to tell you."

They were alone but not, the chilled air and fluorescent lighting making for literally the worst ambiance imaginable. But none of that mattered. Brianna wanted her. Maybe she'd never act on it and maybe life would wind up harder for knowing it. But just like their surroundings, none of it mattered.

Hadley took a step closer, let her hand come up to cup Brianna's cheek. "I'm glad you did."

"Yeah?" Brianna's eyes—big and brown and filled with both apprehension and longing—said everything Hadley wanted to hear.

"Yeah."

A kiss was out of the question. Obviously. But damn if she didn't let her gaze flick down to Brianna's mouth. Her perfect lips parted ever so slightly. Invitation? Anticipation? Hadley swallowed. What was the worst that could happen?

"What's going on?" Brad's voice, harsh and confused, came from behind her.

Hadley jumped back as though she'd been caught with her hand up Brianna's blouse, or perhaps her tongue down Brianna's throat. She hadn't even heard the cooler door open. "Nothing."

Brad stood in the doorway. If his suspicions weren't up before, they sure as hell were now.

"We were just talking," Brianna added, probably making things worse rather than better.

"What kind of talking?" He folded his arms.

Hadley debated telling him the truth. She also debated telling him to fuck off. Especially given their conversation that morning.

"Nothing." Brianna cleared her throat. "Nothing important."

He didn't move and, since he blocked the only way out, they didn't either.

"Why are you hiding?" he asked.

"Because I'm struggling with something, and I wanted Hadley's advice."

She had no idea where Brianna's sudden bravery came from, much less what it might mean. But it managed to be the truth without giving anything away, so she opted to keep her mouth shut.

"What?" Brad's eyes narrowed. "What are you struggling with?"

Hadley opened her mouth, hoping a yet to be formed lie would materialize.

"I'd rather we talk at home," Brianna said. "Please."

Whether he sensed the gravity of the situation or had his own serious matters that needed hashing out, Hadley couldn't be sure. But he nodded soberly. "Okay."

"Let's get out of here and finish service," Hadley offered. Not really a meaningful contribution to the conversation at hand, but whatever.

Both Brianna and Brad nodded, and the three of them filed out. They got a few funny looks, but no one said anything. She'd always rolled her eyes at the drama that seemed to unfold in restaurant kitchens, especially of the romantic variety. More than once, she'd lectured prep cooks and waitstaff alike to keep their heads down and their pants zipped. If the stakes didn't feel so fucking high, she might appreciate the irony of needing a taste of her own medicine.

Chapter Ten

At the soft knock, Hadley hurried to the back door, expecting to see her brother. The guy had a lot of nerve showing up unannounced at quarter to midnight. Even if he and Brianna had finally had some explosive—overdue—argument, and he needed to lick his wounds. If she hadn't been so busy shoveling ice cream in her face and feeling sorry for herself, she'd have been as tucked in fast asleep as her parents were. Or at least tossing and turning in the discomfort of her own skin.

She yanked it open. "Seriously, dude?"

Only it wasn't Brad standing on the other side, looking sheepish and bedraggled the way he did when he'd screwed up. It was Brianna. Beautiful and lovely and with tears in her big brown eyes. "I'm sorry to show up unannounced," she said.

Hadley's mind scrambled for something to say, something to do other than pull Brianna into her arms and never let go. "Don't apologize."

Brianna sniffed. "Does that mean I can come in?"

She leapt back, feeling like an absolute fool. "Oh. God. Yes, of course."

"Thanks."

"It feels dumb to ask if you're okay, because obviously you aren't. But, like, do you want to talk about it? Can I get you anything?" She scrubbed a hand over her face. "Would you prefer if I stopped bombarding you with questions?"

That got a small laugh. "Have your parents gone to bed?"

Dad's snores rumbled from the living room. And Hadley's pulse, already elevated, kicked into full gear. Like on the elliptical and hating her life fast. "Yeah."

Brianna came in and kicked off her shoes. The habit made Hadley smile even as her mind raced, zipping through scenarios and what the appropriate reaction to whatever it was would be. "Can I get you something to drink?"

"Whiskey?"

Her brow shot up before she could stop it. Not that she hadn't drowned her share of troubles in a stiff one. Brianna just struck her as more evolved than that. But she schooled her expression because she wanted to know exactly what had happened to put Brianna in such a state. And perhaps even more, she wanted to be whatever Brianna needed. Now, obviously, but kind of always. Even if it slayed her in the meantime. She tipped her head toward the three-season room that used to be the back patio. "I'll meet you out there."

Hadley poured two fingers into a highball glass from the bar her parents had set up in the corner of the dining room, then decided to pour the same for herself. She might have a vague sense of why Brianna was here, but something told her it was more and bigger than the incident in the cooler.

By the time she returned to the sunroom, Brianna had perched on the edge of the wicker sofa, feet on the floor, ankles and knees pressed together, fingers laced in her lap. It made Hadley wonder if she'd ever sat so properly in her life, which almost made her laugh. Instead, she handed Brianna one of the glasses and joined her, leaving half a cushion buffer between them.

"Thanks," Brianna said.

Hadley nodded. "What's going on? Talk to me."

Brianna took a sip of her drink. "Brad and I broke up."

For the second time since Brianna's arrival, Hadley's mind swirled in a dozen directions—from wanting to kick her brother's ass to a thrill of hope she certainly had no business feeling.

"Well, technically, I broke up with him," Brianna added before Hadley could form a singular thought. "Though based on how he took it, I think he might be more relieved than heartbroken."

Still. Her heart ached for both of them. "I'm so sorry."

"Are you?"

"I mean..." She sure as hell wasn't going to admit to being elated.

Brianna lifted her chin. "This might help. He's in love with your dad's physical therapist."

It answered a few questions and begat dozens more. "I'm so, so sorry."

Brianna's eyes locked on hers, and Hadley genuinely wondered if it was possible for the human heart to explode in one's chest. "I'm not."

"No?" God, was that really the best she could come up with?

Those gorgeous brown eyes rolled with exasperation. "I mean, I'm a little enraged that he would have stayed with me and just kept going through the motions for who knows how long, but that feels kind of beside the point."

Whatever skills Hadley may have possessed when it came to calm in the face of chaos abandoned her. A deafening chorus of possibility blasted in her ears, making it impossible to think of anything else.

"The truth of the matter is I'm relieved. Sure, I wish he'd had the guts to be the one to call it when he realized he had feelings for someone else, but that feels kind of hypocritical."

"Yeah." She hated being the one to put Brianna in the position, but she couldn't bring herself to regret what had happened.

"Besides, I got to be the brave one. That's nice for a change. And I'm in charge of what I do next. I get to, for once in my life, decide exactly what I want and go for it."

A tingling sensation traveled down Hadley's spine and back up. "And what is it that you want?"

"I want you," Brianna said simply.

"Me." Was this happening? Or had she fallen into some hallucinogenic fever dream that would leave her tangled in her sheets, sweating and breathless from just how real it felt? Despite everything that had happened in the last few days, she still didn't trust it. Or herself.

"Yes, you." Brianna took her hand. "I'd hoped the feeling might be mutual, but maybe it isn't. Or maybe it is, but you don't feel like you can act on it, even now. Or maybe you might but not yet. Or maybe—"

"It's mutual. It's so fucking mutual."

Brianna looked at her, eyes finally hopeful. "It is?"

"Brianna Kearns, I've been in love with you since the eighth grade."

For the first time that night, the tables turned, and Brianna was the one rendered speechless. "Shut up," she said finally.

Hadley laughed. "That won't make it any less true."

"Why didn't you say anything?"

She canted her head and blinked.

"Okay, fine. I can see exactly why you wouldn't say anything." Brianna chewed her lip. "That's not, you know, why you left, is it?"

"I'd be lying if I said it wasn't a factor at all, but I promise it was only one reason of many."

Brianna nodded slowly, as though she were an already saturated sponge trying to soak up even more. Then she started. "Wait. I got distracted. You're in love with me?"

It felt so simple now, so obvious. "Guilty as charged."

The nodding became more vigorous. "I want to say I'm in love with you, too, but I only just really let myself entertain the possibility of that, so I feel like I should let it percolate for a hot minute. I don't want you to think I'm anything but genuine when I say it."

That Brianna was even thinking it sent a thrill shooting through her like a jolt of electricity. "I don't need you to say it. And I want your honesty more than anything else."

Brianna smiled softly. "That's something you and your brother have in common. I wasn't sure I was ready, but he needled me to be open with him, and it suddenly felt right. And then he told me about his feelings for Shelby and that he'd been wrestling with what to do."

Rather than breaking the mood, the observation settled over her, almost like a blessing. Brad hadn't broken up with Brianna, but he wasn't—wouldn't be—devastated by it.

"Is that weird?" Briana closed one eye and scrunched up her nose. "Talking about him?"

"It probably should be, but it's not."

"If it makes any difference, he's gone off to see Shelby."

Hadley cringed. "Does that bother you?"

Brianna hesitated, but then a smirk crept in. "It probably should, but it doesn't."

Her heart beat even faster, making her wonder vaguely if emotional roller coasters counted as cardio. "What do you need? What do you want tonight?"

The smirk remained in place. Brianna licked her lips. "I thought I answered that question a minute ago."

The words—those three magical words—reverberated through her. *I want you.* On one hand, they told her everything she needed to know. On the other, they left her at an absolute loss over what to do next. "Yes. Maybe you could clarify, though. Wait, not clarify. Expand. Elaborate."

Brianna smiled. She made a show of taking Hadley's hand and pulling it into her lap. "I want to spend more time with you. I want to explore this zingy feeling, see if it has legs."

Zingy. Such a perfect and yet completely insufficient word. "I like the sound of that."

"I want to go to bed with you."

Not wholly unexpected, but hearing Brianna say it sent Hadley's poor deprived libido into overdrive. "I want that, too," she managed. "All of it."

Brianna's gaze seemed to search Hadley's face, and when she'd finished there, she worked her way down. Thirsty. That was the only word Hadley could come up with to describe it. It left her feeling exposed and, at the same time, impossibly aroused.

Obviously, they should tiptoe into this. There was so much history, so many complications. Navigating things with care and consideration would be best for everyone involved. They could go on a real date, maybe hold hands. Kissing would probably happen sooner rather than later, but it didn't mean they should rush—

Brianna's lips pressed into hers. Not confident, exactly, but urgent. Insistent. Curious.

Adjectives flashed in Hadley's brain, the need to make meaning as engrained as her own name. But just as quickly as they appeared, they vanished. Instinct took over. Instinct and hormones and a decade of longing. She kissed Brianna back, her own urgency taking center stage. The taste of Brianna's mouth—sweet, with traces of vanilla and smoke from the whiskey they'd both sipped but abandoned. The feel of Brianna's skin under her fingers—warm and soft along the line of her neck.

It was everything. It was so much more than she imagined. It wasn't nearly enough.

She pulled back just far enough to search Brianna's eyes. "You probably didn't mean right this minute."

Brianna's brow quirked.

Hadley's clit throbbed. "Or did you?"

"How weird would it be?"

"Going to bed with you in my childhood room with my parents asleep a couple of rooms away, you mean? Not weird at all."

Brianna smirked. "It's not like your brother would be next door."

Hadley laughed, a genuine if thoroughly unsexy snort that burst out before she could stop it.

"Too soon?"

By rights, yes. Too soon to joke, too soon to act on the spark that that had somehow turned mutual. But as she looked at Brianna's sheepish grin, love and desire and some big, glorious feelings that didn't even have names swelled in her. And all that mattered was this moment, this woman. She stood from the sofa and held out her hand. "Come on."

Chapter Eleven

They made it through the door of Hadley's room before making out in earnest, barely. Gone was the initial crush of lips, the announcement of a kiss followed by the search of each other's faces for signs of consent, of desire. It was all urgency now. Tongues and teeth and hands in hair and hands seeking skin and echoes of why the hell had they waited so long to do this.

She managed to shut the door behind them before Brianna pushed her against it, her breasts pressing into Hadley's and hinting at the way their bodies would mold together without the burden of clothes.

So many clothes.

She worked her fingers under the hem of Brianna's sweater, tugging upward until she created just enough space between them to rid Brianna of it altogether. Brianna's breasts—creamy and full and utterly perfect, swelled over the cups of her pink and black polka dot bra. With a growl, Hadley pushed off from the door and reversed their positions. She filled her hands with those perfect breasts and brought her mouth back to Brianna's. When she shifted her attention to Brianna's shoulder, Brianna let out a gasp laced with a yelp.

Hadley jerked her head back. "Did I hurt you?"

Brianna pressed her lips together and shook her head. "It tickled."

"Ah."

Brianna smirked. "But also shot right to my clit?"

She laughed. "I'll take that."

"Honestly, I don't think there's anything you could do to me that I wouldn't want."

Even without anything particular in mind—other than trying to steep herself in Brianna—the comment packed a punch. And to borrow Brianna's line, shot right to her clit. "I still want you to talk to me, though. Tell me what you like, what you want."

"I'd like to get you naked," Brianna said rather matter-of-factly. "I want to feel you, taste you."

She bit back a joke about that being her line. She'd rather show Brianna anyway. Since she'd already rid Brianna of her sweater, she tugged her own henley over her head and tossed it aside. "On the bed. Lie back."

Brianna did as instructed without hesitation. The sight—arms draped over her head in a mixture of invitation and abandon—took Hadley's breath away. She paused simply to soak it in, give herself a moment to bask in the fact that something that had occupied so much of her imagination for so very long was finally happening, finally real.

"You're not having second thoughts, are you?" Brianna's tone was playful, but a shadow of worry shone in her eyes.

"I'm having a lot of thoughts. Mostly about how you are even more perfect than my wildest dreams."

Brianna shook her head. "I'm not perfect."

It was one of those words she used perhaps too lightly, though she meant it in every possible way. But she could also appreciate that it would hang heavy with a woman like Brianna. She'd like to change that, eventually, but it didn't need to be tonight. "Debatable. But I'll settle for beautiful. Sexy. Exquisite."

Brianna blushed, but her smile didn't feel forced. "You're pretty exquisite yourself."

"I haven't done anything yet," she said with a bit more swagger than she'd intended.

Rather than call her out, Brianna merely smirked. "Well, what are you waiting for?"

Not one damn thing. Hadley joined Brianna on the bed, blanketing Brianna's body with her own. She brought her mouth back to Brianna's, though she resisted any urge to hurry the kiss. She might feel like a horny teenager, and they might be rushing things in the grand scheme of things, but she had every intention of taking her time.

And that's exactly what she did. A slow and sensuous exploration with lips and teeth and tongue. A lengthy appreciation of Brianna's neck, the soft curve of her shoulder, and the gentle indentation along her collarbone. A thorough meditation on each of Brianna's breasts, paying the most particular attention to her lush, dark areolas and taut nipples.

Brianna sighed and squirmed. She made these little noises that made Hadley want to ravish her hard and fast until they'd both had their fill. But as much as she wanted that, she wanted to keep Brianna like this—held in that magical balance of pleasure and longing—for as long as possible.

"Why are you still wearing pants?" Brianna tugged fruitlessly at the waistband of Hadley's sweats.

"I could ask you the same thing." She shifted away, just long enough and far enough to shimmy Brianna's jeans down her legs. The polka dot bikinis Brianna wore underneath—that matched the bra she'd already discarded—made her smile. "Those are cute."

"They'll look better on your floor."

Hadley didn't know what she'd expected. Playful sex kitten wasn't it. Not that she was complaining. "Yes, ma'am."

She dispensed with the last of Brianna's clothes, then her own. When she returned to the bed, she braced herself over Brianna, nestling one leg between Brianna's thighs. Brianna arched under her, giving Hadley a hint of the heat, the wetness, that awaited her.

"I'm not sure how long I can wait to touch you."

Brianna arched again. "Why are you waiting at all?"

Excellent question. Hadley slid a hand between them and found Brianna even hotter and wetter than her most torrid fantasies. "Fuck," she whispered.

Brianna gripped her shoulder. "Yes."

She tried to go slow, to savor. Brianna was impossibly soft. She moved against Hadley's hand, conveying exactly what she wanted without having to utter a word. Hadley got lost in the perfection of it.

"Please." Brianna's voice held desperation now. "More. I need to feel you inside me."

Never had a request sounded so wondrous in her ears. Hadley shifted her hand, sliding one and then a second finger into Brianna's wetness. Brianna tightened around her, molding around her like a glove. Hadley's own pussy responded in kind, clenching like a fist.

"Yes. Oh, God, yes." Brianna gripped Hadley's shoulders, and her hips pumped with each thrust of Hadley's hand.

"That's it, baby. I've got you."

She hadn't given any thought to the term of endearment. It simply rolled off her tongue like she'd been calling Brianna that, thinking of her that way, for years. But at the words, Brianna's hold on her tightened, and she literally erupted, spilling hot and glorious into Hadley's hand.

Brianna bolted upright. "Oh, my God."

Hadley soothed her back down with kisses and pets. "Shh. It's okay. I've got you."

"I…I've never come like that before."

"It was insanely sexy. And I'm already thinking about making you again."

Brianna shook her head slowly. "Not before I get to touch you."

"You don't have to—"

In a flash, Brianna rolled, nudging Hadley onto her back and taking the position Hadley had enjoyed only a moment before. "I know you're not arguing with me right now."

It was Hadley's turn to shake her head. "No argument here."

"Good." Without another word, Brianna slinked down Hadley's body, settling herself between Hadley's legs.

Hadley grasped for words, but there were none. And when Brianna's tongue pressed tentatively into her, she was gone.

❖

It was well after one before they came up for air. Hadley scrubbed a hand over her face, even as her other one pulled the soft curve of Brianna's shoulder a little tighter. Holy crap.

Brianna lifted her head. "You're not regretting this, are you? I'm not sure I could bear it if you did."

"No." She pressed a kiss to Brianna's temple. "I'm feeling lots of things, but regret is nowhere close to being on the list."

Despite the reassurance, Brianna frowned. "Like what?"

"How gorgeous you are. How many nights I fantasized about doing what we just did. How despite all those fantasies, reality is better."

Brianna pinched her side. "Sweet talker."

"It's the truth. I'm also thinking a little bit about what happens next because I can't seem to help being that person, but I promise all that pales in comparison to the amazing sex and dream come true stuff." She kissed Brianna, this time on the mouth. "You've legit blown my mind here."

Brianna blushed, which was extra adorable given the sex goddess routine she'd pulled out of her pocket not an hour before. "My mind's pretty blown, too."

"Wait." Hadley sat up, sending Brianna on an ungraceful tumble into the pillows and the covers sliding unceremoniously down to her waist. "Have you ever been with a woman before?"

Brianna sat up, pulling the covers up to cover her breasts. She scratched her scalp briefly, looked Hadley square in the eye. Then she cringed, biting her lower lip and squeezing her eyes closed. "Define been with."

Surely no one could be as good as Brianna had been with zero experience. Then again, when would she have had the chance to hook up with a woman? She and Brad got together in tenth grade. "You tell me."

Brianna opened her eyes and blew out a breath. "Well, I made out with Tracy Montano senior year, which Brad totally knew about, for the record."

She chuckled. Funny he hadn't confided in her at the time. "Okay. Is that all?"

"And I make no secret about being bi, so most of my recreational reading is of the sapphic persuasion?"

"Sapphic persuasion?"

Brianna smacked Hadley's arm with the back of her hand. "Don't make fun."

Hadley lifted both hands. "I'm not. Okay, I am. But it's your choice of words, not the books you like."

Brianna huffed and, again, it was totally adorable.

"I mean it. And you clearly know what you're doing, so if you got that from books, then I'm hella impressed." And oddly charmed.

Brianna folded her arms, a haughty little lift in her chin. "I think I've demonstrated on several fronts that I can hold my own despite being self-taught."

Hadley nodded slowly. "You most certainly can."

"Does it weird you out that you're my first?" Brianna asked.

"Of course not. Does it weird you out that you aren't mine?"

Brianna laughed. "Nah. I'm putting all my freak-out eggs in the sister-of-my-boyfriend-for-the-last-twelve-years basket."

She cringed. "Are you really freaked out?"

"Honestly?"

Hadley braced herself. "I sure as hell don't want you to be dishonest."

That got her an exasperated look, but then Brianna's features softened into a smile. "Honestly, I'm not. Maybe I should be. And yeah, I think it's going to be really awkward when your family finds out. Oh, God, or when mine does, but I'm up for it."

She hadn't expected an illicit one-night stand, even when it was clear she'd be taking Brianna to bed with her. Still, this openness and the implication that what they had would last at least long enough to tell their families made Hadley's heart swell. "I love how ready you are to own it."

Brianna frowned. "Does that mean you aren't?"

"Oh, no. That's not what I meant at all. I just wasn't sure how you'd feel about it."

"I mean, I may not have let myself admit it, but I've been wanting this, wanting you, for a long time. I'm about ready to shout it from the rooftops."

Hadley nodded, allowing that truth to soak in.

"Besides, Brad's already fallen for someone else, so who's going to begrudge me moving on?"

There was moving on, and there was hopping into bed literally the moment it happened.

"Though maybe we should give it a few days."

Hadley laughed. "Yeah."

"You'd be okay with that?" Brianna unfolded her arms and grabbed Hadley's hand.

"I am. I think it's a good idea, actually."

Brianna chewed her lip again. "Does that mean I should go?"

The thought of sending her back to the apartment she shared with Brad left more than a bad taste in Hadley's mouth. Though she'd probably go to her parents' instead. Or maybe a friend's. Still. It was going on two in the morning, and the idea of Brianna going anywhere didn't feel right. "What if we set an alarm for five, then we can get up and start coffee and stuff? We can tell my folks you came over to talk and crashed on the couch."

"Yeah. I like that."

She pushed herself forward, grabbing Brianna and taking them both back down to the mattress. "The bonus of this plan is I get a few more hours in bed with you."

"Should we try to sleep?" Brianna asked without a lot of conviction.

Hadley pressed her pelvis to Brianna's and thrilled at the way Brianna arched to meet her. "Did you want to go to sleep?"

Brianna shook her head, rocking it back and forth on the pillow in what had to be the sexiest denial Hadley had ever seen.

"So, it would be okay if I kissed you?"

The side-to-side motion became a nod of assent. Hadley kissed Brianna's jaw, her neck. She had zero complaints about their first time, but it filled her with so much wonder, it hadn't left her with a lot of attention to simply explore. To delight in each curve and swell of Brianna's body. She did that now, taking her time and basking in each sigh, each soft moan.

They hadn't resolved the questions of what next, but there'd be time for that. Brianna had chased away that initial fear. For now, she had more urgent matters to attend to. She had the woman she loved—naked and eager—in her bed for the next several hours. And she didn't plan to waste a minute.

Chapter Twelve

Hadley reached across the center console and squeezed Brianna's hand. "You sure you're ready to do this?"

Brianna squeezed back. "I'd honestly rather have done it before we slept together, so I think ready is beside the point."

Hard to argue with that logic. And since there was every possibility the conversation would go badly, she resisted the temptation to make a joke. "It might suck, but it might go really well."

Brianna swiveled her head, brow raised. "If by really well, you mean no swearing, crying, or throwing things, then sure."

"Are you talking about yourself? Or Brad?"

Brianna did laugh then, her anxiety no match for the absurdity of the situation. "I'm holding out hope none of us winds up in tears."

Hadley pulled into the driveway of the townhouse Brad and Brianna shared. "It's good to have goals."

Brianna rolled her eyes but didn't hesitate to get out of the car and stride up the front walk. Hadley hurried to follow.

Brianna unlocked the door, but knocked as she opened it. "Brad?"

No response.

"Huh." Brianna dropped her keys in the basket on the console table and headed for the kitchen. "Brad? You here?"

Still no response. Hadley ignored the flash of panic and reminded herself not to jump to conclusions. Before she could admit how badly she was at doing that, the garage door rumbled.

Brad came through the side door just as Brianna reached for it. They both jumped, and Hadley had to swallow a laugh.

"Is everything okay?" he asked.

"Are you okay?" Brianna asked at the same time.

Brad coughed and looked suddenly uncomfortable. "I'm…good."

One look at Brianna made it clear he wasn't convincing anyone. But then Hadley noticed a smudge of lipstick on his neck. It was faint, but there was no mistaking it. "We need to talk," she said with far more confidence than she'd felt only minutes before.

Brianna looked at her with surprise, but Hadley knew this was the right moment. She gave Brianna an encouraging nod. Brianna mirrored the move. "Let's all sit down."

Brad headed for the table in the eating area rather than the living room, a move Hadley respected. They each took a seat and stared at each other for a few seconds. Hadley bit the inside of her cheek to keep from blurting it all out. They'd agreed on the ride over that Brianna needed to be the one to tell him.

Brianna used all the right lines. Wanting to be honest. Discovering feelings. Knowing she needed to end things before acting on those feelings, but perhaps getting to the acting on them part a little more quickly than she'd planned. She kept her cool, and Hadley fell even more in love with her than before.

When she'd finished, Brianna laced her fingers together and rested them on the table. Hadley held her breath.

"You're…together?" Brad looked from Hadley to Brianna and back, blinking rapidly. "As in, together together or spent the night together?"

Brianna's shoulders straightened and her chin lifted ever so slightly. Not defiant, exactly. Just a hint of challenge, like she was daring whoever it was to contradict her. "Yes."

God, she loved this woman. Hadley squared her own shoulders and prepared for an uncomfortable, if not downright ugly, conversation. She gave a nod of her own. "Yes."

His gaze darted back and forth a few more times. And then the hugest grin she'd ever seen spread across his entire face. Like, his ears were involved in this grin. "I love it."

"Wait. You do?" Brianna's expression held a mixture of confusion and alarm.

"Totally." He flung a hand in Hadley's direction. "I mean, I knew this one had a crush on you back in the day, even if she was too stand-up to say or do anything about it." He whipped his other hand at Brianna.

"And you're like the nicest person ever and deserve to be happy. If that happy means you're staying in the family, then I can't think of anything better."

Brianna chuckled nervously. Hadley, on the other hand, laughed. Bent over, tears in her eyes, could barely catch her breath laughed. Of course he was happy for them. Of course this completely bonkers, potentially disastrous situation would fall into perfect place. And her brother, so in love in his own should-have-been-a-hot-mess way, provided the cherry on top. "Okay, then," she said finally, when she'd gotten ahold of herself enough to form words.

"Are you going to tell Mom and Dad?" he asked.

She hemmed. Brianna hawed. "We weren't going to just yet," Hadley said eventually.

"You should. Sooner the better." He nodded that way he did whenever he was formulating a plan.

"Why?"

Brad grinned. "Because they'll take Brianna and me breaking up better."

She shot him a bland look. "You mean they'll take you hooking up with Shelby better."

"I'm not hooking up with Shelby," he said too quickly for Hadley to believe him.

"Yet," she said.

He canted his head back and forth. "Yet."

Suddenly, the pieces clicked for Brianna. "You were with Shelby last night."

A flush crept up his neck and splotched his cheeks. "We were just talking."

Hadley raised a brow.

"Okay, talking and kissing." He gave a sheepish shrug.

Given what she and Brianna had been up to, she was in absolutely no position to judge.

Brianna reached over and grabbed his arm. "You should. Hook up with her, I mean. More than hook up. I'm probably the last person you want advice from, but I think she'd be good for you."

Not to mention taking the pressure off of them in the uncomfortable questions and awkward conversations department.

"Thanks." He frowned. "I think."

Brianna regarded him with affection. "I'm sorry I couldn't be. Good for you, I mean."

Brad blew out a breath. "Don't apologize. We never stopped being good together, but we both stopped being good for each other."

Brianna nodded. "I'm glad we can stay friends."

"Same. And seriously, Mom and Dad will be so relieved not to worry about losing Brianna as a potential daughter-in-law."

Hadley lifted a hand. "Maybe let me take her on a proper date before you start planning the nuptials."

Brad folded his arms. "I give you two a year, tops."

Brianna frowned.

"Till you're engaged, I mean," he added quickly. "I know that's weird given how long we were together without doing that, but I've got a feeling."

Hadley didn't argue since she had every intention of proposing as soon as she thought the answer would be yes. Brianna, for her part, smiled softly.

Brad laughed. "Mark my words."

It still amazed Hadley what a difference six months could make. She and Brianna had decided to move in together. Just an apartment for now, but they'd started talking about looking for a house together. Brad had followed Shelby to Rochester when she was offered her dream job, and he'd landed a gig managing a restaurant not that different from Devine's. She and Brianna had driven up once, and the whole family had plans to go together once Dad got the clearance for that long a ride.

Brianna had changed, too. Not at her core, obviously. More like she'd blossomed. In addition to making Hadley the happiest woman on the planet, she'd come into her own as pastry chef, complete with the white coat and swagger she'd pooh-poohed for so long. It amazed her, too, that she got to spend every night working alongside the woman she loved. No, she wasn't getting writeups in the *New York Times.* But she didn't need to. She made good food with and for the people she cared about most in the world.

That was especially true tonight. For the first time since his accident, her dad was coming in for dinner. He'd finally built up the stamina, but he'd also made peace with taking his place in the dining room rather than the kitchen. And Brad and Shelby were making the trip to celebrate. Sure, she and Brianna wouldn't be able to join for the whole meal, but she'd reserved a table for six anyway.

Hadley made her usual rounds of the kitchen, checking the line and everyone working it, before heading to the corner where Brianna worked her magic. "Are you feeling ready for tonight?" she asked.

Brianna folded her arms and jutted her hip with the sort of playful defiance that left Hadley wishing for a dark closet and an hour left to their own devices. "Do you seriously think I might not be ready ten minutes before service?"

"I wasn't talking about your desserts."

Brianna lifted her chin. "Damn right you weren't."

"I was talking about seeing Brad," she said, though she was pretty sure Brianna knew that's what she'd been asking about all along.

"I am." Brianna frowned. "Should I not be?"

They saw Brad—Shelby, too, for that matter—regularly before they'd moved. But it had been a couple of months, and Hadley thought there might be some awkwardness. "You tell me."

That got her an exasperated look. "I'm happy for them. More than happy. And their being so happy means I don't have any residual ick over breaking up with him to be with you."

Sound logic. It was just that emotions and logic didn't always go hand in hand. "I was only checking."

"You're sweet." Brianna tipped her head. "Should I be checking on you?"

It was silly to be nervous. It was Brad, after all. Literally, the nicest guy ever. And her own "ick" had also been assuaged by the bliss he'd found with Shelby. Even if she might be inclined to worry about the insta-love of it all, they were so damn good together, it was hard to believe they hadn't been together for ages. "Nah. I'm good."

"You know, I wouldn't be surprised if Shelby showed up with a ring on her finger."

"Are you serious?" She'd always assumed Brad's relationship escalator moved at a glacial pace. But the more she thought about it, the less incredulous she became.

Brianna shrugged. "When you know, you know."

Hadley frowned.

"What? You don't agree?"

More like agreed a little too much. She'd known Brianna was the one from that very first night together. Sure, she'd been priming that pump for years, but once everything between them finally clicked into place, everything felt right with the world. So much so that she'd been sitting on a ring of her own for the last three months. Just waiting for the right moment.

"Hadley. What's wrong?"

"Nothing."

Brianna's hands went to her hips. "You're lying."

"Is it true for us?" she asked.

"Is what true?"

"If you know, you know."

"I'd say so." Brianna lifted her chin. "Is that your way of proposing?"

In the least romantic way possible? And without the ring? Not even a little. "I hope I'd come up with something a little more special than the middle of the kitchen fifteen minutes before service."

"I wouldn't care about when or how. The question is all that matters."

And the answer. Could she? Perhaps the better question at this point was how could she not? She dropped to one knee. "Noted."

"Hadley."

"For the record, I planned to do something super romantic. And I have a ring, but I don't go carrying it around because that seems like asking for trouble. But I don't think I can go one more minute without you knowing that I'm utterly in love with you, and I want to spend the rest of my life with you."

Brianna beamed. "Sounds like you know what I know."

Her heart lodged somewhere in her throat, beating like a galloping horse. "I just need to know if the answer is yes."

"You haven't asked a question." Brianna smirked, but her eyes were glassy.

"Will you marry me, Brianna?"

"Yes. Yes and yes and yes again." Brianna grabbed her hand, pulling her to her feet and into a kiss.

Hadley jumped when the cheers started. One look around told her the majority of the kitchen crew had just witnessed her impromptu proposal. So not what she had planned, but somehow, perfect. This was her family, as much as her parents and her brother. "Okay, everyone. A round of drinks on the house, but after service."

A chorus of laughter and congratulations followed, then everyone scattered.

Brianna gave her hand another squeeze. "I'm glad you didn't wait for the perfect moment."

"I think I realized any moment with you is perfect."

"I love you, but no. That's too cheesy even for us."

Hadley laughed. "Fair. Though I'd argue you're perfect for me, and anything that gets me closer to a lifetime with you is pretty damn great."

"Fair." Brianna grinned. "Are we going to tell your folks? I'd feel bad stealing the thunder if Brad and Shelby have an announcement, too."

"Agreed. But now that half the staff knows, I don't think keeping it to ourselves is really an option."

"It's decided, then."

She nodded. "It's decided."

At the sound of the printer spitting out the first tickets of the night, Brianna angled her head toward the main line. "Looks like you're being summoned."

"I'm sorry I can't whisk you away for the rest of the night to celebrate."

Brianna waved her off. "We've got all night."

"All week."

"Always," Brianna added.

Hadley nodded. "Always."

About the Authors

Gun Brooke, author of thirty novels, writes her stories surrounded by a loving family and two affectionate dogs. When she isn't writing on her novels, she works on her art, and crafts, whenever possible—certain that practice pays off. She loves being creative, whether using conventional materials or digital art software.

J.J. Hale has been devouring books since she was able to hold one and has dreamt about publishing romance novels with queer leading ladies since she discovered such a thing existed, in her late teens. The last few years have been filled with embracing and understanding her neurodiversity, which has expanded the dream to include representing kick-ass queer, neurodivergent women who find their happily ever afters. That dream became a reality with her now two-time Goldie Award–winning debut novel. Jess lives in the south of Ireland, and when she's not daydreaming, she works in technology, plays with LEGO, and (according to the kids) fixes things.

Aurora Rey is a college dean by day and award-winning lesbian romance author the rest of the time, except when she's cooking, baking, riding the tractor, or pining for goats. She grew up in a small town in south Louisiana, daydreaming about New England. She keeps a special place in her heart for the South, especially the food and the ways women are raised to be strong, even if they're taught not to show it. After a brief dalliance with biochemistry, she completed both a BA and an MA in English. She is the author of the Cape End Romance series and several standalone contemporary lesbian romance novels and novellas. She has been a finalist for the Lambda Literary, RITA, and Golden Crown Literary Society awards but loves reader feedback the most. She lives in Ithaca, New York, with her dog and whatever wildlife has taken up residence in the pond.

Books Available From Bold Strokes Books

All For Her: Forbidden Romance Novellas by Gun Brooke, J.J. Hale & Aurora Rey. Explore the angst and excitement of forbidden love few would dare in this heart-stopping novella collection. (978-1-63679-713-7)

Finding Harmony by CF Frizzell. Rock star Harper Cushing has to rearrange her grandmother's future and sell the family store out from under her, but she reassesses everything because Gram's helper, Frankie, could be offering the harmony her heart has been missing. (978-1-63679-741-0)

Gaze by Kris Bryant. Love at first sight is for dreamers, but the more time Lucky and Brianna spend together, the more they realize the chemistry of a gaze can make anything possible. (978-1-63679-711-3)

Laying of Hands by Patricia Evans. The mysterious new writing instructor at camp makes Grace Waters brave enough to wonder what would happen if she dared to write her own story. (978-1-63679-782-3)

The Naked Truth by Sandy Lowe. How far are Rowan and Genevieve willing to go and how much will they risk to make their most captivating and forbidden fantasies a reality? (978-1-63679-426-6)

The Roommate by Claire Forsythe. Jess Black's boyfriend is handsome and successful. That's why it comes as a shock when she meets a woman on the train who makes her pulse race. (978-1-63679-757-1)

Seducing the Widow by Jane Walsh. Former rival debutantes have a second chance at love after fifteen years apart when a spinster persuades her ex-lover to help save her family business. (978-1-63679-747-2)

Close to Home by Allisa Bahney. Eli Thomas has to decide if avoiding her hometown forever is worth losing the people who used to mean the most to her, especially Aracely Hernandez, the girl who got away. (978-1-63679-661-1)

Innis Harbor by Patricia Evans. When Amir Farzaneh meets and falls in love with Loch, a dark secret lurking in her past reappears, threatening the happiness she'd just started to believe could be hers. (978-1-63679-781-6)

The Blessed by Anne Shade. Layla and Suri are brought together by fate to defeat the darkness threatening to tear their world apart. What they don't expect to discover is a love that might set them free. (978-1-63679-715-1)

The Guardians by Sheri Lewis Wohl. Dogs, devotion, and determination are all that stand between darkness and light. (978-1-63679-681-9)

The Mogul Meets Her Match by Julia Underwood. When CEO Claire Beauchamp goes undercover as a customer of Abby Pita's café to help seal a deal that will solidify her career, she doesn't expect to be so drawn to her. When the truth is revealed, will she break Abby's heart? (978-1-63679-784-7)

Trial Run by Carsen Taite. When Reggie Knoll and Brooke Dawson wind up serving on a jury together, their one task—reaching a unanimous verdict—is derailed by the fiery clash of their personalities, the intensity of their attraction, and a secret that could threaten Brooke's life. (978-1-63555-865-4)

Waterlogged by Nance Sparks. When conservation warden Jordan Pearce discovers a body floating in the flowage, the serenity of the Northwoods is rocked. (978-1-63679-699-4)

Accidentally in Love by Kimberly Cooper Griffin. Nic and Lee have good reasons for keeping their distance. So why does their growing attraction seem more like a love-hate relationship? (978-1-63679-759-5)

Frosted by the Girl Next Door by Aurora Rey and Jaime Clevenger. When heartbroken Casey Stevens opens a sex shop next door to uptight cupcake baker Tara McCoy, things get a little frosty. (978-1-63679-723-6)

Ghost of the Heart by Catherine Friend. Being possessed by a ghost was not on Gwen's bucket list, but she must admit that ghosts might be real, and one is obviously trying to send her a message. (978-1-63555-112-9)

Hot Honey Love by Nan Campbell. When chef Stef Lombardozzi puts her cooking career into the hands of filmmaker Mallory Radowski—the pickiest eater alive—she doesn't anticipate how hard she'll fall for her. (978-1-63679-743-4)

Bold Strokes Books
Quality and Diversity in LGBTQ Literature